AND THEN THE RAIN CAME

AND THEN THE RAIN CAME

A NOVEL BY

Evelyn Minshull

Thomas Nelson Publishers
Nashville

Published in Nashville, Tennessee, by Thomas Nelson, Inc., and
distributed in Canada by Lawson Falle, Ltd., Cambridge, Ontario.

Scripture quotations are from the NEW KING JAMES VERSION of
the Bible. Copyright © 1979, 1980, 1982, Thomas Nelson, Inc.,
Publishers.

Library of Congress Cataloging-in-Publication Data

Minshull, Evelyn White.
    And then the rain came / Evelyn Minshull.
      p.   cm.
    ISBN 0-8407-3383-6
    1. Noah (Biblical figure)—Fiction. 2. Bible. O.T.—History of
Biblical events—Fiction. I. Title.
PS3563.I476A82 1992
813'.54—dc20   92–16893
                                      CIP

Printed in the United States of America
1 2 3 4 5 6 7 — 97 96 95 94 93 92

For Valerie, whose drawings
give direction to building.

PART ONE

So God looked upon the earth, and indeed it was corrupt. . . . And God said to Noah . . . "Make yourself an ark of gopherwood; make rooms in the ark, and cover it inside and outside with pitch."

Genesis 6:12–14

1

Straightening, Kyral arched her shoulders to ease their aching. One thumb throbbed from an encounter with the rough edge of a rock. Her scalp crawled with humidity. Damp clothing littered the bank, and her arms dripped, attracting mosquitoes.

Still, she smiled.

Here, by the stream, life was good. Minnows darted; slashes of sunlight exposed scuttling crabs and mossy pebbles. A butterfly, intensely iridescent, carved a looping blue path from petal to stone, to a snag of long-dead limb extended like an arthritic arm toward the opposite shore. Birds sang, leaves rustled, and more distant sounds, reaching Kyral dimly, wove a comfortable confusion it wasn't necessary to separate, identify, or interpret—except for the hammerblows.

She knew whose those were. And whenever she heard a sudden spurt of taunting, she knew for whom it was intended.

Sighing, she returned to her work. If only that exasperating man of hers could be more like the others.

No!

Quickly she canceled the thought, not because it was traitorous to the vows she'd spoken before her father-in-law, Lamech, and before Yahweh, but because if Noah *were* like

3

the others, she couldn't respect him as she did, as she always had, as she would, even if . . .

She wouldn't pursue that, either. She would never, even in isolation, join the ranks of those who smirked and tapped their temples meaningfully. She would not—could not—accept their assessment. Too often Noah's lucidity, his intensity, his commitment in the face of ridicule had swayed her to the threshold of believing the unbelievable: great quantities of water would flow from the heavens and gush from the earth; this tiny tendril of the Euphrates would swell and multiply; ultimately the combined forces of the deluge would lift the ark. And the gigantic, monstrous half-boat, half-house, huge and ungainly as a hillside, would float.

"Great waves will carry the ark like a fragment of bark on a stream," Noah had explained when their children were wide-eyed with youth, "and the waves will move it so . . ."

They'd imitated the slow undulations of his hands, and Kyral's thoughts had rocked and flowed with the imagined swells.

"But what if the waves are *huge!*" Ham, flapping his arms wildly, swooped about the small room until Shem and Japheth ducked for cover beneath cushions and rushes. And Noah lunged to rescue an urn before growling, "Enough!"

Ham, deviltry gleaming through lashes lowered in counterfeit remorse, murmured, "It is only, my father, that I worry for Mother. How can she cook and clean when the ark pitches so?"

Ham had ever had the knack of reducing Noah to sputtering frustration. And for the child's sense of propriety, though neither "propriety" nor "sense" might ever be terms appropriate to this middle son of theirs, Kyral tried to smother her exasperated laughter.

It was Shem who answered. "When Yahweh can show Father how to build such a boat, do you think He can't save Mother's cooking?"

And Japheth, emerging with rushes still caught in his hair, threatened soberly, "If you aren't careful, Ham, you won't have to worry. You'll be left here on land to drown with the other bad people."

Undaunted, Ham pulled his face into an expression of scorn. "Then I'll *swim!*" he shouted and, with an exaggerated breast-stroke, thrashed about the house, once more threatening everything from brothers to crockery.

Noah escaped to his building—where the worst dangers came from thrown clods and obscene shouts—leaving Kyral to scold Ham, expel the boys to play, and admit that for her the unimaginable had gained tangibility. Surely she had her sons, with their easy confidence in Noah's dream, to thank for that.

And hadn't Methuselah, Noah's venerable grandfather, his eyes as dark as ancient raisins, asserted that the flood would, indeed, occur and that his own death would be a signal for its beginning? His gnarled fingers imprisoning Kyral's wrists, he'd insisted, "Yahweh decrees it!"

And, for those moments, as well, she'd believed.

Slapping a coverlet against a smooth rock, she shook her head in dismay at her recurrent gullibility. The impending flood was surely only a tale, merely a dream, a folly—her husband's folly.

Still, when Noah spoke of it—his eyes clear and snapping, the timbre of his voice deep and solid—it became a prophecy she could believe, a dream she could embrace, a folly she would gladly share, sometime . . . in the future.

But she cringed from the immediacy Noah increasingly expressed. Just that morning, he'd refused his usual breakfast of cheese, dates, and hot meal sweetened with honey and swirling with milk still warm from the goat.

"No time, m'dear," he'd said, giving her a quick kiss. Into a small pouch he stuffed a handful of raisins and two slabs of bread joined with curds. "The flood's so close, I can almost smell it. A year or so, no more. And where will we be then if the craft still leaks?" His eyes gleamed with excitement.

"But if you don't eat properly . . ." she protested.

"Yahweh will provide the energy required! Only consider, love, how short the waiting. After all these years . . ."

There was no reasoning with him when such fervor gripped him.

Lunacy, their neighbors called it.

But not she. If Noah lost his sanity, she would surrender hers. Without complaint, she would enter willingly whatever unreality possessed him.

And yet . . .

Her mind shrank from thoughts of confinement in the ark. Even when doing essential household chores, she suffered a sensation of smothering, breathlessness, panic, a need to lift her arms and stretch in all directions, touching nothing but air.

Though it meant breaking the rhythm of kneading to scatter flies or gnats, she often moved her pastry board out-of-doors. There was in unshared air a sense of sovereignty, an unrestricted safety in uncluttered space.

Even at the market, crowded by colors and odors and textures and besieged by the whines of beseeching peddlers, she felt oppressed, and at night, searching for sleep . . . Had rapists and murderers not dredged each night's darkness, she would have carried her pallet into the open air.

Once, when the children were still small—when Japheth, a thumb in his mouth, had muttered and murmured; when Ham had chuckled as though remembering some successful joke; and even Shem's gentle breathing had been as tangible as an additional presence—she had done just that. Despite her care in rising, Noah had grunted a question and then flopped over to resume his steady snoring.

She hadn't ventured far. Just to the courtyard, where if she wished, she could reach out to touch the rough plaster of the outer wall.

As she'd known it would, the breeze comforted her. Night insects wove a delicate lullaby designed to exorcise unease. She'd begun to surrender to sleep when, just beyond the hedges, drunken laughter erupted, resurrecting childhood terrors.

In vivid memory, her father, his wineskin cast aside, loomed above her, his eyes like reddened lights, like fires. His huge, rough hands steadily descended; the dirt-rimmed nails, chipped and scarred, impressed her flesh.

She'd almost shouted into her adult night as she had shrieked in those childhood days, "No! Please, Father, *no!*"

Once she'd seen that pleading pleased him, inspiring him to further cruelties, she learned to suppress her cries. Once she'd encased her fear in a quiet chrysalis of hatred, the seasons of torture abated in frequency, if not in the quality of terror.

But her inward hoarding of horror had cost a great price. Even her mother's warm love served as insufficient cushion and ineffective balm.

Kyral's fears had far outlived her father's ability to reach her. Surviving into a marriage rich in nurturing, they challenged even the power of her faith in Noah's Yahweh.

And they continued to oppress her.

But she would brace herself to endure even the ark for Noah, if that was what he required, not because she feared his anger, but because of their love.

Still, if he loved her as deeply as he vowed in those moments when he was actually with her in mind as well as in body, surely he could be more careful in his work!

Grateful for the activity that allowed no opportunity for further thought or memory, Kyral rubbed at a stain of pitch impervious to all her efforts to remove it. Black, inflexible, shiny, it marred the breast of the robe she'd woven just the past spring from the fleece of her favorite ewes.

"Pitch?" Doreya's musical voice interrupted Kyral's annoyance. "Again? When will he ever stop gathering pitch?"

"When he's finished building, I suppose," Kyral answered dryly, not looking up, but moving to make room on the large, flat rock.

Doreya's laughter bubbled. "And that will be . . ."

Kyral scrubbed with new, still futile, energy. "In a year or so, he says now," she answered. Already, the great ship had been taking shape for over 117 years.

Doreya touched Kyral's arm. "You can't know how much I admire you, never saying a word against him—even to me." She sighed. "And I envy you, too, despite the abuse you endure because of him. At least . . ." and her voice grew wistful, "at least your abuse doesn't come *from* him."

Dropping the damaged garment to the shallows, Kyral murmured, "Not again so soon!" but Doreya's swollen face convinced her. Squeezing the hem of her drenched robe, she applied gentle dabs of coolness to the split lip, the darkening eye, the bruised cheekbone (just as her own mother had patted and crooned, treating wounds far too deep for touching).

How does she bear it? How could anyone so capable and perceptive withstand such verbal and physical abuse? How did so many women endure the tyranny, the infidelity, of brutal husbands? And yet, what power had wives to resist? Even as loving as her mother had been, she'd possessed no authority to prohibit depravity; she could only attempt to assuage its effects.

Careful of the swelling, Doreya asked softly, "Did he *ever* strike you?"

With difficulty, Kyral disengaged her thoughts from her childhood. "Noah?"

"Of course, Noah!" Doreya's laughter rippled; then she touched her lip to stanch renewed bleeding. "Who else?"

Sensitive to Doreya's slight flinching, Kyral cooled the cloth again. She hated to answer. "Never," she whispered.

"Never." The word embroidered a sigh. "And he never cursed you, or beat your children, or called you a whore?"

Kyral cringed inwardly at the hateful word, spoken with a casualness she hadn't observed since childhood.

Harshly she straightened herself. She'd surrendered too much of today's thought to her father. Even from his grave, he caused much pain. But he could conquer only when she participated.

"Still . . ." Doreya's laughter recalled Kyral's thoughts to the present. "Noah isn't *quite* perfect! He stains his clothing with pitch!"

They had been friends for years, Kyral and this woman young enough to be her daughter, or her daughter-in-law. How she wished that Doreya were! It wasn't that she'd have had Ham, Shem, or Japheth marry other than their and Noah's choices. Certainly she loved Maelis and Afene and would cherish Tamara as well, should she and Ham suspend quarreling long enough to speak their vows. Still, Kyral had often approached Yahweh in worship tinged with reproach.

If only you had blessed me with this daughter, or if I had borne yet another son for Noah, what delight Doreya would have brought to our household. And what praise to You!

>>> <<<

Dabbing at tears, Tamara ran toward her childhood sanctuary.

She and Ham had quarreled, *again*. And the wedding was not a year away.

Already their home was under construction, her father holding Ham to careful craftsmanship—accurate measurement, attentive planing of wooden struts, cautious packing of clay into molds, all air expelled. Her father added those loving details and comforts he had supplied throughout her life. His "little goddess" he had always called her, speaking softly and with such tenderness that her mother's brow contracted in jealousy and her mouth crimped into a thin line.

It had pleased Tamara to see her mother's envy and even to excite it. It certified her belief that she was very, very special—to her father, at least. And, she had thought more recently, to Ham.

But they had quarreled again.

New tears dribbling, she quickened her pace down the broad, hard-packed street through the center of town. On either side low houses of mud-baked brick, stone, or stucco clustered in what had once seemed a cozy closeness. Now she recognized proximities that stifled and stultified. How wise her father had been to insist on building her home (hers and Ham's) in an area permitting, as he termed it, "elbow room."

Ham's mother had approved, as well. Kyral had stood on the bare lot with the outline of the house already evident, her hands propped on her hips as she swiveled about, drawing deep breaths of contentment. It only added to Tamara's satisfaction that her own mother stood aloof, her face taut with familiar jealousy. Determined to capitalize on her mother's discomfort, Tamara strode slowly across the lot.

"Isn't it lovely, Mother?"

Her mother sniffed.

Tamara dropped an arm casually across the stiffened shoulder. "I think of all those years you've been crammed between Hannah and Em—so close you can't spill dishwater without splashing at least one of them."

Carefully her mother extricated herself from Tamara's touch. "I'm only grateful that I share dishwater with friends," she said coldly, "rather than with a spoiled, vindictive daughter."

Tamara smiled.

Though she'd never consciously traced the roots of their mutual hatred, she suspected they reached into her childhood to early competition for her father's attention and softness. It was simple to see why her mother lost each battle. What man wouldn't melt to prettiness—eyes wide and innocent, lips tremulous—in preference to angularity and hard-edged accusations?

And what daughter wouldn't luxuriate in the worship of such a man and do all she could to perpetuate it?

"You've learned well," her mother had said more than once, "just how to manipulate him."

"Want to take lessons, Mother?" Tamara would ask softly, but never when her father might hear.

"I wouldn't stoop so low. And don't be so haughty, Missy. You may yet meet your match in that foolish son of Noah's."

It was possible her mother was shrewder than she in assessing Ham. Whenever they quarreled, Tamara tested techniques that never failed with her father. But here she was, again, running to seek solace from Ham's selfish, stubborn resistance to her wiles.

And yet, even during the drama of personal tragedy, she was fully aware of the appealing picture she made, her hair streaming behind her like sculpted sunlight. She ran as she did everything: with her appearance in mind and with full attention to the reaction of observers. There was no headlong flight for her—stumbling, stubbing her bare toes, looking foolish. Rather, her long, well-shaped limbs posed gracefully; her arms moved elegantly; her straight posture emphasized suppleness and form.

When a covey of young men lounging in sycamore shade drew to attention, she stored their rude sounds of male appreciation in her mind for later. At the moment, she was grief-stricken.

Cloyren held earnest conversation with an arthritic old man whose head deflected the direct rays of the sun. In contrast, Cloyren's hair was fine and full; his graceful hands shaped eloquent gestures verging on delicacy.

Just as she passed, Tamara's pace faltered, and she felt gratified as he called after her, "Tamara?" with that familiar questioning inflection.

Surely he'd follow.

She must look ghastly!

Let him come later to comfort her. He knew where she'd go when she wanted to be alone—or alone *with* someone, as she had been so often with him, when he'd whispered inflammatory words so close to her ear that even a beetle, crawling nearby, hadn't scurried at the sound. She wondered how her heartbeats, thundering like the wings of doves startled into flight, hadn't charged the surrounding air just as they electrified each nerve within her.

Why couldn't Ham be more like Cloyren?

Ham looked at her with that little-boy smirk, his dark eyes sometimes so glazed that she knew he was merely designing another prank. She'd enjoyed his silliness when they'd first fallen in love, when none of his tricks had yet victimized her. Sometimes then he'd made her a partner, both in planning and in implementation. But now he was as likely to lure her as anyone into a trap where he could guffaw at her expense. Recently his eyes filled more readily with tears of helpless laughter than with the fires of yearning.

But when Cloyren looked at her—even now, since his marriage—his glance was sensual, like smooth hands stroking her. She shuddered with anticipated pleasure.

Ham's hands were like a herdsman's, large, bumbling, calloused, often sweaty. How . . . and why . . . had she convinced herself and her father—and Ham—that she preferred ruddy, raucous awkwardness to smooth sophistication such as Cloyren's? Not that Cloyren had ever suggested marriage to her.

Her thoughts stung with the memory of her disbelief when she'd heard he planned to wed Brea! What could he possibly find to admire or desire in her? Brea's mouth was always puckered as though sensing an unpleasant odor and her bony hands arched toward overblown bosoms—surely, Tamara thought, to draw attention from her thick, layered waistline and swollen ankles. After all the poetic phrases he'd spun about Tamara's physical charms, how could Cloyren have turned to someone so obviously opposite?

It must be her father's wealth, she'd told herself. Such assurance served to soothe her smarting spirit. Cloyren's expensive tastes simply required resources Tamara couldn't tap.

It was enough that he came to her with admiration, with flirtations merging on the suggestive. Never ravishing her physically, he caused her to hope, vaguely, that he'd try. Of course, she'd repulse him. She could never dishonor her father by giving her body before marriage—to anyone.

But she couldn't deny the excitement of testing the bounds of temptation where Cloyren led her with consummate skill.

Long years before, she had claimed a broad ledge of rock as hers. From high on the breeze-swept cliff, sheltered by scrawny branches devoid of foliage, she could overlook the town huddled in its bowl-shaped valley, the thread-thin winding of the river, and a dozen rich fields and meadows with their circumference of woodland and wasteland. At this distance, the forested darkness seemed cozy, an impenetrable wall against intrusion. Behind that protection, she could dismiss whatever roamed, waiting for night. Her mother had warned her as a child—with more spite than concern, she realized in retrospect—that children who ventured into the forest would never return. Their parents would find them, if they sought them at all, torn and bloodied and quite, quite dead.

But from her ledge the world lay at her feet, "as befits a goddess," her father had often said. From there she could shape her own reality, and no one had the power to alter or shadow it. There she could imagine glowing directions for her life. Yet before she could shape the future, she must reshape the recent past.

Ham had quarreled with her. Ham, who said that he loved her, who would soon promise to consider her bone of his bone and flesh of his flesh, had embarrassed her. And then, when she'd drawn herself up haughtily, he'd said . . .

What, exactly, had he said? She must recreate the scene in every hurtful detail, reviewing and revising, before she could consign it to memory and, *perhaps*, if he pleaded fervently enough, offer forgiveness.

And she must do it quickly, before he came looking for her. Or, and she hugged herself against a sudden shiver, before Cloyren came.

Instead, it was her father who found her.

Never a bulky man, he had been her bulwark. No matter what she had done or said, no matter how weak or flawed her reasoning, she could count on him to perceive only her perfection.

She gestured for him to sit close to her. "I'll miss you *so much!*" she said through new tears.

His calloused hand warmed her arm. "Betrothals can be broken as easily as they are made."

But making hers hadn't been all that easy, she remembered, with the formalities, the pledges, the considerable dowry.

"Forget the dowry," he said. It had always seemed that he could read her mind!

So could her mother. But hers was seldom a comfortable reading.

"Shall I approach old Noah? Tell him we've changed our minds?" Her father's voice was husky, and she suspected his eyes also were filled with tears. It wasn't that he'd planned so heavily on this marriage, but that he could feel her pain. "I want only your happiness. Since that first day when they laid you in my arms, it is all I have ever wanted. Such a squirming, rosy little bundle you were!"

Settling her head in the curve of his shoulder, she comforted him with a patting hand and soothing little sounds such as a mother murmurs to her child. How could she bear losing him, especially if that silly business about the ark came to pass? How could she possibly enter that looming, dark ship, to stay for who knew how long, leaving it only after Ham's crazy father was forced by starvation or mutiny to rejoin the world?

But it wouldn't happen.

She was sure of that.

For many decades already Noah had been hammering away. As a child, her father had watched woodsmen fell and strip gopher trees, then scurried beside the ox-drawn carts that carved deep ruts as they moved the logs to Noah's building site.

"Sometimes," he'd often told her, "old Noah would see me struggling through the mud. And when he set me high on a log and steadied me with his hand on my knee, I pretended I was the master of a sailing ship or riding on some gigantic, lurching beast." He would smile gently, contemplatively.

"Despite his craziness, Noah's a good man." And he told her how occasionally, long before his marriage and her birth, he'd served in various crews hired by Noah. Wielding an adze, chip by chip he'd shaped stone-hard logs to timbers sturdy enough to withstand even such seas as Noah described. He'd fed the fire while, with much sizzling and banging, metalworkers shaped huge iron nails, the glowing red-gold metal congealing to dull darkness, the sparks erupting in vivid sprays with each hammerblow. And when the timbers were lifted, steadied, and secured by those nails, when the ship began to take shape, he'd ached to believe. He'd yearned to feel such a craft beneath him, to know its rolling, its breathing as the sea gave it life.

Other smaller vessels plowed the gentle Euphrates. Once riding in a relative's fishing boat, he'd gripped the seat, squinting against the breeze-driven salt air, and grinned his exultant fear. But to sail on such a craft as Noah's!

When Tamara was a child, her father had enchanted her with such tales, such dreaming. But now, when the ark represented a threat to her future, a potential for endless torment by her friends (and especially by Cloyren!), she was no longer bemused.

Still, it wouldn't happen! One of these days old Noah would die, or someone would set fire to the hulking eyesore. She wondered that it hadn't already occurred! Either way, that would be the end of "Noah's Folly."

Then, *if* she decided to become Ham's wife, they could settle into a life like everyone else's. Dressed in scarlet or white or whatever best suited her mood of the day, with gold chains dramatizing the curves of her neck and breasts and the slenderness of her ankles and wrists, she'd move through the marketplace with sedate sensuality, a basket held delicately on her arm. Her expression, both innocent and slightly frowning in concentration, would deny all awareness of the impact of her beauty. She wouldn't seem to notice the hush of admiration and envy attending her progress from stall to stall.

She and Ham would sit in the shade of fig trees. He'd bring her hibiscus blossoms and secure them in her hair as he spoke passionately of his love. Perhaps later she would bear him a child—a beautiful, perfect child, who seldom

cried. And he would extol her virtues as a wife and mother.
And they would never quarrel.

Still, they *had* quarreled.

Breaking into her thoughts, her father prompted, "I could
see Noah this very hour."

Tamara sighed. Her mother had made it clear that she
was welcome only until the wedding had taken place. And
Tamara knew that—should she change her mind now—her
stay would not be extended until a new husband could be
found.

Her father said, "Surely Cloyren would be
approachable . . ."

She pulled away, almost coldly. To be a second wife! To
spend her life in subjugation—and to such as Brea!

Her father sighed.

"Besides," Tamara whispered with a flavor of martyr-
dom, "I still love Ham."

"If he'd only grow up!" her father said tightly.

"Perhaps, if we're patient, he will. Remember, dear Father, he hasn't had the attention or the love that you have
given me."

A comfortable silence stretched between them, and she
knew that whatever occurred, whenever Ham hurt or angered her and however her mother scorned or belittled her,
she would have an ally in this dear man who had centered
his whole existence on her.

When he had gone, when the sun-warmed ledge was once
more hers alone, she breathed a deep sigh of satisfaction.
Gazing with a sense of proprietorship over the valley and
woodlands, she pulled her knees to her chin, laced her fingers before her, and traced the line of the river until an awkward bulk blocked its silver flow.

The ark.

Dwarfed as it was by her present perspective, she could
reduce it to its rightful placement in her life, to a miniature
presence, a hurdle of minuscule proportion. Once she had
molded Ham to become more like her father, the ark and its
significance would cast only a fragile shadow across their

future. If, indeed, it should ever be completed, if Noah should insist that Ham and she become players in his crazy scheme . . .

Well, she would simply refuse.

And which of the two—distracted father or desirable wife—was Ham most likely to choose? There wasn't the slightest doubt! Ham would be like a puppy, wriggling and salivating for her caresses.

Noting the sun's position, she stood, stretched luxuriously, and began her descent. It was somewhat disturbing that Ham hadn't come to find her. Nor had Cloyren.

Both of them, she determined, would pay for their neglect.

It was obvious that Ham was sulking.

But then, everything about Ham's moods was obvious. When happy, he was ecstatic, hilarious, rowdy. When he was sad, no tragedy had ever delved so deeply toward calamity. When he was angry, every red hair sparked and crackled, and his beard wobbled in such an endearing, outrageous manner that—except when his displeasure targeted her—Tamara dissolved into giggles. And so eventually would he.

At such times he would lunge, imprisoning her in his arms, and she would find herself fired by a passion that Cloyren's attentions, however suave, had never excited. What a burly bear of a man Ham was when his love for her consumed him and her hunger for him was a tangible flame, licking along her veins. But it was impossible to picture him as anything but a spoiled child while he sat there, his lower lip jutting, eyes aggrieved, arms tightly crossed.

"No wonder you're drawn to him," her mother snapped one day as she wove table linens while Tamara dreamed above a coverlet for the wedding bed. "You're just alike."

Her needle suspended above the white expanse with its growing bouquet of embroidered flowers, Tamara braced herself.

"Both spoiled," her mother elaborated, her tone, as always, spiced with dislike. "Both determined to have your own way. Both immature, with little chance of changing."

When a child, such exchanges had wounded Tamara, had sent her crying to her father for his solace. But now, her father's preference deeply entrenched, she was long past caring what her mother thought of her. And now she had Ham . . . and *his* mother.

Quietly she retorted, "If I'm immature, whose fault is that?"

Her mother's eyes sparked with malice as she gave the predictable answer. "Your father's. There was no stopping him, no convincing him that he groomed you to be an impossible wife . . ." her voice grew weary, "as you have, the gods all know, been an impossible daughter."

Tossing her head, Tamara jabbed viciously with her needle—and impaled her finger. "My father seems to find me possible enough!" Idly she wondered if she should soak the blood spot from the coverlet or merely build another flower around it.

"It's easy enough," her mother snapped, "to convince a blind man that the night sky is green. But should he ever regain his sight . . ." With a sigh of defeat, she left her loom and began to rattle cookery in preparation for the evening meal.

Ham, still sulking, was studying his fingernails. *I can't see why,* Tamara thought uncharitably. *They're always foul with dirt and sawdust.*

Dirt and sawdust, she remembered a bit shamed, from her future home, more elaborate and spacious even than the one Cloyren had commissioned for Brea. She threw Ham a glance of dislike. She hated feeling that she might have been wrong! And there he sat, sulking, expecting her to grovel.

Well, she wouldn't—not for him; not for anyone. And yet how she yearned to nestle in his huge embrace!

Cloyren's arms seemed unmuscled by comparison. While his whispers inflamed her, his embraces seemed almost tentative, his kisses anemic. With some superiority, she considered haughty Brea enduring those kisses—too soft and too wet for pleasure. It was Brea, as well, who must wince each time she saw her husband's arm draped familiarly across the shoulder of a young girl, their faces kiss-close.

Tamara drew a deep, quivering breath. Ham would never apologize. Obviously enduring his immaturity was the price she must pay if she planned to become his wife.

What could she say that would break his sulk, yet assure her, within her heart, that *she* was the victor? Shaping phrases in her mind, she opened her lips to speak.

They spoke at the same moment, their words mingling in a murmur, erupting on tearful laughter, then quieting with a kiss made fiercely sweet by the alienation of the endless afternoon.

⁍⁍⁍ ⁌⁌⁌

Straightening from the kneading board, Afene pressed the back of her hand to her forehead and sighed. She was so tired, and not only physically, not even *primarily* physically.

As her parents lay dying of pestilence, she had learned that emotional draining was more wearying by far than any physical work. When there was nourishment to be given, painstakingly, drop by drop; when wastes must be dumped, then buried to prevent the spread of disease; when there were fouled clothing and bed clothes to be laundered and laid in the sun for drying, for warming, for sweetening, she'd felt energized. It was when there was nothing physical to be accomplished, when she must simply sit, and watch, and grieve, and remember, and wait, that she felt defeated.

It had been difficult to see her mother's bloom deteriorate to the parchment of dried petals; to watch her father's cheeks sink and crease like old, cracked leather; to look for remembered luster in their eyes and read only dullness; to search unsuccessfully for some sign of energy in those atrophied limbs or some symptom of strength in those wavering voices. But the waiting had been worse.

This current waiting, this emotional draining, was the same, yet not the same.

Father Noah and Japheth firmly believed that the time of the flood was near. When her loneliness was most acute, she fervently hoped so. However, until then the tension that affected Father Noah, increased Great-Grandfather Methusaleh's ramblings, and deepened the lines of Mother Kyral's forehead also afflicted Afene.

Of course Japheth was most directly to blame for her disquiet. Not, she hurriedly amended her thinking, that "blame" was an accurate term. Japheth, like each of them, simply followed Yahweh's directives.

Well, not Ham. Ham was too busy hiding sandals under sleeping pallets and courting silly little Tamara to show any true grasp of Yahweh's plan, or any real conception of how it was speeding toward fruition.

When Japheth had spoken with Ham, it had been like trying to reason with a mischievous child. Besides, as Yahweh's appointed evangelist, Japheth had his own work to do.

"Speak to all you meet," Father Noah had exhorted. "Warn of the approaching disaster. Plead with our neighbors to change their ways, to give their allegiance to Yahweh, and so find a haven on the ark."

But it was a waste of time. Japheth hadn't won a single convert. And, in the meantime, what of her? She could only work in the house, readying their most important possessions for what might well be a speedy departure.

Sometimes she even talked to herself. Who else was there?

Japheth had forbidden friendships with the ungodly women living on all sides. And she hadn't really minded. It sickened her to hear of their "religious" practices—orgies, more accurately. And even though she tried to shut her ears to the sordid details, they lingered in her mind like decaying food, sullying her thoughts, even when she and Japheth spoke of love. Because her parents and then Japheth and his parents had carefully sheltered her from the darker evils of their surroundings, she had rested, all of her life, in protected innocence. Perhaps that was why, when some detail of perversion intruded into her consciousness, she couldn't easily discard it.

She was eager for the end . . . and the beginning.

The flood must come.

Japheth must be restored to her to share long periods of deep, loving conversation. He must work with her as Maelis and Shem worked—side by side, constantly. Maelis often prepared the tablets of wet clay, wiping clean a stylus grown awkward by drying clumps, pausing to rest a hand on Shem's shoulder as she leaned beside him. Whether she was actually reading or simply admiring the evenness of the symbols, Afene couldn't know.

But how she coveted Maelis that closeness!

Had Shem's duties taken him afield, as Japheth's did, she might have spent more time with Maelis, whose bulk made her own angularity appear almost feminine. With Maelis there was no threat as there would be with dainty, pretty Tamara, if she ever grew less flighty, more willing to be involved in women's talk.

Certainly Tamara and Ham were well-matched, although what life on the ark with those two would be like was something Afene couldn't begin to imagine. Even in the breadth of the city, their foolishness intruded. Their clamor annoyed. On the ark the temptation to tie them together— squalling and still squabbling—and throw them overboard might be too strong to resist.

But she would endure even their childishness simply to be done with the waiting and the loneliness.

Whenever she described her aloneness, Japheth urged, "Visit my mother. When you complain to me, I feel powerless. Besides, it breaks my concentration. And my work is difficult enough." Daily, new bruises attested to that.

Of course, she hadn't been complaining, only informing. She never complained.

Once Mother Kyral, sipping peppermint tea, had sighed, "Afene, my dear, never have I known anyone more long-suffering." Afene had felt that she was sincere, just as when she said that she'd never seen floors scrubbed so close to extinction as Afene's. Cleanliness, Afene knew, was her greatest virtue.

That, and never complaining.

But when Japheth could see, day after day, that his efforts were wasted on the infidels, didn't it seem reasonable that he spend more time with her, the one he loved above life itself? "But if we reach one soul, my love," he would say, his dark eyes eloquent with pleading. "To save one soul for Yahweh is worth any sacrifice I can make."

And, apparently, it was worth any sacrifice of hers, as well.

Well, she wasn't too certain she'd trust a conversion, at this point. How many hundreds of years had Noah been lecturing and exhorting, all to no avail?

And if they should, by some chance, allow others on the ark, where would they find the extra room? And mightn't some wag, pretending conversion, enter the ark to cause mischief? What would Father Noah do then? Throw him overboard?

Hardly!

Knowing he could profit from her insight, she'd tried to discuss many of these possibilities with Japheth. But "visit Mother" he would insist, mechanically, each time she mentioned almost anything.

And she had, at times, visited Mother Kyral and, quite truthfully, enjoyed their time together. Mother Kyral, leading Afene to the herb beds and even into the verges of the woods, had taught her to recognize the best roots and berries for drying and to preserve them in casks and pouches for storage later in the ark.

The shared work had encouraged Afene, one day, to confide to Mother Kyral her deepest, most desperate fear. It was something she'd have hesitated to share even with her own mother, had she lived. It spoke of a woman's most wrenching sadness, her most wretched failure.

It had been a wonderful day. Feathers of cloud brushed the blue, blue sky. A warm breeze caressed, and the scent of summer's rich ripeness evoked thoughts of fragrant lotions.

"On such a day," Mother Kyral exulted, "life can be nothing but good!"

Afene made no answer. The quiet tears of a sleepless early morning still weighted her heart.

"What is it, my child? A burden shared is a burden cut into bite-sized chunks."

"I fear . . ."

"Yes, yes. We all fear something."

"It seems certain . . ."

"Little is certain, my child."

"I know, or think I know . . ." Afene drew a harsh, trembling breath, then blurted, "Mother Kyral, I am barren."

Her disclosure could, Afene knew, give cause for divorce—or worse, the taking of a second, fertile wife. And how could she ever surrender Japheth or share him without complaint? Not that there was much of him to share, with his evangelistic obsession . . .

But Mother Kyral, patting and crooning, held her close. "Oh, my dear, dear child," she soothed. "There are years and years in which Yahweh will grant you children! Only consider how difficult it would be to care for little ones when the flood comes! Why," and she chuckled comfortably, "we'd be fishing them out of the water, soaking wet and sniffling, only to have them go overboard again, and again!"

Afene was startled into laughter.

Following that visit, it became almost habitual to seek her mother-in-law's comfort in this sensitive area. And their deepening relationship allowed her to see herself as a fuller partner than either Maelis or Tamara.

Still, Afene yearned for companionship with women nearer her own age. But even if confinement on the ark made friendship with the other young wives improbable, she wouldn't complain. There would be no reason for complaining since Japheth could never be far away.

⫸ ⫷

Shem, surrounded by sunlight but rigid with displeasure, stood in the doorway.

Maelis breathed a silent sigh. *What now?* she wondered, not deeply concerned. She was accustomed to her husband's moods and resigned to her role as pacifier.

From the beginning, from the moment she'd first known that she and the other young wives had been chosen by Yahweh, she'd recognized in each of them qualities required during the time in the ark, and beyond. On dull days, when depression settled about them, clarifying loss, Tamara's little-girlness would brighten their gloom.

Certainly, with the four couples, Grandfather Lamech, and who knew how many others confined in such quarters, clutter could soon become filth. But Afene would never tolerate that.

Maelis had always known that she herself was not beautiful, like Tamara. Nor would she ever be a compulsive housekeeper, like Afene. But her own less obvious role, Maelis knew, would be fully as essential in a cramped environment.

She would moderate Shem's arrogance.

It wasn't that he meant to be insufferable. It was simply that he indulged his calling, as he understood it, as Keeper of the Faith. Japheth's evangelistic zeal could never neutralize Shem's cold disdain for those who refused to believe. In the area of service to Yahweh, Shem tolerated no vacillation, conceded no progression or gradation of devotion, recognized no possibility for forgiveness.

At times he directed his vexation even toward members of the family. She could understand his frustration with Ham. Her own calmness was ruffled often by Ham's unswerving immaturity. But Shem also mumbled at his mother's refusal to delight in the prospect of life aboard the ark. He

grumbled that it would be better if Japheth memorized Enoch's inflexible edicts concerning the godless than continue
his vain efforts to save them. And, only moments earlier,
he'd disputed Father Noah's approach to building.

At such times Maelis must smooth Shem's bristling. She
must reason, cajole, plead when necessary—whatever was
required to keep peace.

Catching her glance on him, he turned, "You think me too
harsh," he accused, but gently. He was always tender with
her.

"I find you . . . perhaps . . . overzealous."

"But when can zeal for Yahweh be a fault?"

"When it wounds. When it diverts the devotion of
others," she replied as gently as he had spoken.

"Even pagans are . . . 'devoted' in their worship of idols."

"In their case, then, be zealous. But your *father* . . ."

"He goes to the ark after eating," his tone had saddened,
"without cleansing his hands!"

She allowed herself a smile. "Father Noah, too, is zealous.
His work calls him. He has no time for washing."

"But, the *ark!*"

"The ark isn't an altar for worship."

"Still, it is *Yahweh's* ark! Yahweh will visit us there!"

She asked softly, "And who gave Father Noah instructions
for its building?"

"Yahweh, as you well know," Shem mumbled a bit pee-
vishly.

"And what were those instructions?"

He sighed, indicating that he knew her knowledge to be
as broad as his; she was simply putting him through a cat-
echism as though he were a younger brother.

"He specified dimensions. Materials."

"And what was His rule about the washing of hands?"
She waited.

Another sigh would denote simple defeat. A smile would
prove his restoration to good humor. But his surrender was
less complete.

"It's unseemly," he insisted.

Only rarely did she fail to intercept his displeasure before it reached its targets. Then, she must rush in, not to argue or to challenge, but to petition for forbearance with glances, an expression or a cautionary hand to his shoulder or forearm.

After such confrontations, she would walk slowly to the house, dampen a cloth, and lie with its coolness against her forehead until the tension eased.

She was careful that Shem never know the toll his domineering demanded of her emotions. And she felt that none of the others had guessed—except for Mother Kyral.

Not much missed Mother Kyral.

Maelis smiled. Shem, relaxed and moving from the doorway, patted her in passing. She could suspend her role as mediator—at least for the moment.

❧❧❧ ❦❦❦

Kyral breathed deeply of flower-scented air. She could identify rose fragrance, leftover lilac, and—gardenia? Perhaps. If she had a favorite time of the day, surely this would be it, when the sun angled downward from its zenith, promising quiet, inviting laziness, allowing her to anticipate those gentle moments of evening when Noah and she would sit together conversing quietly. Those times when sharing was too deep for speech were better still.

Dear Noah . . .

Unbidden, the remembrance of Doreya's bruises shattered her quiet joy. A prayer without words swirled. Was she expressing gratitude that she'd been spared a husband's abuse? (She shut her mind to memories of those childhood abuses she hadn't escaped.) Or was she pleading that Doreya might yet know a husband's tenderness? (Then what of the countless other women who suffered? And what of those men equally victimized by their lusts and angers? What of the children . . .)

The prayer disintegrated into sighing, as she'd come to expect when her load of concern grew unwieldy. When approaching Yahweh with the cares of her own small world—Noah, the boys and their wives, Tamara, Doreya and her little Grena—she felt almost competent.

But the pressure of heartache overwhelmed when she added that larger, more threatening society.

Forgive my weakness, she prayed inwardly. *It's only . . .*

"I understand," came the answer.

Sighing, she yearned to lean into Yahweh's omniscience and be content.

But I don't understand, her thoughts protested.

There was humor in His response. "Can't it be enough that I do?"

Of course it couldn't. He'd fashioned their minds for questioning, for growth. Spreading her arms, she strained to convey the confinement she felt. It was as though her fear of closed spaces had turned inward, as though she yearned to burst from the shell of self.

He interrupted her groping for expression. "You can't save them all. Only think how Noah has argued, and for so long a time! Only watch Japheth, as he reasons against their evil." A sigh. "And I . . . *I* have pleaded, and threatened, and agonized . . ."

She had never heard such pain in any human voice.

O my Lord! She longed to comfort Him, as He had so often soothed her fears, eased her pain, answered her uncertainties. Here was a new dimension of understanding—that Yahweh, who was all-powerful, could also experience defeat.

"Their hearts are stone," He sighed, "harder than stone. Their eyes are blind. Their ears dull, clogged. Their emotions congealed."

Not all of them, she began.

"I, too, love Doreya and Grena," He said.

Unexpectedly, she sensed a withdrawal of His presence. Frowning, she wondered why, then shrugged. Perhaps He merely wanted to be alone.

And she had work to finish.

She had always loved the fragrance of freshly dried laundry, smelling of sun and breeze. On such a day, the fibers seemed to capture the aroma of blossoms, retaining them for hours. She worked slowly, savoring the sunlit task, storing its flavors against that time when she must go inside to prepare the evening meal.

Coverlets, robes, linen cloths, each had adopted the contours of the particular bush where she had draped it. One woven scarf caught on a thorn, snagging. She stretched the fabric, easing the pulled thread into place. Last of all, gathering Noah's robe, she laid it softly atop the pile. The cloth shone with the luster of the fleeces from which it had been woven.

And the pitch . . . well, the pitch would likely be there forever, a reminder that, in Doreya's words, even Noah wasn't quite perfect.

Breathing deeply, storing green and blue, birdsong, and fragrance in her heart, Kyral smiled.

"Perfect enough," she murmured, and was content.

2

What a perfect day for a wedding, Kyral thought as she bustled from her oven to the outdoor tables to the small arbor she and the daughters-in-law had decorated with ferns and vines, with bright blossoms of hibiscus, rose, and poinsettia, and with twined garlands. Even the birds seemed to sing more joyously in the morning quietness, devoid—for once—of the sounds of adze-strokes and hammerblows.

On rising Noah had dressed in his finest robe. Its embroidered border of dark purple grapes, magenta and crimson pomegranates, and leaves of deep blue-green testified to Kyral's skill in rich dyes. Doreya had suggested, and added, the fine twining tracery of delicate gold thread.

He turned slowly, and Kyral approved his appearance with a smile. "The ark can wait through one more wedding, my dear," he said shyly. Loving him with such intensity that her vision clouded with tears, she leaned into his embrace.

For Shem's wedding day she'd had to beg Noah to suspend work. For Japheth's, he'd grumbled, "I suppose I'm expected to waste the day, again."

Perhaps not quite perfect yet, she thought fondly, *but getting closer, every day.*

"I'd have worn the new robe, m'dear, but somehow someone stained it with pitch."

She smiled. "You look very handsome. They'll think you're the bridegroom."

His laughter was hearty, booming, warm. "Not likely I'd take another bride," he growled, his fingertips pressing into her back, straining to draw her closer still.

What a waste, she thought, that this mood must surrender to baking, spreading wedding linens, and sputtering over guests. She murmured, "So much to do."

They separated lingeringly.

"How can I help?" he asked.

She tried to think of a way where he wouldn't be underfoot. Dear man, he was more at home with the broad blows of a mallet than with delicate pots and plates.

"Help Shem with the trestles," she suggested, at last. She turned at the doorway. "Poor Tamara, poor child," she sighed.

"With me for a father-in-law?" he teased, "or with Ham as a husband?" Then he, too, sobered. "Her father and she were so close. He'd have been proud to see her as a bride." He paused. "Though I always fancied he preferred Cloyren to our Ham."

"He only wanted Ham to grow past foolishness, as we do."

Noah's voice deepened. "And sometimes I despair . . ."

She returned to touch his arm. "Never despair, my love. And especially not on a day such as this."

❧❧❧ ❦❦❦

Maelis stood apart, her lips pursed, to view Tamara from all angles. What a beautiful child she was! Once she'd grown past posturing and pouting, what a lovely woman she would become!

In ordinary times, a mature Tamara would have been assured of lifelong admiration from men and women alike. But now, necessarily, her circle of future admirers must be limited to those few the ark could carry.

Whenever thoughts of that future forced themselves upon

her, Maelis felt no vindication or smugness that she and Shem would be among the saved. Rather, she knew a drenching sadness, a draining sense of loss. She had a certain knowledge that, evil as they might be in the sight of Yahweh (and of Shem), each of those people who had brushed her life had left her richer. How could she discount such moments of touching, such shared humanhood, as a smile, a soft word, a snatch of melody hummed by a child, a tear excited by laughter or celebration, a spot of sunshine shared, kindness shown in tragedy. How could she not grieve for the lives to be lost in that terrible flood!

She thought of Ainna, clumsy with the infirmities of age, disease, and drunkenness. As she careened along the narrow streets, Ainna threatened those who ridiculed with swipes of her club, yet never broke stride or bawdy lyric, and seldom anything else more serious than a nose or collarbone. Despite Ainna's obvious failings, Maelis recognized her courage, her refusal to bow to adversity.

And there was Kaben, as twisted in his mind as in his expression. One side of his pale face was frozen into a perpetual sneer; spittle drooled from the useless half of his mouth. Trapping unwary young girls with a net and wooden paddle, he declared his intentions in garbled but graphic detail. Since his useless arm curved inward and one leg dragged behind him like a wounded snake, the weakest maiden could have escaped. However, surely for the sake of attention and excitement, they often screamed and thrashed and threatened.

Still more than once Maelis had seen Kaben pause to help an amputee whose crutch had slipped from beneath him, or to steady an old woman who'd stumbled into a ditch, her bowl of apples swimming in sewage, or to comfort a child lost from its parent. Once, his grotesque face further twisted by empathy for a coyote pup caught in a trap, he'd solicited aid from hooting passersby. Only she had paused, had freed the coyote, and tugged Kaben to his feet. And for her trouble, he'd caught up his net and tried to loop it over *her!*

There were so many others, those in whom she'd seen

chinks or glimmers of goodness. If *she* were aware of them, then surely Yahweh . . .

Shem would have pronounced such thoughts blasphemous.

Are You displeased with me, Yahweh? she often asked. *These people are Your creations! However diluted it might be, however adulterated or abased, they exhale Your breath. If they would turn to You, You would still embrace them, wouldn't You? Couldn't the ark expand to hold as many as would reach out to accept Your safety? I cannot hate these people, my Lord, nor can I bear it if You do! Though You hate their sinning (and I must, too, since it grieves You), please, as the waters cover them, as they cry out in dying, assure me that You, too, will feel anguish.*

All had been children once, born into that sweet innocence. Even Ainna had once cooed lovingly against a mother's breast. And surely Kaben had once tried to catch butterflies and falling stars with the same fervor he now turned toward young women. Surely the most depraved among them had once touched a flower with wonder at its softness and color, and felt a sad loss when its petals drooped. Yahweh knew better than she the corruptive, corrosive elements that twisted and damaged. If they'd been blessed with her rearing, mightn't the others, too, have developed in a manner more akin to His will?

She grieved especially for the children who were still children. They retained that flexibility, that tenderness, that scarcely tarnished innocence which would allow their souls to melt in love and their knees to bow in worship.

There was one in particular—she had never known his name—who when Noah moved building materials was often first in the pack appearing from nowhere. Shouting, shoving, claiming any available space, most would launch themselves toward the cart. Swinging their legs from the sides and back, calling to Noah to "giddyap," they scuffled and sang their tuneless songs.

This one waif—not content with that—would, when quite young, walk close beside Noah. With one thumb tucked in his mouth, which somehow managed to smile in spite of the barrier, he tugged at the hem of Noah's tunic. Noah had taken to carrying the boy on his shoulders, occasionally jouncing a bit, to the child's delight, or prancing, bucking, even braying. That had continued for perhaps two years, until, laid on his pallet with a wrenched back, Noah was at Kyral's mercy.

"When will you learn?" she scolded, her hand dripping the ointment that filled the house with its eucalyptus odor.

"He's just a child, m'dear."

"Yet growing all the time."

He winced under her probing fingertips. "There. There's the spot." And then, "He grows only a little each day."

"As you grow older and more decrepit 'only a little' each day."

"Decrepit, m'dear?"

Maelis, helping about the kitchen area, smiled at the pain in his voice. Carefully not turning, still she could sense Kyral's reaction, which communicated itself in soft murmurs and chucklings.

"Then I'll promise," she heard him say.

But Kyral, not quite mollified, tut-tutted until she'd completed the odorous massage. With a final pat, she ordered, "And here you stay, for at least three days."

"Who'll do the work," he grumbled, "if I lie here harking to the laments of women?"

Smiling, Maelis knew that she'd been lumped into the complaint only for Noah's protection.

"Fortunately Yahweh's patience is much broader than yours, my lord. It's not that you must complete the ark before the flood comes, but that the flood will come when the ark's complete."

Noah grumbled something that closed with the word *riddles*, and Kyral joined Maelis in preparations for baking.

"He loves the children so," Kyral said later, as she stood by the oven. "And I think he keeps hoping that this one and that one will yet come to Yahweh. How it pains him—and annoys me—when a few short years beyond his enduring their play, they're pelting him with clods and pebbles."

But the one nameless waif, whose increasing weight had troubled Noah's back, never joined the gangs of hecklers. Maelis had seen him crouching beside Noah, holding wooden pegs between his teeth, then producing them solemnly, while Noah received each with equal ceremony. She'd smiled at the boy's desire to help, though progress on casements and shelves slowed in the process.

And then there was the day when the child caught a splinter in his lower lip and, blinking back tears, held steady while Noah removed it. And, not much later, a woman, dragging the boy behind her, had spewed oaths while she battered Noah about the head and shoulders with a wooden ladle.

As far as Maelis knew, the child had never neared Noah or the ark again. Once or twice she'd noticed him hanging pensively on the fringes, though never with the mobs who ridiculed or harassed. Eventually she hadn't seen him at all.

"Maelis! Why do you stand there like a stump! The wedding's today, remember!"

Starting, Maelis suspended such thinking for later, when she fully intended to approach Yahweh on that nameless waif's behalf. She smiled an apology, and Tamara's pique melted into bright-eyed enchantment.

"*Today!* I can't believe it, can you? Were you this . . . this . . ." Tamara trembled.

"On our wedding day?" Maelis asked, lifting Tamara's golden hair and allowing it to drift as it would. "Yes, of course I was excited—and frightened."

"And . . ." Tamara turned to study Maelis' expression, "doubtful?"

Maelis weighed her answer with as much care as she weighed the wealth of curls. "Doubtful of Shem's love? Never. Doubtful of my ability to be a worthy wife? Constantly."

Giggling, Tamara shrugged.

Of course, Maelis thought comfortably. *When you're this*

beautiful, it isn't your own worth you question. She began brushing the web-like hair, twisting it, experimenting.

"Ham's mother suggested that I ask you," Tamara confided. "She said that no one else could do hair half so well. And *you* have beautiful hair, too! Did you realize that?"

"I've been told so," Maelis answered mildly. Someday, when she knew Tamara better, she might confide that in those awkward growing years she'd been able to tolerate herself only because of her luxuriant hair.

"It's the color of polished chestnuts," Mother Kyral had insisted many times. "It's like the movement of gentle waves," her own mother had whispered, drawing frail fingers down its length as she lay dying. "It has the texture of cords to bind my heart forever," Shem sometimes said, in their moments of deepest love.

"Maelis," Tamara scolded, apparently too happy to be truly sharp. "You're such a dreamer today! Are you thinking of how lovely my wedding will be?"

"That, among other things," Maelis murmured, and gave total attention to the improbable task of making Tamara more beautiful than she already was.

Later, as Tamara craned her neck to see more of herself than was humanly possible, Maelis decided, "There was never a more beautiful bride!"

"You're certain?"

"I'm positive!"

"It's because of my hair," Tamara exulted, and hugged Maelis around her ample waist.

Maelis felt bulky and awkward, as she always did in the presence of smaller, lighter girls, but only mildly so. Years before she'd come to terms with herself, and just as she'd never think of shunning others on the basis of appearance, neither would she shun herself.

And Tamara's hair *was* beautifully dressed! Ignoring its flyaway fullness, Maelis had brushed it to an even richer sheen, braided it with a delicate flowering vine she'd found tracing a stone wall, and coaxed the thick braids into a coronet. Because the formal style defied a natural tendency toward curling, small tendrils of fine hair had escaped to lie in damp ringlets at Tamara's temples and at the nape of her neck.

Her always bright coloring heightened by excitement, Tamara seemed incapable of quietness. She turned, danced, twirled. The gossamer whiteness of her robe floated, rippled, flared. And small, fragile shells, gathered on a golden thread and draped about her neck and tiny waist, reflected iridescence in the bright sunlight.

"I'm so happy," Tamara began, then suddenly stilled. Her shoulders slumping, eyes wide and dewy, her lower lip trembling, she whispered, "If only my dear, dear father were still alive."

And Maelis, careful of hair and shells and dress, caught and held her tightly and comforted with small pats and crooning.

It had been ten months since Tamara's father had fallen to his death from the ledge that was her sanctuary. Both Tamara and Ham had been with him.

"There's a special stone," he'd said excitedly. "It's silver-gray, but streaked with pink and black. And when the sun shines from a certain angle, the rays ignite sparks of mica. It would be perfect for my little girl's front entrance."

Tamara knew the stone. She had, in fact, pointed it out to her father years before. And while she'd forgotten, he'd remembered.

So like him . . .

Ham, in an expansive mood that day with the house so nearly completed, smiled indulgently. "Will we need a cart?"

"Between the two of us, we can carry it."

"And I could help!" She gave a skip of excitement.

They regarded her with matching smiles of amusement, and Ham bent to kiss her. "You always help me, my love, simply by lighting the world around me."

Her father chuckled approvingly.

He's beginning to like Ham, she thought. *Marvelous! My two favorite men in the whole world!*

Tolerance diminished, however, as they worked to pry the flat rock from the hardened soil.

"You'll break it!" her father grumbled, pushing Ham to one side. "Why must you attack everything? Whenever will you learn that gentleness can be stronger than force?"

His look of concern touched Tamara, who tried to reassure him by smiling, by moving into Ham's arms—once she'd maneuvered them from their position of sulking. Still, her father frowned as he pried patiently and tested, lifted, and pried again at the unexpectedly stubborn rock. Perhaps it was because of his preoccupation that he forgot care, the narrowness of the ledge, the sheer plunge to the valley floor.

Why hadn't Ham thought to warn him, as the soil finally surrendered its prize? Why hadn't *she?* There'd been time enough.

The rock had come free slowly. His feet solid on the ledge, her father stood there holding it. With a glowing expression he regarded her, surely anticipating her pleasure.

And then . . . he turned toward Ham, and stepped backward.

Ham reached to steady him, but his fingers touched rock, brushed cloth, clawed air.

Thousands of times the next moments, each seeming an eternity, had replayed themselves in Tamara's memory. Her father, tipped off-balance, his arms flailing, never relinquished the precious rock—her doorstep—until both feet had lost their moorings. While he'd turned and twisted in midair, like a spinning toy, growing smaller, she stared in disbelief—clutching Ham, and he her. Their startled screams merged with her father's . . . his dying in echoes far below in a rattle of loosened rocks.

She had wanted to hide her eyes, but couldn't. She had yearned to follow this man she loved best of all, but Ham caught her, held her, comforted her with uncharacteristic gentleness.

"Oh, my sweet, sweet love," he said brokenly. "All the houses in the world aren't worth such a loss!"

At last, he had coaxed her from the ledge. They must get

help to retrieve that dear, shattered body before wild animals could desecrate it, he insisted. They must grieve with her mother and neighbors, he explained. They must bury the lifeless form . . . and try to suppress the memory of those terrifying moments.

Tamara's mother was resting in the courtyard when Ham approached, tentatively, with Tamara, sodden and unstable, stumbling behind him.

"So you got her pregnant," she accused coldly. "I never expected she'd make it to your marriage bed intact. So, what am I supposed to do about it? Tell her father. He shares your blame." And she turned as though to enter the house.

Tamara, bursting into fresh tears, plunged ahead, and cast herself blindly at her mother's feet. Carefully, lips curled with distaste, her mother stepped aside. "Take your whore to your own house," she ordered Ham. "I'll send her things."

Ham, frowning, frozen, seemed incapable of response.

"He's dead," Tamara blurted. "Father's dead."

Silence pulsed. Then, in a slow-drawn breath, her mother whispered harshly, "How did you . . . finally . . . manage to kill him?"

Ham jerked forward, then, his hand extended, but her caustic glance impaled him, stopping him in mid-movement. Her eyes were wide, but dry. "She's been killing him for years," she said tonelessly. " 'Do this for me, Daddy.' 'Do that for me, Daddy.' " Crumpling, she sank to a bench. "Was it . . . his heart?"

Ham shook his head. "He . . ." He cleared his throat to try again.

"He fell from the ledge!" Tamara shrieked. "And *yes!* He was doing something for me! He was getting a rock . . . a rock . . ." For a moment, only, she found the strength to stand, to arch over her mother's shrinking form in a parody of triumph. Then, sobbing bitterly, she fell into her mother's arms, murmuring in heartbroken monotony, "I killed him. I did kill him. And I loved him so . . ."

And her mother—for the first time and the last—held her, stroking her back, soothing, "Oh Tamara. Oh, darling. It's all right, child. We'll see this through together . . ."

But only moments later, coldness restored and distance intensified by the momentary warmth, she turned away, dismissing them by her silence.

During the funeral and the flurry of condolences, she might have been alone in mourning. That same day immediately following the burial, Tamara's belongings were heaped on the doorstep, and the house barred against her. "How can I care?" Tamara asked Ham, but her eyes were haunted. "That woman was never my mother. She was only my father's wife."

She found quarters with an aunt, her father's widowed sister, and in a few hours had nearly erased her mother from her thoughts. But it was many months before her dreaming could replace her father's dying screams with the gentler memories of his love.

There had never been a day more suited to a wedding! The sky, as blue as deep, deep waters (but no match, Ham insisted, for the color of Tamara's eyes), arched above a world of verdant foliage, exotic blossoms, and the wedding arbor. A gilding of sunlight lit Tamara's braided hair to the brilliance of burnished brass.

Her remembered grief had been short-lived; her laughter was light and excited, a music which—she noted with pleasure—brought smiles to all lips but her mother's.

Unexpectedly her mother had attended, arriving alone, sheathed in mourning clothes, her lips and cheeks garish with cosmetics. She had come, not to share her joy, Tamara was certain, but more likely to blight it.

Shrugging, Tamara flitted about, charming everyone else. She especially needed to charm Cloyren—if he came—to teach him, once and forever, that she was a prize men would die to possess.

Their most recent meeting still rankled. She'd been picking berries for a special wedding pastry. Actually, she'd been *plucking* more than picking, since she and Ham had just fought another small skirmish. It seemed better to snag her fingers on briars and damage a bush or two than to risk another extended sulk so close to their wedding day.

Thinking herself alone, she snarled at the birds who challenged her right to the patch, glowered at the sunshine that blinded her just where the fruit was thickest, and cursed decisively when blood oozed from a fingertip.

"Ah! The happy bride." The words dripped with sarcasm. She scowled beneath a shading hand. Cloyren regarded her with his head to one side. The quirk of his mouth threatened laughter.

"Happier than if *you* were the groom!" she snapped.

Moving closer, he captured her arms. "Are you so very sure?" he whispered, his breath warm in her ear. And those thousand images recurred—of their times together, of her racing blood . . .

Resolutely, she jerked away, and the berries spilled. "Now, see what you've done!" Tears stung her eyes. She swiped at them angrily.

"Tears," he said tenderly, "over a few berries?" And then, "Berry stain becomes you."

He gathered her into his arms. And she stayed there, feeling comforted, and shamed, as she permitted him to kiss the berry juice from her eyelids and his fingertips strayed from shoulder blade to waistline.

"You beautiful little whore," he whispered through laughter. "I could take you now, if I wanted you. I can take you whenever and wherever I please, no matter what vows you make to that red-bearded boor."

She struggled against him then, battering ineffectually at his chest with her fists. "No one . . . ever . . . called . . . me . . ." but she couldn't bring herself to repeat the hateful word. "*No one!*" Despite her struggle, he held her easily, and she wondered why she had ever thought his arms weak.

"Perhaps not in your hearing," he scoffed, and released her so swiftly that she stumbled backward into a bush, sprawling there.

His laughter excited new anger. No one had ever treated her with such scorn. Were her father still alive . . .

"And yet . . ." his long, cool fingers caressed her cheek, "I could still enjoy you, I think. When you tire of that oaf, just let me know, my sweet, and I'll welcome you . . ."

"As a second wife?" she spat. "*Never!*"

"Never as a second wife," he agreed, and amusement warped his parting words. "Only as a concubine."

She had never felt so diminished, so stained. She'd wanted to rush to the river to wash there, to scrub away his touch. But she'd realized, even then, that it would take more than water or sand to erase the wound to her pride. Even as the memory spun through the brilliant sunshine of her wedding day, she felt her face warming.

"My darling little girl."

It was Ham, looking handsome in his new, cream-colored robe, its hem embroidered in purple and gold. His beard was neat. (She had seen Maelis trimming it.) His eyes were shining. And, yes, his fingernails were spotless.

"You are most beautiful," he said, "when excitement brings that color to your cheeks." And he kissed her warm blush, while she allowed him to believe that his nearness had caused it.

As the music began, as conversation hushed, as Grandfather Lamech, Father Noah, and Ham took their places in the latticed shadow of the arbor, Afene nestled against Japheth. His hand sought, found, and clasped hers.

A flush of warmth swept through her. This was the closeness she craved, the closeness that would never diminish again once they'd entered the ark.

Soon, Yahweh? she prayed.

For Afene any wedding ceremony melted away the years, supplanting the current scene with the remembered. How excited she had been the day she and Japheth spoke their vows beneath an arbor much like this one. Her breathing had quickened to the music of harps plucked softly, throbbingly. The occasional rattle of tambourines created a rhythm that her pulse repeated. The scents of flowers—nicotiana, gardenias, roses, lilies—had drugged her senses. The gentle longing in Japheth's eyes began a soaring sensation that raised her to her tiptoes and rippled through her heart. Like lifting foliage, she was caught in an upward breeze. The power of her joy was like the surging of waves approaching shore. Her words were transformed to unintelligible buzzing; excited laughter trembled on her lips.

She felt beautiful.

"You are beautiful!" Japheth said, capturing her hand in his until she thought the bones would crumble.

She felt desirable.

"I desire to share my life only with you," he whispered.

Bone of his bone . . . flesh of his flesh, they would cling only to one another, sharing all that life offered, whatever its joy or sadness. Yet how could life ever be sad with Japheth at her side, with Japheth loving her?

Her parents had still lived, although the shadow of death already lay in her mother's wanness and the slight hesitation of her walk. Already she leaned heavily on any available arm. Afene's father stabilized and affirmed her. Instinctively, it seemed, he sensed when support was required.

Japheth would be as sensitive to her needs once the flood came.

Soon . . . soon? Yahweh?

Then, of all women, Afene would know herself most blessed, just as she had realized at the moment of their marriage vows, just as she recognized now with Japheth's firm hand on hers. And just as she fully suspected even when he was out of sight at his work. She smiled as Tamara approached the altar.

Japheth's absences would soon end, now that the ark was fully under cover. Layer after layer of pitch coated every timber, inside and out. Once they were in the ark, once their new lives had begun, nothing could mar her joy in her husband, and in their children.

The familiar constriction caught in her throat.

But they *would* have children. Mother Kyral was convinced. And it wouldn't make sense, would it, for Yahweh to select a barren woman, since His new world must be populated?

She hugged herself with excitement, and Japheth squeezed her arm.

"It's a beautiful ceremony, isn't it?" he whispered.

She hadn't noticed. But observing, she had to admit that it was, perhaps nearly as beautiful as hers and Japheth's had been. Of course, Tamara was such a lovely thing, she'd beautify any setting. A pity she was so flighty.

Afene was glad that Cloyren had shown the decency to stay away. What a foul, unnatural man he was! She'd wondered, sometimes, just what he and Tamara had been to one another.

"*Yes!*" Ham shouted to a question usually answered in whispers. Afene blushed for Japheth. How embarrassing to be related to such a fool! Others smiled, but she didn't find it amusing in the least, nor apparently did Methuselah. Shocked from his napping, grumbling above his thin, wobbling beard, he shuffled away in his stooped, shambling gait toward the ark.

Once the questions had been answered, the harps played again—a sprightly tune vibrating with joy. And Ham and Tamara, embracing, twirled round and round until Ham staggered with dizziness and Tamara's braid loosened.

Well, Afene had hoped there would be children in Yahweh's new world. And until someone smaller came along, Ham and Tamara would have to do.

Young people, their laughter vivid and carefree, danced beyond the arbor. Most of the older neighbors had gone home, pausing first to kiss Tamara's radiant cheek, thump Ham on the arm, thank Kyral for the lovely food, and—a trifle warily—nod to Noah.

Kyral smiled at their diffidence. They reacted to Noah with mingled fear and respect, as though he were an extension of the ark rather than merely its builder. And perhaps he was. Both stood undaunted in the face of ridicule. Both wore Yahweh's aura of impregnability.

Sighing, she studied the littered low tables and benches.

She'd tend to them later. First, she would take a moment to absorb, to remember, to consider.

How would Ham and Tamara weather the problems ahead? Today, they were like two sprites, prancing to the music, their faces flushed, their eyes bright. They might be as light as flower petals, they moved so effortlessly, nearly airborne. Could they understand that they might never again experience a day so fully their own? So wholly joyous?

Did any of them realize—truly—what lay ahead? Perhaps it was better they didn't.

Even Noah seemed freed from his weight of responsibility. Not once, except when Methusaleh stamped toward it, had she seen him glance toward the ark. Surely they'd all needed this day of music and laughter, this respite from which, later, their souls could feed.

She could no longer dismiss the flood as a figment of Noah's dreaming. Yahweh had told her firmly, unequivocally, what to expect. All these people—these friends— would be lost.

She closed her eyes in anticipated pain. Those young people, sharing with Ham and Tamara, perhaps planning their own weddings, their own lives together, would be lost to the flood.

All those young mothers and fathers, laughing as their children—their faces smeared with sweets—created new dance steps with wild loops and spins.

They, too, would perish.

And Tamara's mother, would she be lost also? She sat alone, arms crossed tightly against her thin chest as though to hold everyone out. Or was she holding something in, perhaps her dislike for this daughter? All these months she had grieved alone for the husband whose love she'd alienated by striving to hoard it. Poor, sad woman. Was it possible she'd welcome the deluge to wash her from such a dissatisfied existence?

I should go to her, Kyral thought. The mothers of the bride and groom . . . But even as she was willing her feet to move, Tamara's mother looked up and straightened haughtily. Gathering her mourning robe more closely about her, she left. Kyral sighed.

"Never mind," a soft voice spoke at Kyral's elbow, "happiness makes her ill." Doreya, stooping to gather crumpled linens, salvaged a lost crumb of spicy cake and murmured approval. "It was a lovely day, my friend."

Kyral smiled. "It will be as lovely, one day, for Grena . . ."

She broke off. The flood would occur long before Grena was of marriageable age. But in any event there would be no such joyful day for Doreya's child. In a drunken stupor, her father had promised her to Shumri. Kyral shuddered at the thought.

Shumri was a tradesman, oily and lecherous, his puffy face pitted with the ravages of social disease. Three of his six wives had already died of its effects.

"I will kill myself—and her—before I'll see him take her," Doreya had vowed quietly, more than once. Then she added, "But that will be years and years from now!"

Kyral was less certain. She had seen the grace with which Grena moved and the sweetness of her expression. She had noted the shaping of waist and thighs and the suggestion of breasts. But, worse, she had noticed Shumri's noticing.

"Doreya, my friend . . ." Though she tried to make her voice light, concern defeated her efforts.

Doreya paused in the act of brushing crumbs from a bench.

"Come with us," Kyral urged.

Doreya frowned. "Where?"

"On the ark."

Doreya smiled. "I'd *like* to see it one day! Of course, I *see* it, every day, but I haven't been on board since I was a child. What a lovely place it was to hide! Grena's there now with some of her friends."

"I don't mean just to tour it." Kyral caught Doreya's arm. "I've yearned to ask you for years! I love you as my own daughter. And I can't bear the thought . . ." The tears came, followed swiftly by sobs that shook and choked her.

Embracing Kyral, Doreya crooned, " I was afraid of this, that the preparations would be too much for you! You've been under such strain and for far too long. But there, there, cry all you want. Salt tears will set the dye in this new scarf." Laughing softly she whispered further fond nonsense.

Kyral had never loved her more. How could she bear to lose her to the flood?

Dear Yahweh, she prayed silently, *help me to make her understand.*

Resolutely she dried her tears, pulled slightly away, and forced her voice to calmness. If she expected Yahweh to help her, she must be lucid.

"I want you to go with us . . . on the ark, before the flood comes." She paused, then emphasized, "And *stay* with us— you and Grena."

Doreya's lips moved, as though to form speech, but no sound resulted.

"Grena would be safe there," Kyral insisted. "So would you."

"But only for a while! And when we came out . . ." Doreya's eyes widened with terror. "Oh, Kyral, dear friend, I know that you mean well! But Saert wouldn't just beat me. He'd kill us both!"

"But Saert will die—in the flood."

Doreya, her composure regained, once again became the confident caregiver. "You're overwrought, dear Kyral. We'll speak of this again, perhaps. But come, now. Lie down and rest. I'll get a cool cloth for your forehead. And I'll clear the tables."

Sighing, suffering herself to be led, Kyral apologized numbly to Yahweh.

When she was feeling stronger, more rested, more in control, she'd coax this dearest friend to safety.

3

Kyral loved Seventh Days. When she and Noah were newly married, she'd thought it simply a delightful way to ensure more time with her husband. He'd been so handsome then. When she told him so, he colored almost like a girl, neck to hairline. Clearing his throat, he accused her of not being as intelligent as he'd supposed.

She'd admired his expansive shoulders, with no hint of the stoop that distinguished them now, and his strong hands, unmarred then with chisel scars or nails blackened by misplaced hammerblows. But perhaps most intriguing, right from the start, had been his eyes, that mossy brown of a pool's depths when the sun rays slant, igniting sandstone and tortoiseshell and algae. And she loved his broad brow, ever furrowed in thought, which she hoped might, at least sometimes, bend toward her.

Other girls had envied her then. She could read their pouting. Some obviously hoped to sway his attention to themselves. She allowed them to think that his lack of interest stemmed solely from adoration of her rather than, even then, from distraction. Perhaps Yahweh was already planting in Noah's mind germinal plans for the ark. Certainly she recognized early that she must either share Noah's mind and heart with Yahweh or surrender every portion of them. And the more she learned, once she'd grasped the concept

47

of a truly loving Father—one who would never brutalize, as she had once thought all fathers did—the less she feared the competition. Noah was a patient teacher. Seldom fluent or impressive, he was always enthusiastic. Her immediate grasp of the Creation Hymn had delighted him, and when she wept at the tragedy of their earliest ancestors, he caught her to his broad chest and comforted her.

"Only think," she had sobbed, "but for the serpent, we might still live in that marvelous garden!"

And he replied, "But for the willfulness in the hearts of men and women, the serpent would have failed."

That had given her something to think about. For weeks afterward, as she struggled with early housekeeping, she watched for symptoms of willfulness in her own behavior—and found them.

Only willfulness could have caused her, once her mother-in-law had rearranged her kitchen utensils, to restore them to their earlier order, when she knew that some suggestions had merit.

And what but willfulness had caused her to lie one entire sleepless night with her rigid back to Noah simply because he'd neglected her goodnight kiss? When he turned in his sleep and reached for her, she carefully avoided him, then wept because he didn't waken and, guessing her distress, ask its cause.

If that wasn't willfulness, what was?

"I've decided," she said one day, when construction of the ark still lay far in the future and she'd carried their lunch to a field fragrant with grass and wool and fresh-turned earth, "I would almost certainly do as Eve did."

Grinning, he raised an eyebrow. "You like fruit so well?"

"I like flattery," she admitted. "And . . . and I'm willful."

"Hmmm." He observed her with those laughing eyes while he tasted a slice of fresh bread spread with freshly churned curds. "Wonderful bread!" he said. "Surely it's the best I've ever eaten!"

She colored with pleasure.

"You *do* like flattery, don't you?" he teased, and his laughter was so robust and her spluttering so startled that other workers turned to observe them.

She ducked her head to hide the flaming of her face.

"You blush beautifully," he said.

"More flattery!" she muttered into her shielding hands.

"Now . . . how can we test the 'willful' part?"

"If you don't quit teasing, and tell me you love me," she murmured, "I'll feed the rest of this 'wonderful bread' to beggars."

"So quickly proven!"

Tossing her head, she gathered together the basket in which she'd carried the lunch and the linen cloth she'd used to wrap it. But, before she could rise, he caught her, and told her all she'd hoped to hear.

Such times together had deepened their love, but Seventh Days molded their marriage.

She loved them when the children were small, when she could sit to one side and observe Noah as he taught them. Their expressions altered momentarily, as only children's do, with understanding, questioning, excitement, and worship.

But perhaps she loved the Sabbath even more now that the children were grown. At sundown, she would smother her baking fires, the hot stones hissing with bouncing droplets of water. Noah would lay down his tools with a finality that seemed to be almost an act of worship. Then the boys and their wives, all of them scrubbed and freshly-clothed, would join them for prayer and praise.

Of all the week, that evening and the next day were the most peaceful and the most precious—not only in the family's quiet togetherness, but in their remembrance of Yahweh's power and goodness. And they were peaceful despite the fact that all about them life progressed, often more raucously than on ordinary days. Some of the neighbors delighted in disrupting their prayer with taunts and loud clanging sounds and in overriding their hymns of praise with bawdy lyrics. Some even brought their priests to perform ritualistic rites of magic or sacrifice within easy sight.

Others openly performed frenzied dances with one another and with temple prostitutes, while timbrels initiated or imitated the movements of throbbing breasts and gyrating thighs.

"Ignore them," Noah would instruct. "May Yahweh forgive and enlighten them."

Ignoring was more easily said than accomplished, especially when the children were still young and naturally curious. Ham had been the most susceptible, of course. Once, after a particularly obscene dance, she found him examining his naked body and moving his hips experimentally.

She explained that while his body was wonderfully made by Yahweh, and certainly nothing of which he must ever be ashamed, it was also sacred to the uses for which Yahweh had intended it. And she explained that many people—some not necessarily evil, but certainly misguided—didn't or wouldn't understand. In the midst of framing her arguments, she floundered, finding them unconvincing at best and personally embarrassing to the point of panic.

What kind of mother are you? her thoughts demanded harshly, as she knelt before small Ham, adjusting his tunic about him, stilling his thighs with a pat, and suggesting that he have a talk with his father about such things.

Later, feeling helpless and woefully inadequate to the task of motherhood, she asked Noah, "How can they expose themselves so shamelessly? And before impressionable young boys?"

"The sad truth is," Noah sighed, "that they don't spare even their own small children."

With searing pain she remembered her father those several times when cruelty had not been sufficient to satisfy, and he had . . .

"My dear. What is it?" Noah's hands were shaking her arm, his eyes scanning her face. "Are you ill?"

She dragged herself back slowly. "No, not . . . ill."

"Are you certain? You're pale as moonlight."

She nodded, but her knees were as weak as bread dough as he led her to a bench, eased her down, and sank before her. "My love," Noah said gently, "I've explained to Ham, and I think he understands now. And since the ark's begun, soon surely Yahweh will lead us from this evil place. . . ."

His words faded off in concern, and she knew that no ark, no distance, no amount of time could heal completely the wounded memories her father had bequeathed her. And, much as she loved Seventh Days, delighting in their family worship, she approached the next few with trepidation, dreading what fresh obscenities the cruel or depraved might thrust upon them.

Not all their neighbors were callous, though. Some, like Doreya, noted those weekly sunsets and quietly went about their own tasks and conversations. Often, in that relaxed period of waiting for sunset to end Seventh Day and signal another week of work, Doreya would come to sit with Kyral and visit.

"Dear friend," she would often begin, frowning, "please don't be offended by our rituals."

"I scarcely notice," Kyral would usually answer, sometimes even truthfully. "Yahweh fills our hearts and minds. Our ears hear only His words."

More than once, with longing in her voice, Doreya sighed, "Our gods speak only to our priests. Of course," she hastened to add, "the priests tell us what they've said, and it's very exciting sometimes! And . . . sometimes . . ."

"Sometimes?" Kyral prompted.

Usually Doreya shuddered and changed the subject. But once, she ventured, "I was remembering . . ."

Kyral touched her hand. "Tell me."

"No. The gods . . . might be offended."

But Kyral, hoping for an opportunity to tell Doreya of Yahweh, waited. The stillness hummed with distant voices, the music of a lyre, and a sweet, flutelike instrument. There were the sounds of children playing near the ark and the breeze moving gently through foliage.

"It was . . . when our firstborn was sacrificed," Doreya whispered.

Kyral gasped. She'd been told that Doreya's child was

stillborn! "It is tradition," Doreya spoke softly, yet a slight tremor in her voice denied a true belief. "I knew that if it were a son, and if he were perfect, he would be . . ." She cleared her throat. "And yet I grieved. It is not traditional to grieve," she said wryly, "when one has been so honored."

Awkwardly, her mind reeling with the enormity of what she'd heard, Kyral patted Doreya's arm. To lose any child was surely the greatest pain a mother could be called upon to bear, but to see it laid, living, on a blood-spattered stone altar . . . to hear its cries and the thud of the knife . . . and then silence . . . or the chants of worshipers . . .

She flinched. Feeling her hand tighten on Doreya's arm, she willed it to relax.

"Everyone tried to help me. I yearned to tell *you*—my dearest friend—but the gods told the priests that if I did, my womb would be closed forever. Some of the other women spoke of their own early feelings, how they'd passed quickly because they had honored a god, and he would bless them with many children. And he had, of course, so I knew they were right. And yet . . . I cried. Night and day, I cried."

Kyral stifled a small moan.

"All I could think of," Doreya continued tersely, "was that lovely, small boy. His large eyes and soft, soft skin. His tiny, perfect hands, cupping my breast, while his mouth worked—seeking the nipple . . . just before they took him away . . ."

"Oh, my poor, dear friend!" Kyral's arms enfolded Doreya. But Doreya righted herself, leaned away, laughed nervously.

"How foolish I am, even now! After all these years. And when I have Grena. It is surely because I continue to grieve that the gods snatch my other babes long before birth."

There had been countless miscarriages, Kyral knew. But they were more likely caused by a husband's brutal beatings than through the displeasure of a "god."

"Dear Doreya," she whispered. "Please let me tell you of Yahweh . . ."

"No!" Doreya thrust Kyral's hand away. Then more softly

she said, "Your god is cruel in other ways. And even if he weren't, how could I risk the loss of still more children?"

In the still of deepest night, when Noah's snores were soft, contented rumblings that somehow comforted, Kyral often lay awake, dreading what lay ahead for Doreya and Grena if the flood were delayed, and what would surely occur when the flood finally came. Unless . . .

Yahweh, she prayed, *give me the words to speak to this friend, words that will touch her with knowledge.* Though many of Kyral's other petitions grew into conversations, no answer to this prayer became audible in her mind. She knew she must trust.

Doreya had said that Yahweh was cruel "in other ways." Surely she referred to the flood. All her life, she'd heard Noah speak of its inevitability. Such a plan for mass destruction must seem the ultimate cruelty to those unable or unwilling to consider Yahweh's parallel provision for safety.

Therefore, when she spoke to Doreya again, Kyral must focus on the way of salvation, rather than on the end result for those who rejected it.

During the year following Ham and Tamara's wedding and in those months after Father Lamech's sudden death and burial, Kyral often tried to broach the subject of Yahweh, always with the same result.

"You ask that I turn my back on the gods of my father and mother," Doreya would say. "Often when they were still alive we worshiped together. And even now, I attend the temple, praying to the gods that they are happy, well-fed, and cared for in the afterlife. If I reject these gods, then I lose all hope of seeing my parents again. Even worse, the gods will remember and—as my punishment—doom my father and mother to starvation and disease. I know this is true, dear friend. It has happened to others. The priests often speak of it."

At other times Doreya said, "My dear friend, you despise the gods of my husband, the gods to whom I entrusted my infant son! If I say they are false, how can I bear the guilt of my baby's death? Better that I plunge a knife into my own breast than live with such anguish!"

And Kyral, both hating to upset Doreya and lacking confidence in her own skills of persuasion, would retreat from further discussion. Then she'd plead with Yahweh that the proper time would come, that Doreya would listen, that she and Grena *would* become Yahweh's.

But the ark neared completion. Time would soon run out. *This next Seventh Day,* Kyral promised herself, if Doreya came to visit, she would make an opportunity. And she would not draw back.

Doreya came while Kyral's mind still clung to the comfort and praise of Noah's closing prayer. As the flood neared, it seemed their closeness to Yahweh deepened, sweetened, intensified.

I feel so close to You, my Lord.

"I am with you and within you."

I know such peace.

"I am peace to those who love and serve me."

I feel so unworthy.

"Are you not one of my children?"

And Doreya? Grena? Are they not Your children, as well?

"They could be, if they would."

And then Doreya came softly, sinking to the bench beside Kyral. "Will I disturb you if I stay?"

Smiling a welcome, Kyral suppressed a small annoyance. If only Doreya had hesitated for a moment longer, she could have asked Yahweh for convincing words. Perhaps He would instruct her, anyway. Certainly He knew her need and hesitancy.

Softly Doreya confided, "Last night, I dreamed we were on the ark. Afloat."

Kyral's breath shortened with surprise. *Thank You, my Lord!* How could she have doubted?

"There have been many times when I've thought about it as a safe haven." Smiling, Doreya leaned back, catching a knee between her laced hands. "I look at the stars, sometimes. How distant they are, how . . . clean and bright. And I yearn to be safely away from shouting and anger and cruelty, to be separated from the demands of people—of the gods." She turned. Even in the dimming light, Kyral noted the warmth, the sweetness of her expression. "When I was little, when I could run into the ark and hide and think myself all alone in the world, when I could shut out all other sounds and squeeze my eyes tight . . ." She sighed. "But I'm no longer a child. I realize that I can't hide from life." Laughing, she said, "You'll think me foolish."

Gently Kyral murmured, "Never, my dear friend."

"I think *myself* foolish when such thoughts beguile me. I know what they lead to." Doreya touched a fresh bruise on her chin. "And," she said heavily, "I know what they *may* lead to."

Kyral asked hoarsely, "What has Saert done?"

"He's taken another wife, for one thing. The gods told him to." She spoke matter-of-factly. "And I don't mind, if she can give us sons. And, if she can't, at least the beatings will be divided between us." She paused. "She's pregnant, already. And so he needs me *now*. But, once the child is weaned . . ." Her voice broke on a sob.

Kyral caught her close. *Yahweh! Show me what I must do!*

He was silent. Or perhaps she was too shocked, too preoccupied, to hear an answer.

"What will happen," she urged, "when the child is weaned?"

"Saert threatens to . . . give me to the temple."

Kyral's arms tightened convulsively. Her mind reeled. She had known of girls and women delivered by fathers or husbands to that massive edifice of stone, its towers rising dizzyingly, glittering with gold. She had heard of carved altars, set with jewels and sprayed with the blood of older women who were no longer useful in kitchens or orchards. But women like Doreya, who were lithe and beautiful, had other uses, at least for a time.

"Perhaps they'll allow me to work in the kitchens," Doreya said, but she didn't sound convinced.

"Of course I'm no stranger to the ceremonies," she continued. "I have danced in the temple." She hesitated. "Dear friend, I pray you won't think less of me, but I have lain with the priests in worship. Surely you would have guessed that. It is . . . traditional."

Kyral closed her eyes. She breathed a quivering sigh.

Doreya said sensibly, "It isn't like giving my body to men! The priests become gods." She sighed. "It's hard for you to understand because Noah is both priest and husband to you."

"Stop!" Kyral whispered hoarsely. "Please, please stop."

"As I feared . . . I've upset you."

Within Kyral's mind, words formed. "Listen to me," she said. "Listen closely."

Obediently Doreya quieted.

"Yahweh, our God, is . . . not like other gods . . ."

Doreya stirred.

"You must listen," Kyral insisted, "this one time, perhaps this time only. You *must* hear me!"

Doreya was gone. Unconvinced.

Still, Kyral comforted herself tiredly, she hadn't protested that her gods would be offended. In fact, she'd reacted scarcely at all.

All lost, Kyral thought, yet a tremor of hope survived. Surely it was significant that Doreya had been attentive . . . that any arguments had been tentative, even thoughtful. Perhaps she only needed time for testing these new concepts.

Merciful Yahweh . . . I can't even recall those things I told her!

"You said that I was unlike other gods . . ."

Yes. Yes, I remember now.

"He isn't lascivious," Kyral had said. "He wouldn't enter the bodies of His priests, or of anyone, to entice young women into sexual acts. Rather, He enters the minds and the hearts of all His people and guides them in righteousness."

But Doreya had frowned at the word.

Yahweh reminded her, "You explained what it is to be righteous."

Yes! To seek good. To love others . . .

And Doreya had protested mildly that her gods simply expressed their love through sexuality, rather than by instructing someone in the building of an ark, for example.

"But such sex is selfish!" (Kyral had carefully avoided the word *carnal*.) "It sacrifices the body and subjugates the intellect purely for the pleasure of another . . . or of oneself—not that sex is always evil. Yahweh Himself fashioned it for the uniting of man and wife, for the shaping of children . . ."

I floundered badly.

"Her priests would have been much more practiced in their opposing arguments."

She sighed.

"I prefer your rather awkward innocence."

But when I fumble . . .

"She knows your humanity, your caring."

Still, how could I not confuse her? "Sex is bad;" "sex is good . . ."

"What can*not* be used either for good or for evil?"

But how can Doreya understand?

"She has a mind. She loves and hates. She sees that her love for Grena is good; that Shumri's lust is evil. You demand too much of yourself, my child. She must come to a knowledge of me as *she* decides."

I am presumptuous . . .

"You are human."

And other points I made . . .

"Concerning Creation."

Oh, yes.

She had told Doreya of Yahweh's power, that He had created the world and all that was in it.

"But, dear friend," Doreya insisted quietly, "so did our many gods do those same things! How can this be?"

Kyral shook her head. "Yahweh did it—He alone," and she began to recite the Creation Hymn as it had come through Enoch and Seth, from the parents of the entire world.

"Two people—parents of us all?" Doreya had smiled. "My friend, I think you're gullible."

"Not so gullible that I believe a priest when he propositions me by saying he houses a god!"

I nearly lost her there, my Lord.

"Perhaps you touched a chord of doubt, of guilt."

Don't You see . . . I spoke in judgment! I . . . forgot friendship.

"Perhaps she touched a chord of doubt in *your* mind?"

Never, my Lord! Yet Kyral knew that, at times, she'd found it incomprehensible that in six days . . . *But I grew to believe. And now I know that it doesn't concern me* how *it was done, only that it was You who did it. If only I could convince Doreya* . . . Then, remembering His chiding, she prayed, *Touch her mind and heart, my Lord.*

The petition became a constant prayer for the week, and all during the next Seventh Day, she continued to pray.

❧❧❧ ❦❦❦

Early the next week, Noah came to her, eyes glowing, mouth quirking, hands clasping with such fervor that the knuckles paled. It was obvious he could barely restrain some momentous news.

"The ark . . . " he said, finally. "I have only to install more cages. Yahweh has told me that already birds and animals have set out from distant mountains and valleys. My dear . . . the time has come! At last!"

She yearned to echo his excitement wholeheartedly. Instead, she felt the same hesitation she had known when a youthful Ham presented some newfound, squatting animal friend for her touching. Or when she'd accepted young Japheth's breathless gift of crimson berries—almost certainly poisonous—that he fully expected to see baked into tarts and eaten.

She hugged Noah, giving him, she hoped, affirmation

enough that he would never guess the sudden chill possessing her spirit as all the old fears roared back—her terror of closed spaces, her horror of day after day after day after day . . . confined.

The morning was clear and lovely. The fragrance of hyacinth hung thick and sweet on the air. Closing her eyes, Kyral inhaled deeply. She'd always loved hyacinth—not just its perfume, although it had often served as a narcotic to her unease. She admired its personality, as well, with its straight, independent blossoms curled tightly on themselves.

She hugged herself, then stretched her arms to the vastness of the morning and opened her eyes.

The ark.

Always, it was there—hulking, huge, dominating the horizon as it ordered her life. When it was skeletal, she'd been able to ignore it. Even when the hull was complete, but the decks unfloored and the tier of windows unroofed, she could control its effect on her emotions.

But not now.

When she deliberately turned her back, its shadow surrounded her if the sun were beyond it. When the sun lay with her, or stood directly overhead, the ark exerted its particular power. She could sense its bulk, its solidity, its enclosing, stifling presence—a presence that, all too soon, would possess her. Totally.

Familiar fears, invading her mind, assaulted, constricting blood flow and breathing. Suddenly, the scent of hyacinth grew oppressive and smothering, the tight-curled blossoms a reminder of shackles, barriers, spaces closing in, closing down, compressing.

No. *No!* She couldn't allow this to continue—this legacy of fear, this debt she owed her father. Once and forever, she must face it. Deal with it. Defeat it. But how?

Yahweh, she prayed frantically, *show me how!*

And the answer came firmly. She must enter the ark. She

must stay there, until she had mastered her fear. And Yahweh would help her.

She gasped, almost choking on air.

"There is no other way," His voice was gentle.

She nodded jerkily.

But first, she thought . . . she knew . . . she must escape,
just for a little while, to prepare for her ordeal. And she
wouldn't solicit His approval for that.

Scarcely aware of movement, she ran, compelled by her
need to avoid stricture, structure, the essence of the ark.
Heedless of dangers scarcely diminished in early morning
hours, she stumbled, panting, toward the most expansive
openness she knew—a hilltop meadow, so raked with
breezes that slight growth survived. It was a favorite grazing
spot for slim, swift antelopes and mountain goats even more
obsessed with space than she.

Even though she hadn't invited Him, Yahweh went with
her. She tried to resist His presence, to find it restricting. Instead, it breathed a soothing coolness, a healing warmth, an
expansion of lightness, an assurance of safety.

She paused (*they* paused) to watch a trio of goats, self-
assured, almost arrogant in their joy of certainty and swift-
ness. One, his head up and his expression smug as he
surveyed "his" world, posed on an outcropping of rock. She
laughed softly. (*They* laughed softly.)

Then Kyral frowned. Trying to avoid an air of challenge,
she eased a question toward Yahweh. *How can his kind possibly survive the ark?*

"They will think themselves at home."

She pictured the stalls—dark and close. Dare she ask
Him? She must!

How is that possible?

"The fragrance of meadow grass and open air will surround them. They will be blinded to the bars and the timbers. Dry hay will become moist and fresh, tender with
spring's juices. Space will surround them, and the sounds
of the sea, of people, of other animals will convert to breeze,
to flowing streams, and to the voices of their own kind."

She breathed deeply, at peace—for a few moments; then doubt intruded again.

"It's all right, my child," He assured, even before she could frame an apology. "We'll work together on your fears as well." (A pause.) "Would you have me alter your senses, as I will touch theirs?"

She was tempted to nod, to avoid confronting her lifelong dread.

But, no. She wasn't a goat incapable of translating speech and grasping responsibility.

She straightened, squared her shoulders, felt her jaw tightening in resolve.

"You have chosen well," He assured her. Then sighed.

But she already knew that before they could attack her unreasoning fears, they must recall the reasons.

They must deal with the memory of her father.

ͽͽͽ ͼͼͼ

He had always been a big man, all rippling muscle and wide, strong hands, and eyes that never warmed to smiling or love.

He was incapable of love. And Kyral, huddled in her mother's cushioning arms, had listened to her crooning and wondered how such gentleness had survived his cruelty. Perhaps her mother's softness required contrasting iron. Certainly it had attracted it.

When Kyral was small, she'd had to look up and up and up, as though viewing a nearby mountain, to see her father's face. She seldom took the trouble, unless it was to read the intensity of some current displeasure. And she could tell that from his hands—whether they convulsed, contracting and reddening; whether they reached for the lash or reached for her, clamping her upper arm, thrusting her roughly to some bench or corner or propelling her to the place of harshest punishment, the shed.

A low building, its slanting roof admitted only slashes of light more frightening than total darkness because of what they partially revealed. It was better not to realize the presence of rats, nosing into rubble for some small fragment of food. Especially while she, with the scent of breakfast still on her clothing, grease on her fingers, crumbs clustered on her skirt, cowered in the semidarkness.

Sobbing, she would shake her skirt and scour her hands on the littered dirt floor, would try to ignore the certainty of other filths waiting there, would watch warily as nose whiskers twitched and bright eyes observed her.

And there were scorpions, almost translucent, traversing fallen timbers with seeming innocence. Yet curved tails attested to their poisonous power deliverable at the slightest sign of intrusion.

Kyral quivered at the menacing memory, felt again the crawlings of fear, the tightness of breath, the imagined touch of those poisoned tails. Once again she could see them dragging, questing, then impressing their potent loads on other victims. She heard again her own shrieking, saw its impact on the rats—startled, scurrying—while the scorpions, insouciant, performed their rites of courtship and challenge and play and confident ownership of the space they, and she, shared.

"They can't hurt you now," Yahweh murmured, "not the scorpions, not the rats, especially not your father."

It was true. She had been safe since her father lay dead, and her mother, ungrieving, gathered dried rushes and withered bark and other tinder and stacked it near the leaning shed door. Ceremoniously she lit a fire. Kyral could remember her own numbed reaction as fire engulfed the shed—her near-mourning for the rats, surely squealing within, as the inferno grew and set whiskers and fur aflame. She identified with their mindless panic. But she pictured with cold indifference the scorpions, first scampering from the heat, then trapped, flailing ineffectually at the flames with those venomous tails and crumpling at last, their translucent bodies twisting in soundless death.

She felt no more sympathy for the scorpions than for her father, lying dead near the house where he'd fallen, still holding the ax he had raised to kill their only donkey for daring to balk. Petting the donkey aside, Kyral's mother eased the ax from those still, broad fingers. Bending above her husband, she murmured, "He seems to be dead. Can any of you see movement?"

As the timbers of the shed reduced to ashes, her mother patted Kyral's shoulder with absentminded fervor. And then, the ashes scarcely cooled, she commanded the oldest son to dig deeply enough for a grave.

"You can forget him now," her mother had assured, when the body had been dragged to the edge of the grave, dumped in and covered—first with ashes, then with a layer of stones. "We can all forget him. He can never threaten or hurt us, ever again."

Kyral had known then, as she knew all these years later, that her mother was right. But learned terror lay deeper than knowledge. While knowledge could shape itself into words and phrases, the meaning was negated by fear.

"He was an evil man," Yahweh said. "Anyone who abuses a child is evil."

How he had enjoyed her terror! When she cringed, his mouth gaped in soundless, humorless laughter. His eyes glinted when she begged, sobbing, kneeling before him, clutching his ankles.

From the day she had refused to cringe, to plead, to cower, he had bound as well as confined her. It was while she was bound that he had approached her, almost softly, those most terrible times. With confusing gentleness, he had drawn a finger down her cheek. Then, his lips twisting with some unreadable message, his glance never leaving her face, he dropped his tunic.

In this moment on the hilltop, decades past her father's power to wound, to terrorize, even with Yahweh near her, the fear and horror paralyzed her.

"We must retrace," Yahweh whispered, and she felt His soothing touch on her shoulder.

"Yes." She said it aloud, more for herself than for Him. Yes, in her mind she must reenter that shed and relax there. She must watch the rats and reach out to touch their soft fur, must allow their whiskers to tickle her hand. She must even laugh at the sensation! She must see slivers of sunlight on the scorpions' translucence and admire their grace and beauty. She must see her father . . .

She shuddered.

"Recognize him as the victim of an abusive spirit," Yahweh said, "and forgive him."

She sighed. It would be simple to forgive him as she remembered him last—dead.

"You must remember him alive, and still forgive him."

Then, as clearly as though the scene occurred before her, the images came. Her father as a child—cringing before looming adults, screaming and pleading beneath their lashes, closing his eyes against the words hurled at him: "Whelp of a diseased coyote bitch!" "Carrion!" Each epithet was punctuated by another slash of the whip, each slash empowered by the epithet. He crouched, striving with thin, raised arms to protect his face and head.

I never knew, she whispered in her thoughts.

"You never knew that you knew, but remember."

She saw him again as he had stood before her, long whitened scars lacing his upper body. "Poor little boy," she sobbed aloud and knew that forgiveness had already begun.

There was no turning back. This very day she would conquer the panic and the dread that cast black shadows over her contentment and paralyzed both mind and body.

She stood and straightened. "I will need to go to the ark," she said. His touch remained steady on her shoulder as they went together.

PART TWO

Then the Lord said to Noah, "Come into the ark, you and all your household, because I have seen that you are righteous before Me in this generation."

Genesis 7:1

Tamara had never believed that such a time would truly come. Even when old Noah said the ark was ready for occupancy and she assisted Mother Kyral with storing supplies in the various bins and cubbyholes between the ribs of the vast hull, she'd been able to label it all a childish game. It was merely a prank, outranking any Ham had ever designed. Never had she actually thought that Ham would ever order her aboard.

But he had.

How could he expect to imprison her within those dark, odorous walls, to limit her to only a few possessions, and deny her all conversation save with him and his family! How could he doom her to that inevitable time of contempt and gloating when they must emerge, smelly, rumpled, shamefaced, perhaps even ill from unwholesome confinement in darkness with animals, fleas, ticks . . .

She shuddered. She couldn't bear it. She *wouldn't* bear it! She just wouldn't go. It was that simple.

Surely if Ham were less stone-headed, if he could, even momentarily, still his impetuous flow of prattle, if he would listen, really listen, he could see the wisdom of her remaining behind to monitor what was being said and to soften the ridicule. She could place the blame squarely where it belonged—on the shoulders of one foolish, hard-minded old man, who ruled his family with rigidity intensified by obvious insanity.

She was *glad* that she'd never called him "Father Noah" as Maelis and Afene did with apparent ease. She would never again bestow the tender title of "Father" on anyone, especially not on such a fool! She, who had basked in the warm wisdom, the unquestioning adoration, of a peerless man, would not sully his memory in such a way. An ache settled in her heart, buzzed in her mind, incited her to tears. Never had she missed her own dear father more!

If only he still lived, no one would try to force her onto a dark, dingy, pestilent ark. No one would *dare!* Her father, though peace-loving by nature, would take up arms at such a threat! And how he would hold her, soothe her, love her, protect her, even from Ham. Hadn't he offered to dissolve the betrothal? Even now, he'd annul the marriage, repudiate it. Declare it unconsummated. And who could question his grounds? Despite the nightly harbor of Ham's arms and the ardor of his passion, she would swear to anything to escape a musty prison! And who could prove otherwise, since she was not yet with child? And even if she had a dozen babes toddling at her heels, who would ever blame her, given her present quandary?

Her father would make her his goddess again until the ark episode had failed and, perhaps, even beyond that. She might never return to Ham to share his disgrace.

What an unfathomable creature he was. How could he join with his father, insisting that she participate in the stupid venture? At their marriage, she'd been certain that *she* would sway *him!* Surely, he'd given her cause for such an assumption—hadn't he? But now . . .

What foolish arguments he'd offered! She might have understood if he'd merely continued to order her with that pigheaded male insistence on domination in the home. She knew that to be a farce. Wives could always get their way. But not this time.

She'd tried pleading, flirting, reasoning. And, when all else failed, she'd wept.

"You are my wife," Ham said for the hundredth time.

"And you. Are you not my husband, the one who promised to love me as his own flesh?"

"And I do." His expression wavered from confusion to helplessness. "You're the center of my world," he protested limply. "I worship you."

"And to prove your devotion, you expose me to ridicule?"

He reached as though to touch her. "I strive only to . . ."

"Subject me to poisonous snakes?"

His hands dropped, his shoulders collapsing. He sighed. "I've explained, my dearest love. They won't be poisonous for the term of our journey."

"Ham! Listen to yourself! How can anyone believe something so . . . so . . ."

He dared to smile! "Improbable?"

There was no reasoning with the foolish man! "So *impossible!*" she snapped.

"Yahweh has told my father," he reached again as though to embrace her, then shrugged as she evaded him. "It's essential that we all go. It is from us—Shem and Maelis, Japheth and Afene, and you and me, my love—that the world will find its new beginning."

She simply threw her hands to the heavens in mute appeal. Catching her in his arms, then, he whispered against her cheek, "Can't you feel honored?"

She thrust him away, taking perverse pleasure in his startled stumbling and the raw anguish that reddened the rims of his eyes.

"*Honored?* Honored to be made a joke to everyone who's ever hated me?"

She stopped abruptly. That was it. Those who loved her would absolve her, because forbearance was an element of loving. And yet, except for Ham, who loved her? She admitted grudgingly that his family did, although Afene had insisted, one afternoon as they rested on a stone bench near the marketplace, that the ark would never survive such slovenly ways as Tamara's.

Tamara had tossed her curls. "We aren't on the ark yet."
Nor will we ever be, she'd completed in her thoughts.

"Bad habits are stubborn," Afene said, "nearly impossible to break."

"There are bad habits and *worse* habits," Tamara teased. She tugged an apricot from her marketing pouch and wiped it on her sleeve. "I'm wondering who you'll drive overboard first with your obsessions and complaints."

Afene sniffed.

Complacently, Tamara compared her expression to a rabbit's, exploring decayed clover.

"I don't complain," Afene insisted, rising. "However, if you're upset by a little constructive advice . . . ."

Tamara caught Afene's arm and tugged her into a half-hug. "Dear Afene, *I'm* not the one who's stalking off in a huff! Come," she urged, "we could make a pact. I'll promise to fold our bedding, if you overlook a cobweb or two."

Afene shuddered.

Giggling, Tamara lifted the apricot to her lips.

"You're not going to *eat* that, are you? Without washing?"

"I . . . cleaned it."

"And just look at the stain on your sleeve!"

Tamara took a slow, deliberate bite. The fruit was sun-warm and succulent, brimming with juice that ran languidly down her chin. That, too, she wiped on her sleeve.

Afene seemed close to tears. "If that stain ever comes out . . . ."

"Who'll notice," Tamara asked, "or care, if we're on the ark?"

"*If* we're on the ark?" Afene's voice was strangely hollow, sharply rising. Tamara realized, for the first time, how intense was Afene's longing. How opposite their yearnings. Swift pity caused her to cast the apricot away, though rich flesh still clung to the seed. If only she could as easily erase the tension from Afene's expression.

"Dear Afene," she began. "Of course I meant *when* . . . ."

It had occurred to her that day, to a point exceeding any expectation, that she had grown to love Ham's family, that she'd miss them. Even his father was likable, despite his stubbornness—and his insanity.

Beyond them, she was acknowledged only for her face and figure. With men, the admiration too often shaped itself as lust; with women, as jealousy. Even the few friendships surviving from girlhood had become shallow, spasmodic.

Her mother had always despised her, as much now as ever, and perhaps even more since a week or so ago, when she'd chanced across Ham and Tamara in a tender moment.

It was near the verge of town, where a slim waterfall spilled freshets of a peculiar purity and coldness. They'd gone there, she and Ham, to fill a waterpot and—enchanted with a cloud of small indigo butterflies wobbling above the iridescent spray, sometimes venturing to the point of disequilibrium—had remained. First they watched, then they exclaimed and delighted. Finally they waded, hand in hand, their sandals tumbled to the mossy bank and their bare feet growing quickly inanimate as their hands extended cautiously to coax the cloud-like creatures closer. One landed in Tamara's hair.

She hadn't sensed its slight weight, but knew from Ham's awed silence that it was there. "It thinks you're a flower," he said, his quiet voice heavy with emotion, his fingers tightening on hers, "as I do."

Reluctant to dislodge the insect, yet needing Ham nearer, she eased into the bend of his arm, then turned. Her love for him was a warm tangibility, urgent and aching, and she wondered that it failed to ease even the frigid stiffness of her feet. Giggling, she imagined herself and Ham there, hours or even days later, frozen in place, and content. She nestled against his breast.

"Is it still there?" she whispered.

"Why would it leave the sweetest flower on earth?"

Carefully, she lifted her lips to his and felt their quivering softness firming against hers. She heard his shuddering sigh and knew its implications. Only then she saw her mother, or perhaps she heard first the sound of a waterpot dropping from her mother's stiffened fingers.

Startled, they pulled apart, then—spurred not by passion, but by the hatred in her mother's eyes—closed, or nearly closed, the distance.

"Mother," Tamara said, almost pleadingly, and tried to move a step toward the bank.

"Whore." The word was inaudible against the joyous riot of the waterfall. But the scornful twist of the lips and the superior arch of eyebrow and shoulder were unmistakable.

Ham stiffened. He would have responded, but Tamara quieted him with the urgent pressure of her hand.

For a tense moment, the women regarded one another. Then, without even retrieving her cracked waterpot, Tamara's mother left, walking stiffly straight, arms rigid at her sides, her hatred remaining almost a presence by the stream.

"Is it still there?" Tamara asked brokenly.

"Hnnnh—" It seemed an effort for Ham to free himself.

"The butterfly?" Tamara tensed against the certainty that it had deserted her.

"It's gone. They're . . . all gone."

She sighed, shaking her head against tears. The celebration of the waterfall seemed mocking. "How can she hate me so?" she asked, neither needing nor expecting an answer, but requiring the solidity of the question. It hung between them. "But how could anyone with a real mother possibly understand?" A deadness, colder than the stream, more rigid than her feet, had settled against her heart. Only her father had ever truly, unconditionally loved her. Only her father . . .

Tamara, more convinced even than before, reviewed Ham's unreasonable demands on her, his insistence that she submit to the ark. Surely the love of Ham's family, moving to enclose her, could never compensate for imprisonment, however temporary. If Ham truly loved her, he'd never make demands so contrary to her well-being.

But if Ham *didn't* love her . . .

She tightened her arms across her chest, wanting to crush

the aching voice within. Without Ham, there was no one.

Once she had thought that Cloyren . . .

Her lip curled with distaste as she recalled the incident in the berry patch when he had reviled her, and his expression of mingled amusement and scorn whenever he'd seen her since. Heat invaded her cheeks.

And yet . . . thoughts of the ark hung like a swarm of gnats in her mind.

She'd heard that Cloyren had set Brea aside, and divorced her. But he'd invited no new wife into his household. Still, considering the notoriety and breadth of his sexual appetite, she knew he wouldn't abstain.

She shuddered. How had she ever fancied herself in love with such a glutton, how risked her purity to such foulness? Not that he'd ever requested such a sacrifice.

In the beginning, Ham's passion had been bumbling and raucous, affecting in its innocence. And there was in his lovemaking still an endearing lack of polish that communicated honesty and spontaneity. But Ham had condemned her to the ark.

Should she consider groveling at Cloyren's feet and offering herself as his concubine, merely to escape that cave of an ark? Did she truly prefer to subvert all that she was and had hoped to be rather than endure temporary ridicule?

Shallow, miserable, unworthy wretch, she accused herself, and accepted the assessment.

Whore, the indictment continued. And she knew that, despite Cloyren's opinion, despite her mother's condemnation, she had never been that. Though that was exactly what she would become if she pursued such thinking, if she carried such planning to reality, as she fully intended doing.

❯❯❯ ❮❮❮

Tension dampened her forehead and the curls clinging there. Impatiently, she thrust them back. Surely Yahweh was with her, she thought, striving to calm her inward fluttering, since she had so easily found Cloyren.

Reclining on a massive boulder near the carved gates of his house, he was scanning the boughs of an olive tree. There was such studied grace about his position that she knew he'd been well aware of her approach. One tooled leather sandal swung casually by a single strap.

"Nearly ripe," he murmured, his glance never shifting. The tree, she thought uncharitably, was scarcely worth such appraisal. Dusty and unkempt, it promised a harvest of only a handful of fruit.

"And you, Tamara," he asked with that insidious smirk she now found so detestable (Oh, how could she ever come to terms with her aversion or mask her abhorrence!), "are you nearly ripe, as well?"

Fresh shame engulfed her.

"I think you may be," he said, regarding her at last. "I think before—*long* before—the ark finds itself afloat, I shall have plucked these olives for my table. And, if I wanted you, I could pluck you, quite as effortlessly for my bed."

If he wanted her. *Of course* he desired her! Only his pride, wounded by earlier spurning, caused him to cut at her now. Yet what civilized slashing! And how much more grievous the wounding when there seemed no motivating anger. His words oozed with ennui. Where Ham's rejoinders, when she incited him to red-faced wrath, pelted like pebbles, only bruising, Cloyren's indifference probed with a rapier's precision. And she preferred such sophisticated cruelty to Ham's bearishness?

Never!

Yet she preferred anything to the ark. Still she musn't allow Cloyren to lacerate her further or even to imagine that he dared. Having been her father's "goddess" and then Ham's cherished bride, she had learned her value.

Straightening, she lifted her chin. But before she could speak. Cloyren moved to face her. His movement was studied even then; his robe cascaded in graceful silken folds to the tops of his sandals. Did the man do nothing without first evaluating its effect?

Nausea rose in her throat, and when he reached as though

to cup her chin, she steeled herself against his touch, resisting an urge to squeeze her eyes tightly shut as when she was a child and a splinter had to be removed.

He withdrew his hand.

"So you've tired of the red-bearded fool," he said.

She couldn't answer. She still loved Ham. How would she ever, ever maintain a façade of preference for Cloyren?

It was that or the ark.

Forcing a coy smile, and feeling herself as counterfeit as he, she seated herself with careful grace just beyond his reach. The boulder was large and cool and as smooth as though it had been worked by a stonemason. She breathed slowly, deeply, silently.

"I have come," she said with a downward sweep of her lashes, "to accept your offer of marriage."

He hooted.

Inwardly she sighed. How could she flirt when he refused to cooperate?

"I never offered you marriage," he said, with only the hint of a sneer, "nor do I accept used . . . or damaged . . . goods."

Wincing she felt her resolution draining. She should slap his smug face and stalk away while any shred of pride remained. But the ark . . .

She forced herself to meet his mocking glance with honesty. "You offered . . ." she swallowed with difficulty, "to take me as your concubine."

There. It was done. She had shamed herself, had invited his scorn. Nothing he could say or demand could diminish her further.

Or so she thought.

Arching his neck backward, he began a dry chortling. If only she'd brought a dagger, she could so simply slash his throat, could contentedly watch his foul blood etching a line down his body, while his eyes widened in horror and his contempt for her degenerated to pleading.

The pleasure of the thought renewed her courage, but

only for a moment, until tears curved down his hateful cheeks, and he dabbed at them with a square of silk.

"That offer has been withdrawn," he managed, between spurts of laughter, "though I might accept you now as a whore for my stable slaves—if you prove yourself worthy."

Closing her eyes, she whispered wretchedly, "You loved me once."

His answer was coldly controlled and frighteningly devoid of feeling. "I *pretended* to love you once."

New anguish forced her to look at him, to extend her hands in pleading.

"I enjoyed the game," he said callously. "You were merely entertainment, diversion for an afternoon when someone more adventurous had already filled my needs. Later, we could laugh together at your clumsy overtures, your posturing and trembling . . ." He sneered. "You're such a child!"

Yet his eyes scanned her speculatively. Shivering, she fumbled the folds of her robe more loosely across her breast.

He reached out a hand then, and, powerless to summon resistance, she allowed him to draw her to her feet—standing stiffly as his fingertips stroked her hair, slipped down her shoulders and her arms, lingered at her waist. Tugging her suddenly off balance, he pulled her close, and when she jerked to free herself, whispered on soft laughter, "Have you learned nothing? You're no more pliant than before! I look to my women for boldness, for innovation. And you come, prim and prideful—as though you hadn't been fouled by that awkward fool—and expect me to treasure you!" His eyebrow arched. "Shall I teach you what my slaves expect from their whores?" Roughly he caught her hair, exposed her throat, and dragged his parted lips heavily down her neck. Patterns of panic swirled in her mind and somehow she managed to scream.

Later she retained no memory of her escape. Had she broken free or had Cloyren released her? She remembered only that she ran from his hateful, mocking laughter, that her breath came in painful snatches, as—vision dimmed by tears—she stumbled across uneven ground, dodged low-hanging branches, her thoughts bent solely on the sanctuary of the ark.

Once it was in sight, she leaned against the bole of a sycamore panting, trembling with humiliation. Wordlessly she praised Yahweh for her undeserved deliverance from the natural results of her foolishness. Too ashamed to seek Ham, wondering if she would ever again be able to face him, she thought to find a corner deep in the ark's belly in which to hide. But just within the entryway, Mother Kyral was sweeping and Afene, scouring the floor with sand, was singing a song Tamara remembered from her childhood of a bird who, building its nest of its own softest feathers, died of the cold.

When her father had sung it to her, Tamara cried. Holding her and patting clumsily, he promised never to sing it again. But when she and Tamara were alone, her mother had sung it often. And when the three of them were together, she'd hummed the tune, smiling with half-closed eyes as Tamara clamped both small hands against her ears and shook her head until her curls flopped wildly. *Vicious woman*. How pleased she'd be when she heard of Cloyren's rejection!

Tamara slumped against the doorjamb and the broom's swishing ceased.

"Are you well, child?" Kyral asked so softly that Afene, continuing both work and song, never looked up. Tamara nodded, then shook her head and swiped as hot tears coursed down her cheeks.

"Come."

Mother Kyral led her through the cooking area, down a steep stairway, and into a shadowed nook where only a few things stood: the largest loom, disassembled, a churn, a crate of carpenter's tools more fitted to house building than to ark mending, and three sizable benches.

"Sit."

While Mother Kyral settled on a bench like a contented hen in warm dust, Tamara perched awkwardly on the far edge. One hand clutched and pressed and prodded the other. Mother Kyral's soft fingers covered both, stilling them.

"Tell me," she ordered softly.

A sob tore at Tamara's throat. How could she admit her foolishness? But Mother Kyral, bulky, encouraging, smiling, presented a more comfortable confidante than any other Tamara had found since her father's death. How could she not confess?

"Mother Kyral, I'm so ashamed."

"Dear child, we all know moments of shame."

"None so great as mine!"

"There is nothing you could imagine we wouldn't willingly forgive, and Yahweh is even more compassionate."

Tamara pressed both hands against her flaming cheeks. "I could *never* confess this to Yahweh!"

"But, my dear, whatever it is, Yahweh already knows!"

Dropping her hands, clasping them again, rocking back and forth, Tamara moaned, "Then He'll send me away."

Gently Kyral drew her close. "We feared you *wanted* to leave."

Tamara looked up, startled. But Kyral's smile was warm, her tone inviting.

Tamara nodded. "I felt that way. Before."

Patiently, Kyral waited.

"I thought nothing could be worse than the ridicule when we'd leave the ark. Now I *never* want to leave!"

Kyral held her quietly.

"I . . . I went to see Cloyren, to ask him to take me back."

There was no signal of reproof in Kyral's voice, only sadness. "Poor child! How you must fear us!"

"I could never fear you, Mother Kyral!"

There was no answer, but the soothing comfort continued.

Tamara said tightly, "I hate Cloyren; I hated him even before."

"Yet you went to him." Kyral sighed, then added, almost joyously, "But you returned here! To us!"

"It was only here I could feel safe." And how strange, she

thought, that what she had most dreaded had become her place of tranquility! She said raggedly, "He'll never forgive me."

"Ham?"

"Yahweh." She sighed. "Either of them."

Kyral chuckled. "You underestimate both, Tamara dear. Yahweh forgives all who ask sincerely. And Ham, well, Ham is so foolish about you that if you tried to cut out his heart, he'd ask if he were holding still enough."

They laughed together.

Then Tamara said quietly, "Of course I'll have to tell him."

Kyral pulled gently away. "You'll find him by the stream, I think, fishing from his favorite rock, one last time."

One last time. As she bent to kiss Mother Kyral's soft, wrinkled cheek, Tamara turned the words over in her mind. They sounded so final. *One last time.*

As it happened, Ham was so busy disentangling his line from a snag that at first he gave only a portion of his attention. But she recognized that moment when fishing ceased to be important. It was when she spoke Cloyren's name.

His hands stilled, then dropped. Dark color rose to his hairline, blending red with red-orange. As he continued to listen, the color gradually faded, and she cringed as fully from his pallor.

"My love," she vowed around the obstruction in her throat, "I will spend my life atoning for those moments of stupidity!"

He shrugged, "You were afraid."

She shook her head in disbelief. "Then, you may be able to forgive me?"

He turned to her, taking her in his arms, holding her close. "There's nothing to forgive!"

How wise Mother Kyral was!

"All my life," he said against her cheek, against her ear, against her hair, "I've known that one day the ark would be completed. And even I have known feelings of fear and rebellion; at times I've wanted to escape."

"But, Ham . . . love . . . I went to *Cloyren!*" It was essential that he realize the enormity of her sin. It must be settled this moment, forever. She must leave no crack for recriminations later.

Another shrug; another caress. "Where else could you go? Your mother has always spurned you! And your father . . ." His voice softened. "When you felt I was against you, who else remained but Cloyren?" His hands firmed. "I should go there now, and . . ."

"No, Ham. Please!"

Sighing, he released her. "You still have feelings for him."

"I *detest* him!"

He raised an eyebrow. "Surely you're not afraid *he* could hurt *me!*"

She burst out laughing at the possibility.

"Then . . ."

"It is only," she said, yearning to be held again, "that I wouldn't have you stain your dear hands with such carrion."

Leaving the tangled line where it lay, they strolled arm in arm along the bank. Seen between trunks of scabrous sycamores and slender, arched coconut palms, glimpsed among swaying masses of the foliage of citrus and olive and scrub palmetto, the houses and people seemed fragmented, unreal. "I grieve for them," Maelis had said, more than once, but until this moment Tamara hadn't understood.

A flurry of sound—giggles, scufflings, and a startled half-shriek/half-shout—rose from a patch of bare earth where three children struggled to encircle a bouncing pup. A flood would be as merciless to children and half-grown dogs as to the most evil of adults.

Wanting to block memories of her own childhood play—thoughtless and self-centered—and of Armya and Elose, whose friendships had altered with maturity to survive in diluted form, she closed her eyes briefly against unexpected pain.

And what of young couples, newly married, anticipating joy such as hers and Ham's, hoping—as they hoped—for children? Would they perish, their dreams snuffed as waves encompassed them, perhaps even separating them in those final, frantic moments of drowning?

Could such a fate be any less terrifying for old people, those who were infirm, nurtured only by memories and expecting death to come peacefully? Tears of compassion stung her eyes.

She thought again of Cloyren. If the flood truly occurred, she'd never grieve for him. She'd hope only that when he sank beneath the waters, when he clawed the air in panic, she'd be close enough to see.

No, that wasn't true.

She could not enjoy anyone's death—not even his. If the promise of the flood was more than an old man's crazy mumblings—as Ham believed and as she was beginning to accept—and if Yahweh was indeed determined to purge His world of those who had closed their ears and minds and hearts to Him, her own heart would break at the necessity. Compared to tragedy of such magnitude, her earlier fears of humiliation seemed insignificant. And just as Yahweh's providence had saved her from Cloyren's lustful scorn, so Ham's love would save her from the engulfing waters of the flood. How fortunate she was to have his bearish affection!

"I too have chosen you."

Pausing, frowning, unsure of a small stirring in her mind, she squeezed Ham's hand more tightly, and he nuzzled her neck.

Dear, sweet Ham. Foolish, playful, impetuous Ham. There were times when she shared his family's impatience with him. But Shem could never forgive Maelis such betrayal as Ham had so quickly forgiven her. Not that Maelis would ever dream of so degrading herself.

And Japheth—well, Japheth might forgive Afene, but never so readily, and not without recrimination.

They were past the town, and she saw, with some misgiving, that they neared the hills.

"I'd thought," Ham said gently, "that you'd like to climb to the ledge once more."

She stiffened, then relaxed, nodding. It was only fitting that she submerge the negative that had occurred there— her dallyings with Cloyren and her father's tragic death.

She must remember only that she had grown, there, from her father's love.

Often, climbing the slope, she'd been crying, requiring solace and peace. Often, sitting there, surveying the meadows and the forests, she'd felt proprietorship, superiority. But now a quiet sadness enveloped her. Never again would she see that particular blending of rock and foliage and meadow grasses. Never again would that precise folding of hollow and hill, that unique etching of horizon against blue sky, enchant her.

Tucking her knees beneath her chin, she considered how much the past few hours had changed her. Not only had she come to welcome the protection of the ark, but through some strange emotional alchemy, she now truly believed that the flood must come, that Yahweh would destroy the earth as they knew it, and that she would, indeed, have a part in His new world. Her heart swelled to find Him.

And He answered, "My child."

She looked to see if Ham had heard, but he was hunting among fragments of shale on the ledge, flinging one after another into space. Their tiny patterings and pingings induced a sleepy lethargy. She heard Yahweh promise, "You are loved."

By Ham, I know that.

"By me."

Oh, my Lord! Tears blurred her sight, and she found herself kneeling, her hands extended toward the heavens. And Ham still hadn't noticed! How could he *not* have noticed? Yet her thinking expanded beyond him, beyond the importance of his presence, beyond the significance of their oneness. Yahweh loved *her!* Had chosen *her* to be one of His saved ones! Her heart expanded to enclose that love, to solicit His forgiveness for all her doubts, her fears, her pride, her reckless appeal to Cloyren . . .

I'm sorry. How inadequate that was!

Yet Yahweh answered as simply. "I know."

Ham grasped her shoulder roughly. "Tamara! *Look!* There!"

A smudging on the horizon—rising dust? And movement, slow but insistent, and a slight heaving, like gentle waves, but dark. Were storm clouds approaching? The rains coming, already? Half-standing, hand to her throat, she whispered, "Must we go?"

"The animals!" Ham said, his voice almost exalted. "The animals are coming! Praise Yahweh!"

She settled back on her heels, carefully, as though any sudden movement might dispel the sight.

"And there! Another flock!"

She followed his pointing.

"And another! Representation of all species in the world! Strange creatures never seen before! Two of each kind, at least, that Yahweh may preserve them, on the ark!"

On the ark.

Scarcely breathing, Tamara watched, wondering where they might all fit. What would old Noah feed them? How had Yahweh instructed them to find the ark, with no one leading and no one herding?

Spellbound, she watched as indistinguishable shapes developed humps, horns, stripes, spots, and tails.

"Do you know all their names?" she asked softly.

He shook his head. "Not yet. Yahweh will teach us."

5

Kyral clasped her hands to keep them still. Even when she'd pledged her love to Noah, her heart had thudded more sedately; she'd been able to control her feet, and giggles had bubbled to her lips with less frequency.

Tamara stood on tiptoe, color throbbing in her cheeks. Even Afene, though she still clutched a dripping cloth, had suspended her cleaning to watch. And Maelis? Where was Maelis?

Oh, yes. She'd gone to visit her parents' graves—one last time.

But what a shame to miss this exciting parade of animals, some so strange and beautiful they defied belief! Some so awkward and ugly, Kyral wondered that Yahweh hadn't simply admitted error and erased their species.

Never had she seen, or imagined, anything remotely like the moose! With his misshapen jaw and small, mean eyes, he seemed a figment of some drug-induced nightmare. How could he hold those enormous platter-like, fluted horns aloft? No wonder a dowager's hump had formed at his shoulders! And how could his legs *not* wobble as he walked?

"What *is* it?" someone asked—Doreya, who'd just arrived.

Patting her friend's arm in welcome, Kyral compressed

herself, giving room. "A moose. It lives in colder climates than ours."

"Thank the gods! How hideous!" Then, "How do you know?"

"Yahweh told Noah."

"Oh." It was a small sound.

Not noticing, Kyral explained, "Yahweh's telling us the names of all the creatures we've never seen before. And we're trying to remember."

A hopeless task, she thought, even though Shem, his eyes narrowed in concentration, marked tiny wedge-shaped characters on a wet clay tablet, similar in size and shape to those passed down through the generations from ancestor Enoch. Kyral wondered how Shem would be able to make sense of his scrawling later, and how he'd know which scratched name belonged to which animal. But, and she shrugged comfortably, if they forgot or got confused, Yahweh would simply tell them again.

Undaunted by the hoots of an ever-increasing assemblage, the moose and his mate clumped forward, slumping and uncoordinated, and stooped to enter the ark.

Doreya was asking, "Have you seen Grena?"

Kyral nodded and pointed. Observing Grena had been nearly as interesting as watching the animals approach, wait patiently, then, at Noah's nod, mount the ramp, two by two. Though it was difficult for such a slight girl even to remain upright in the pushing, pressing crowd, Grena had somehow kept herself close to Noah, "helping," Kyral supposed.

In a way, the child *was* helping. Though none of the animals, even the suspicious hyena, the surly cougar, or the shy grouse, seemed the least wary of Noah or reluctant to enter the ark, still, some of the smaller species skittered from the heavy hooves of water buffalo or the crushing feet of elephants. Especially when the smaller animals were wide-eyed and furry, Grena held and stroked them before depositing them on the ramp among less-bulky creatures.

"I was worried about her," Doreya said, her voice so dull that Kyral turned to search her expression.

Doreya smiled without conviction. "Silly, I suppose. But everyone's here."

Kyral knew Doreya wouldn't be worried about "everyone." She'd be concerned only about Shumri.

Yahweh, Kyral thought, *what can we do about Shumri?*

And even though He was keeping the animals under control and giving Noah names, He whispered, "Shumri's downfall will come at his own hand."

And Grena. Will Grena be safe?

"Elk!" Noah shouted above the bleating, cawing, trumpeting, barking. Above the staccato and thunder and rumble of hoofbeats. Above the crowd sounds.

Though most watchers seemed enthralled with the strange parade, it was unrealistic to expect so many to watch such wonders quietly. Sometimes they laughed, as when a monkey climbed a giraffe's wand-like neck and waved, chattering, from his swaying perch. Sometimes they cheered, as when penguins waddled with crisp pomposity behind the rolling rumps of the hippopotamuses, still mud-encrusted. Sometimes they hooted, as when a dodo and his mate, obviously proud of their unlikely shapes and colors, marched pertly.

Often though, the onlookers simply shaped sounds of awe, as when the peacocks, justifiably haughty, spread their iridescent feathers, and when the stately llamas, their sunlit pelts aglow, regarded the crowd with disdain. When blue herons, red-tailed hawks, snowy owls, and songbirds of every conceivable hue and melody glided, wheeled, drifted, swept, and fluttered to the ark's upper deck, the collective sound of the crowd was a lingering sigh.

Occasionally people stepped back, as when a crocodile yawned. They opened a large zone of safety when a group of laughing boys pattered stones among the lions and cheetahs and a lioness belched a startled growl, then turned narrowed, golden eyes to search out the culprits.

"Stop that!" Grena shrieked, pushing a ferret into Noah's startled grasp before pounding down the ramp. The crowd opened before her. "How dare you! Those are *Yahweh's* lions!"

Kyral gasped her surprise, perhaps more at Grena's casual use of Yahweh's name than at her anger.

Yahweh, she prayed, *will Grena go with us?* (Dare she hope for that?) *And Doreya?*

"Panther!" Noah announced.

The creatures seemed to flow up the ramp. Rippling muscles altered sleek black coats with moving patterns of light. A murmur of appreciation swept through the crowd, many of whom worshiped such beasts that priests kept snarling, secured on golden chains, in their temple. And, or so Kyral had heard, they often fed the beasts limbs torn from human sacrifices.

Grena shook a forefinger beneath the nose of a chubby, dark-eyed boy twice her height. "If you do that again, Calet, I'll . . . I'll . . ."

"You'll do what?" he asked sullenly and straight-armed her against an elderly couple, who stumbled and most surely would have fallen had the crowd been less dense.

Grena was flailing, pounding, kicking before Doreya or Kyral could reach her. To the amusement of nearby adults, Calet and his friends backed off. And the bully, Kyral was pleased to notice, nursed a bloody nose. Grena's eyes fairly sparked as she watched their departure. Her posture spoke both triumph and pleased surprise.

"I've always admired spirit in a woman." The words, spoken softly, silkily, made Kyral's pulse congeal. Somehow Shumri had maneuvered himself touch-close to Grena.

Moaning, Doreya clutched Kyral's upper arm with a grip certain to leave bruises.

Yahweh . . . please.

Grena's glance of curiosity turned to disdain. She wiped her bloody knuckles down her tunic, and stepped away.

"A moment, only." Shumri raised a hand in what might have been a graceful gesture of command, but for his bulbous fingers. He reached into a pouch, hanging by a braided golden cord from his bulging waist.

"A reward," he said pretentiously, "until something more fitting can be found."

But Grena, seeming not to notice, had hurried back to Noah in time to stroke the striped mane of a zebra.

If possible, Doreya's grip tightened. Kyral had noticed, too.

Returning the coin to his pouch, Shumri regarded Noah with an expression of cold fury.

Oh, Yahweh, Kyral mourned within herself, *Shumri can never let this insult pass. Save the child. And protect Noah.*

⸎⸎⸎ ⸎⸎⸎

Walking slowly home, Maelis felt at peace. The warmth of the day, the quietness of the meadow—stirred only by lulling insect voices and the throbbing of a sleepy thrush—echoed in her spirit.

For the last time, she had knelt by the graves of her parents. For the final time, she'd placed fresh flowers there, their favorites. There were gentle arbutus for her gentle mother and vivid oleander for her father. One last time she'd tidied the stones laid to discourage the tunneling of moles and mice and the tendency of grass and vines to overrun. Once more she'd renewed the memories she must store in her heart as carefully as seeds and seedlings had already been stored in the ark.

Such loving people her parents had been! Surely, had they lived a decade longer, they'd be joining Father Noah on the ark. She'd never seen them bowed in worship to idols. Though, to her knowledge, they'd never mentioned Yahweh by name, they had unfailingly reverenced purity and honesty and compassion, in much the same way Father Noah and Mother Kyral taught.

When Shem had chosen her as his bride, both had rejoiced. Her father, already failing then, his stature bent and his once-deep voice quavering, had hugged her wordlessly, his tears wetting her cheek. Her mother, who was seldom wordless, rattled on and on in excitement and relief.

"Never, my dear," she bubbled, "will you be forced to submit to lustful priests. Never will you be beaten! Never supplanted by younger wives and cast into servitude! Oh, my child, how I praise whatever gods there may be that you join such a household! I shall inform the sunrise each dawning and the moon each night of my gratitude! Now I can die in peace, knowing you are safe from evil. For I'm convinced that Noah, mild as he is, when left to himself, and—as some insist—a bit wavery in the mind, would use his huge hammers to smash the skulls of any who might threaten you! Not that anyone would dare, so bulging are the muscles of those three young men from helping their father. But *should* a rapist ever approach you, surely one look from those eyes of old Noah—fierce enough when there's cause— would produce second thoughts."

Remembering, smiling, enjoying the stroke of breeze through her hair, Maelis paused at the edge of the meadow. They'd so loved her and she them. Her father had thought her perfect. And her mother, never seeming to notice her bulk, her ungainliness, had always pronounced her beautiful.

"Can this young man of yours possibly realize," she asked as she draped and pinned and gathered fabric for a wedding dress, "what a prize he's getting?"

Walking again, still slowly, Maelis chuckled. She'd never counted herself a prize. Yet how triply blessed she had been in parents and a husband who did!

❯❯❯ ❮❮❮

Time and again, Afene caught herself singing as she packed—not the "cold bird" song that filled her mind in moments of sadness or contemplation. Or the lullabies that produced sadness because of doubt that remained unquenchable despite Mother Kyral's repeated assurances that Yahweh would expect each of them, including Afene, to bear children.

With the move to the ark already in progress and the flood almost upon them—thus assuring perfect, uninterrupted unity between her and Japheth—only happy songs would do: those rollicking tunes of childhood's play, rhythms that had paced a jumping game or counted out the time allowed for hiding. Many were melodies whose words had been warped by misuse and tangled by time, and so could be altered with lyrics suited to any emotion.

At last, we're leaving! Praise Yahweh, we're leaving! We're leaving, we're leaving, we're leaving! Praise Yahweh! Praise Yahweh!

Looking about the small house, she searched for anything she would truly miss. The cot where she and Japheth had slept since their wedding night hugged a wall given to mustiness and nearly scraped an opposite area of sagging shelves. Even their sleeping quarters on the ark would be less crowded than here. Afene regretted only that the bed covers, which had known too many tears of loneliness and despair, could not be left behind.

Her cooking shelves were already emptied, some crocks and baskets moved to the ark, the rest, in various stages of protective wrapping, littered about the floor and uneven table. The best benches would go with them; the table would remain behind. Her hard-packed dirt floor had always been brushed to a sheen, but at such cost to her muscles and temper! There was no question; even rough wood was more easily cleaned, more durable, far less prone to dampness.

What about the wood on the ark? she asked herself wryly. Wouldn't the water all about, and stretching beneath them—perhaps to the height of mountains—introduce overwhelming dampness?

Still, the pitch and the barrier of air between floors would give protection. And no longer would dew rise in the night, creeping from the ground beyond the door to that within, dampening her woven carpets, the soles of their sandals, and any errant fragment of cloth or piece of clothing that

chanced to touch it. Endless water would surely be preferable to the sour odor of damp dirt, and should offer more
dramatic surroundings, as well.

Here her window permitted a limited view—a narrow
thoroughfare traveled primarily by produce carts or animals on their way to market or the temples. On the far side
stood a stone wall in need of repair. Even as she watched,
two carts, both donkeys swerving, careened from opposite
directions. One cart struck the wall with a clatter; the other
overturned in the road. Gourds and coconuts flew every-
where, one thudding even against the house. Curses flying,
the drivers dismounted and tangled in a dusty brawl, while
their animals brayed plaintively for release from the clutter
of wheels and stones and splintered wood. And a pig, caught
beneath the rubble, squealed until Afene's ears rang.

No, she was certain, as melody rose to her lips again,
there was absolutely nothing she would miss!

⇒⇒⇒ ⇐⇐⇐

Kyral swiped the back of her hand across her damp forehead. She'd thought the moving nearly complete, until
she'd tabulated how much food it might take, not only to
nourish them while they were afloat, but until flooded
fields could be drained and plowed and soggy soil coaxed to
growing. And they'd need additional seed, in the event some
rotted or fell to hungry birds and animals—what few there
would be of those.

"Better too much than not enough," her mother had said
when finally freed of a husband's tyranny. But Kyral, remembering unused bread greening with mold and softening
to mushy blackness, had never adopted the maxim—until
now.

She sent Ham to buy extra supplies wherever they might
be purchased, while Maelis ground and stored flour and
baked countless loaves for cooling and wrapping. Afene, up-
rooting, washing, and drying tubers, stored them in netting
to admit the air. Kyral rooted seedlings in deep trays packed

with rich soil from beneath a gopher tree. She took Maelis and Afene in search of more herbs, more wild berries, more ripening fruits and vegetables while Tamara, still too embarrassed to risk facing friends, remained in the ark to arrange casks, pack shelves, and prepare fruits for the drying racks.

And Kyral fretted that still they might lack enough.

"Yahweh will care for us, my love," Noah reasoned.

But though she gave the appearance of relaxing into Yahweh's providence, she trembled inwardly. When a household was undernourished, on whom did the blame fall? The wife and mother, of course! Kyral had always prided herself on the bounty of her home. How could she bear it if anyone pointed accusingly, whispering that she had failed?

"And who will be there to point?" It was Yahweh's voice, warm with humor.

She flushed. Of course. There would be no one but her own family. Everyone else would have perished in the flood. But how could she gain comfort from that when thoughts of Doreya and Grena always intervened?

➽➽➽ ❦❦❦

Dusk was gathering. Soon it would be time to leave work in the ark and return to their homes. Laying aside her mending—impossible, anyway, in the fading light—Maelis breathed deeply of the evening's beauty.

Footsteps pattered on the pier. Grena, running ahead of her mother, called as she scurried up the ramp, "Will Tamara show me what you've done today? May I visit the animals?" Without waiting for an answer, she gave Noah a quick hug and skipped through the darkened entryway. Kyral, sitting without, shelling lentils into a stone crock, heard her shouting Tamara's name.

Now that the animals were enclosed in their pens and many of the ark's caverns filled with grain and foodstuffs and extra sleeping pallets, voices no longer reverberated with quite that echoing quality of a few months earlier. And even though Kyral had expected the accumulated animals to produce deafening hubbub, they seldom made uproar, and their gentler sounds were largely absorbed, as well, by the walls and contents of the ark.

Doreya seemed quieter than usual. More solemn. Loading a double handful of lentils in her lap and beginning to shell with an air of abstraction, she said, "I have something to ask of you, my friend."

Kyral smiled. "Anything," she promised softly.

Doreya seemed to give full attention to the lentils. "Last night Saert asked . . ." she cleared her throat, lowered her voice, "if the manner of women had yet come upon Grena." She added miserably, "My falsehood won't long deceive him."

Kyral shook her head sadly. How her heart ached for the child, and for Doreya.

"When he was drinking last night, he mentioned he'll be seeing Shumri soon."

Kyral placed an arm across Doreya's shoulder in comfort. "What would you have us do?"

"Hide her. On the ark."

Oh, Yahweh! Could this be the answer to her prayers? No reassurance came. "Gladly," she answered, then asked, "Tonight?"

"Not tonight. Saert would miss her and guess at once where she had gone."

"At any time you choose, then." Emptying her lap of limp shells, she covered the stone crock. "There are niches even Noah hasn't discovered!"

Doreya managed a slight smile. "I surely explored most of them when I was Grena's age." She frowned. "Perhaps Saert did, as well. And Shumri."

"Then we'll find a tiny space!" Kyral forced her voice to lightness. "Shumri will be like an old boar, pushing his snout against a mouse hole." But the comparison, with its contrast of voraciousness to vulnerability, was not a happy one. And, Kyral remembered, *Saert* was slim and agile— and cruel. *Even to a daughter?*

Swift memory of her own harsh father left her no doubt.

"And one further request."

"Anything," Kyral repeated.

"Pray Noah's god for our protection."

"Oh, my friend!" Kyral caught her close. "Noah and I both pray for you continually!"

Doreya drew back in surprise. Her face crumpled. Tears, unchecked, slid down her cheeks.

Patting absently, Kyral asked, "Haven't you guessed how dear you are to us?"

Doreya's response was drowned in sobbing.

"Never mind. Never mind," Kyral comforted, knowing from years of mothering that the phrases weren't nearly as important as the tone. "Everything's going to be fine."

But of course it wouldn't. It couldn't, unless, by some miracle, Grena and Doreya joined them on the ark.

Yahweh? she asked inwardly, tentatively.

There was no reply. Why did he answer in less vital matters, yet ignore this concern closest to her heart? She felt a wash of annoyance, but it dispelled with Doreya's next words.

"Give me Yahweh."

Kyral inhaled deeply. At last!

Doreya mopped at her tears. "Have you an image I may take with me?"

"But—there *are* no images of Yahweh."

"Then, how do you know his appearance? How can you worship?"

Kyral lifted both hands to her heart. "He is here. Within us. He speaks to us."

"Yet if you can't *see* him, if you have nothing to hold in your hand, how can you be certain it is he who speaks?"

Kyral had never felt more incompetent! Frantically, she searched the decks, the pier, for Noah or Japheth. Dusk, enclosing the ark, pressed so densely that she might not have discerned them had they stood only cubits away. She sighed. "Yahweh tells us," she said lamely.

Doreya's expression remained heavy with doubt and disappointment. "I had hoped . . ." She sighed.

Kyral urged, "Let Noah teach you how to approach Yahweh."

"But when he has no body, no face or eyes," she shook her head, "I would feel I was praying to air."

Yahweh, Kyral pleaded. *Give me direction.*

"I am a spirit," He whispered.

"Yahweh is a spirit," Kyral said.

"As are our gods! But they also have forms we can see and touch."

"There is no body large enough to contain Yahweh," Kyral said, unsure whether the words were hers or His. "He embraces the whole world. While He speaks to us here, He is on the other side of the earth. He is in the deepest ocean, even as He moves the clouds through the heavens."

"All at once?" Doreya's voice was pregnant with disbelief. "We have many gods for the sea alone! One for small fish for eating; one to pacify the waves; one who powers leviathan . . ."

"Yahweh controls all."

"And yet," Doreya said sighing, standing, "he can't give himself a shape that we can see and hold!"

Desperate, Kyral insisted, "It isn't that He can't."

"Just that he won't?" Doreya asked bitterly. "Then he cares no more deeply than do the other gods."

As though she could physically impress a belief she seemed powerless to convey in words, Kyral caught Doryea close. "Please. Please kneel with me now and ask Yahweh to enter your heart."

But Doreya was pulling away, straightening her clothing, pushing at her hair. "Perhaps another day," she said. "For now, we'll go to the temple."

To the temple? Kyral's heart lurched. To lie with a priest, hoping to exact from such carnality protection for her daughter's purity? And Doreya had said "we."

Kyral protested, "You won't take Grena with you!"

"I must!"

"But the priests will . . . lust after her." Her last word faltered into hopelessness.

Doreya hugged her reassuringly. "My friend, our priests can't lust. Our *gods,* perhaps, but our priests are pure."

"Oh, Doreya!" Never before had Kyral shown such anger to this sweet friend. "They've already sacrificed your firstborn! Will you give them Grena, as well?"

Doreya sank to the bench in a dejected heap, her foot striking the crock, rattling its imperfectly-fitted lid. "Is there no god who can help me?" she sighed.

Again, Kyral strove to comfort by her closeness. "Yahweh can!"

"Then let him show himself to me!" Doreya challenged. The deepening darkness spun with silence. Kyral didn't raise her thoughts in prayer for such a miracle. As far as she knew, despite their closeness, Yahweh had never shown Himself even to Noah.

"Well, then," Doreya said, stiffening again. "Will you at least take Grena with you to your house until I return from worship?"

➽➽ ⬅⬅

Sometime much later, Kyral woke to hear Noah scrambling from their pallet. Frenzied animal screams and shrieks filled the night.

"What?" she gasped.

"Get the boys," Noah called over his shoulder.

Tugging a coverlet about her, she hurried outside. Darkness, only slightly lifting, outlined the ark's looming bulk. If anything, the cries of terror had intensified. Hurrying along winding dark streets, Kyral subdued thoughts of who might lurk there—murderers, perverts . . . No matter.

First, she sought Shem. But it was Maelis who answered her frenzied knock.

"He heard," Maelis said simply, "and has gone to alert Ham and Japheth." She stepped aside, and Kyral, shivering from more than the night's chill, entered. But how could she rest there when Noah and their sons might be facing danger?

"A moment, and we'll both go." Maelis reached for a shawl. Barefoot, they hurried along the dirt path impeded by houses and jutting garden walls. Kyral's first impression, as they gained a clear view of the ark, was of fire.

Why hadn't she noticed when she'd left the house? Perhaps it had only now started. Yes, there, darting through distant darkness, streaming light like ribbons unfurling in wind, were three running figures. Three figures, three flares, while three small fires licked at the pitch-protected exterior of the ark's hull.

The animals were screaming in terror, their hooves pounding until it seemed they would shatter even those sturdy walls. Kyral's breath came in sharp, sobbing bursts. Her voiceless prayer spoke more of panic than of belief.

Oh, Yahweh. Oh, Yahweh. Oh, Yahweh . . .

"Shhh. I am here."

Then how? Why?

"Only think. Would I allow my servant Noah to progress this far, only to be defeated?"

You could have stopped them!

"I could have," He agreed mildly, and she sensed His withdrawal.

Now wasn't the time for argument. They'd reached the ark. Using her shawl, Maelis was already beating at the flames. As her wooden fingers fumbled with her coverlet, Kyral considered how surprisingly hot the fires had grown so quickly. Maelis's wedding shawl would never be the same. Nor would Kyral's own coverlet, and it was one she'd carried from her girlhood home, so long ago, the one beneath which she'd often huddled while her mother comforted—gently, wordlessly—following the horror of the shed.

Shrugging, she held firmly, lifting the precious coverlet high, feeling the breeze catch and billow it as she thumped it down, and down again—watching with momentary satisfaction as sparks scattered, as a small area blackened, briefly, before springing into flames again.

Noah had already drawn water from the stream and extinguished some small portions of flame.

"Shem?" Maelis asked, nearly breathless.

"In the ark," Noah answered, puffing.

He'd work himself into an attack, Kyral was sure. Why wouldn't he ever take care of himself? Why didn't Yahweh tell him that he must? Empowered by frustration, she continued to batter ineffectually at flames.

Groping his cloak about him, Ham hurried up, his bare legs flashing.

"Animals," Noah panted, heading for the stream again. And Ham scampered off, his footfalls thundering up the ramp. But already, the animals seemed calmer.

And Japheth, arriving soon after, removed Kyral's coverlet from her cramping grasp and slammed it into flames, time after time, scattering a few sparks that fizzled near the blackened pier.

"Infidels!" sputtered Shem, emerging from the ark when at last all was quiet. But Noah seemed not to hear. His face was turned upward, his hands uplifted, his expression rapt.

"It is time," he said, relaxed and smiling. "Yahweh invites us to complete our move into His ark."

As they intensified their preparation, the frequency and viciousness of the taunting increased each day. And, although there were no further fires, during each of the next three nights, refuse was thrown at the ark. By the time Noah or one of the boys could investigate, the vandals were always out of sight, if not of hearing. Each night, as dusk gathered, Kyral braced herself against what darkness might bring.

Yahweh, she asked, more than once, *how soon?*

"Soon," was His only answer.

She hoped that Yahweh's "soon" would be soon enough.

In the early afternoon, they began arriving—singly, in pairs, in giggling groups, to set up impromptu tables and benches in the grassy area beyond the wooden walkway near the pier. The women brought baskets and trays draped with handwoven linen cloths of brilliant hues, while the children staggered beneath the weight of reed or wooden bowls piled high with fruit and tubers, cleaned and wedged. Tots proudly carried long loaves of bread, once symmetrical, now squeezed and crunched wherever small hands had clutched or small elbows anchored them.

Two young men carrying a skinned goat, secured by heavy, charred ropes to a sturdy pole, strained to maintain their balance. Once their burden was suspended between leaning, pronged braces, they set about the serious business of good-natured scuffling and the gathering of kindling.

From many baskets and decorated clay pots, savory aromas wound into the ark where Noah was fastening a final hinge. Kyral, slumped at last to a cot, fanned herself with a palm branch. And the young couples stored last minute bundles and packets wherever space allowed.

They had emptied their homes, had framed silent good-byes appropriate to spaces that had witnessed their deepest joys and starkest agonies. Closing their doors with firm finality, they'd mounted the ark's ramp with no thought of descending it again until the flood waters had come and receded.

But now the sounds of people gathering, the high, sweet laughter of children, those aromas . . . all of it beckoned. It was Tamara who scurried to the gangway, perching there to peer out.

"They're covering tables!" she called, turning, her eyes dancing. "And there's so much food!" Quickly she pulled back, whispering, "Someone's coming."

Frowning, laying aside his awl, Noah eased his shoulders and knees, preparing to stand. He stalked, stiff-legged, to the doorway to greet their visitor, a plump, red-nosed official with incredibly filthy feet in spotless sandals.

"Morgine." Noah's tone was even, noncommittal.

"Noah." The man ducked his head and harrumphed nervously.

"Come in." Noah stood aside.

Morgine hesitated, shuffling his feet. Kyral thought wryly he looked as though he suspected they might shackle and forcibly add him to their group. She stood, laying aside her spray of palm.

"Morgine." She advanced, her hand extended. "And how is your dear Sereda? I've never forgotten how, last winter when Noah was ill, she brought hot soup and freshly baked bread. Please carry my best wishes, if you will, and tell her that I'll always cherish her thoughtfulness."

He accepted her hand, bowing over it, murmuring, "My lady, perhaps you might tell her in person." His head bobbed, Tamara thought, like a child's toy fastened inadequately on the end of a slender stick.

Kyral's warmth had done its work. Morgine, at ease, surveyed the ark and its furnishings. "Surprisingly comfortable," he said, "and far from the way I remember it when we were small mischiefs, sneaking in to avoid our parents." He straightened, as though reminded of his present exalted position in the town.

With an air of officiality, he began, "Noah. Since it might

be ah, some time until, uhmmm, you enjoy a good meal again, and company . . ." He broke off, shifting heavily. Bowing in Kyral's direction, he purred, "No offense intended, m'lady, I assure you, concerning your culinary abilities, but rather the . . . er . . . uh . . . mmmm . . ." He seemed to be assessing the cooking facilities within the ark.

"And I take no offense," Kyral assured him, and so freed his tongue for the remainder of his message.

"Noah, your neighbors have prepared a meal in the hope that you and your family will join them."

Noah seemed shaken into friendliness.

Morgine continued, "Many of us are troubled by the fire, y'know, and the increased taunting . . ."

Kyral said gently, "How very kind! As for me, I'd be happy, after what we've been through these past few days, to let someone else do the cooking."

Morgine bowed deeply. "Thank you, my lady," and he looked to Noah for confirmation.

Noah nodded.

"They'll be pleased, then," Morgine said with another bow. When his footsteps no longer rattled the gangway, Kyral exhaled with some satisfaction. "Well . . ."

Giggling, Tamara executed a little dance step of delight, but stopped short when Shem insisted scornfully, "We can't break bread with them!"

"*I* can." Maelis spoke in quiet, firm tones. Turning, she dabbed at her eyes with the shoulder of her tunic.

"Maelis, dear. You're crying!" Tamara's expression blended concern and amazement.

Maelis smiled through her tears. "Don't worry, dear," she said. "It's just that when I meet unexpected goodness . . ."

"Goodness!" Shem was startled to gruffness. Then, as though to make amends, he placed his arm across her shoulder. "You're tired, my love. And too good yourself to recognize treachery."

"Not treachery!" Japheth's eyes gleamed. "Can't you see, Brother? Yahweh grants us a final opportunity to convince them!"

"Perhaps," mused Noah. "Perhaps not. Certainly their gesture has caught me off guard. But we *will* eat with them." He glanced at Shem. "*All* of us."

Shem seemed about to refuse. Then, his jaw tightening, he grumbled, "As you command, Father."

"Are you afraid, Shem?" Tamara asked tremulously. "Ham, they won't poison us. Will they?"

Noah smiled. "My child," he said, "only think. Would Yahweh lead us this far, and then allow us to become victims of His enemies?"

"Then you admit, my father, that they *are* Yahweh's enemies." Shem's tone was still vexed.

"I have never said otherwise, my son."

"And Yahweh has instructed you that we should eat with pagans?"

Noah seemed suddenly weary. "My son, of those writings I have placed in your care, do you read only our ancestor Enoch's warnings to the ungodly? Haven't you studied the Creation Hymn, as well, and learned with what care Yahweh formed our father, Adam? With what hope and expectation He placed humankind in the garden?"

Shem's head was up, his nostrils flaring. "And have *you* forgotten how Father Adam and Mother Eve were expelled for their disobedience! And Cain cursed . . ."

Maelis touched Shem's shoulder, massaging it gently. Already she could sense the shadow of that familiar throbbing just behind her eyelids. Still, she willed her fingers to absorb Shem's anger and transform its energy into her own pain, if that were the price of peace. She was willing to bear anything that might ensure an enjoyable leave-taking from this place. Without feeling the martyr, she'd gladly buy this evening for Tamara, who was poised for adventure, and for Kyral, beaming anticipated pleasure, and Afene, who would surely transform this mingling into an opportunity for sharing recipes.

Shem subsided, sighed, bowed his head in acquiescence. And Maelis, once she sensed his capitulation, pressed exploratory fingertips to her temples and judged the evening saved for her, as well.

Noah was saying, "This is our final chance to witness to relatives and neighbors who worship false gods. Who knows? Perhaps some soul among them, hungry for more than food, may still join us in the safety of the ark." His faded eyes sought the heavens, as though searching for a sign.

Shem grumbled quietly, so that only Maelis seemed to hear. And Tamara, twirling and smiling, obviously recovered from Cloyren's spurning and her subsequent shame, asked breathlessly, "Could we go, now? I haven't said good-bye yet to Armya or Elose."

"Go, child," Kyral said fondly. She fluffed at her own hair, straightened the hem of her robe, and gathered her skirts for the unsteady descent down the ramp.

❧❧❧ ❦❦❦

Tamara sighed, convinced that there'd never been a meal more sumptuous or more varied—a banquet for the eyes, as well as the nose and palate, with sprigs of fresh herbs adorning many dishes. Colorful woven cloths camouflaged rough, makeshift tables, and wildflowers, caught into any available jug and jar, excited a delight possible only with creative disarray.

Thankfully, Cloyren hadn't come. She wondered if he'd been invited. After such a meal, she was glad not to be troubled by reminders of her shame.

Contented, she sat in the shade of a sycamore with friends gathered about her and a final sweet cake still sticky in her fingers. Sighing, she lifted it to her lips, sighed again and offered it to a fat dog lolling nearby. But even he was replete! He rolled his eyes and whined, as if in pain, then ducked his head, covering one eye with a paw. Tamara and her friends giggled as they had when children—before they'd experienced disappointment or rejection, save for those searing agonies of the very young.

How had they grown so far apart? How could her thoughts have so casually consigned these friends to the flood, how forgotten they'd once shared mutual joy and pain? Recently she'd ignored their centrality to her young world when her father was busy at work and her mother already practiced in her coldness.

With such warm thoughts tumbling through her mind and a sad smile trembling on her lips, she looked about the circle. If Yahweh loved them half as much as she did He could never . . .

Elose, her eyes suddenly spilling tears, placed her hand over Tamara's. "I'll miss you," she said softly. "We all will."

There were murmurs of agreement, and a series of pats and assurances broken at last by Nurilla's spiteful words. "Well, we won't miss her for all that long, will we? Just until food runs out on the ark, or someone dies from the foulness of the animal cages."

Into the awkward silence, Tamara urged, "Oh, please, please believe me! For a long time, I thought as you do, and I was determined not to be shut in there."

"So Cloyren told us," Nurilla snickered.

The others hushed her with frowns and nudges, with forefingers to their lips and sputtering hisses.

"I love you." Tamara's voice quavered. "*All* of you." Her glance included Nurilla, whose flashing eyes would not be stilled.

"I can't bear the thought of your dying," Tamara said gently.

Nurilla's stare hooded, slid away.

They stirred uncomfortably, but most expressions were kind.

"Friends worry about friends," Tamara whispered.

"As we are concerned for you!" Armya offered a small packet, tied with a golden cord. "Here. This amulet is made of cloves and garlic and the seeds of some secret plant only Katisha knows. Promise you'll wear it to protect you."

Tamara caught all within reach into a teary embrace so fierce that some wriggled to be free. The fat dog, startled from his slumber, tried to rise, then inched his bulk to comparative safety on the far side of the sycamore.

"Yahweh is truly going to do this terrible thing!" Tamara cried. "Please believe me! Come with us, please!" But they had drawn back. Through her tears, she read their expressions—unbelief, pity, and, except for Nurilla's, forgiveness and compassion.

"I always knew you were gullible, Tamara," Nurilla said crisply. "Else how could Cloyren have duped you for so long! But you must think *us* fools as well, to recite such a tale!" Stretching, she stood in one, smooth, catlike movement, then, laughter trailing behind her, strode away to join the dancers.

Only then was Tamara aware of the music. Thready, at first, as strings and flutes were tested, it tangled in that strange un-melody of instruments being tuned.

"Please," Tamara begged as she looked from one to the other.

Each shook her head—some regretfully, others purposefully.

"You're braver than I am," one said.

"I could never endure the ridicule!" said another.

"To reject our gods!" spoken with a shudder, a look of horror, a frightened glance over the shoulder.

Still another spoke lightly. "I wouldn't mind abandoning our gods nearly as much as leaving the fun and music. And the nights of love." She hugged herself in mock ecstasy.

A ripple of laughter deepened Tamara's despair.

"Enough of solemnity!" Keerin was on her feet, already executing a dance step. The music had become firm, rich, compelling. One by one, like petals peeled from a flower, they left—some with a blown kiss or a quick, thoughtless hug, others not even looking back.

Only Elose remained. "Please, Tamara. It makes us sad to see you sad. Come, dance with us!"

Tamara forced a smile. "This one last time," she whispered, and allowed herself to be led toward the laughing, singing, whirling group. As a hand reached to include her in a circle, she realized that she still clutched the sticky cake.

Kyral had never seen such dancing—so vibrant and so fluid that, despite her heavy knowledge of what the future held for these neighbors, her own feet yearned to yield to the rhythms.

How they twirled, those youngsters, leaning far, far back, their feet barely skimming the ground! If any single pair of hands were to break loose, surely all would fly off into space, like ribbons swirled by a running child!

Her own childhood had not granted her such memories. For her there had been no ribbons or music or dancing. She submerged such thoughts. Yahweh had cancelled her grief.

It pleased her to see Tamara with her friends. Although her eyes were wide and her mouth small with sadness, she seemed to draw all glances.

Such grace she has! What a lovely child. Thank You, Yahweh, for leading her to belief.

Tamara was growing up. Surely with the discipline the ark would provide, she could be only a stabilizing factor for Ham. Certainly he required all the stability anyone could furnish, or, indeed, what all of them together could provide. She'd been gratified with his easy forgiveness of Tamara's flight to Cloyren. Surely that had been a mark of coming maturity.

Wasn't it? she asked Yahweh, but didn't wait for a response. Quickly she remembered Ham's boyish delight in the strange animals: how he'd tried to ride a rhinoceros, until it had bucked and finally launched him—barely grazing that vicious, upthrust horn—into a pile of manure; how he'd baited a wild boar by hunkering down, bouncing on hands and feet, and grunting a challenge. But for Japheth's quick thinking, those tusks could well have split Ham like a fowl prepared for stuffing.

Kyral shuddered. After all these years, Ham was still a reckless child. But she knew he retained, as well, some of the more admirable traits of childhood. His quick smile broke after a sulk like sunshine. His enjoyment in nature's smallest wonders caused others to pause in delight as though for the first time. Perhaps his warmth was his most endearing quality, or was it his enthusiasm in new endeavors? She sighed. Once novelty faded, so did the childlike interest.

Will he ever become fully a man?

"Enjoy the music," came the answer.

Chuckling, she quieted her thoughts and gave attention to the soft, melodic flow as it led the dancers into more stately movements. Flutes harmonized with pipes and harps strummed softly, like the gentle fall of water. Under it all lay the pulsing beat of muted drums.

I shall miss music.

"But you've stored instruments in the ark."

Yes. A small harp, a drum, a child's whistle, a flute carved of some hard, dark wood—she had put them there herself, although she'd wondered if something more important deserved the space.

Noah and I aren't blessed with the gift of music, nor are the boys. And, as far as she knew, none of the young wives was musical, although Afene often sang—more tunelessly than she could possibly have guessed.

Perhaps they'd simply been too involved in their daily tasks to concern themselves with song. Perhaps, during the long days on the ark . . .

No. No matter how long the days or how many there might be, none of them possessed the skill to make music that elevated and exulted, that coaxed and implored and commanded the obedience of dancing feet, that could spin elaborate fantasies and weave melody on melody until the spirit soared.

"I will not let music die."

But we can't store its roots or bulbs for planting later. We haven't the ability—the God-given . . . Oh!

"Exactly. Music is mine. For now, store all the sounds your heart can hold for later remembering."

She walked apart, one segment of her mind soaking in the rich, lovely harmonies, another dwelling on loss. She would miss the melodies of birds, soaring in flocks, and the herds of deer and wild ponies poised in alertness at the edges of the forest. How long would it take to rebuild herds and flocks from those few animals on the ark?

And children—how desperately she'd miss their prattling and laughter, even their quarreling. How long would it take to grow a cluster of children again with only three young women and none even pregnant yet?

She scanned the crowd, finding each. Tamara, wand-slim, was dancing, her color heightened, her sunlit hair floating. How beautiful Tamara's children would be, hers and Ham's. And Afene, looking a bit stern and withdrawn and so very thin. How desperately anxious she was for children. When she became pregnant, they'd know by the second week—both by her joy and her altered profile. But Maelis— there was one whose pregnancy could be hidden for months. Perhaps . . . No, of all the girls, Maelis was closest to Kyral. Maelis would have told her.

So, no children coming now, at least not for another nine months. Even then they'd be too small for enjoying. If only Grena . . .

She must release that concern. Whether Grena and Doreya joined them on the ark was in Yahweh's control. Still, she hadn't seen them all evening! Where could they be? Could Saert already have . . .

The music, she reminded herself sternly, *listen to the music. Store up its melodies, its lightness. There will be time enough, later, for worry and for grieving.*

Afene sat, listening to, but not quite hearing, the music. She was thinking of the food. She'd never tasted such delicious food! Even though both Shem and Japheth had frowned at her, she'd requested recipes, repeating them until they were firmly fixed in memory. Of course, on the ark she'd have so few spices . . .

"We'll give you spices!" several of the women promised. Moments later they returned with vials and packets and small covered urns. Smiling warmly, Afene accepted each gift with slow ceremony, with a careful lifting and a deep in-halation of each pungent fragrance.

"Thank you," she whispered, wondering why it should be only at this final parting that they'd discovered a common ground. But she knew the answer to her musing. Japheth had forbidden her to make friends among the pagans.

And yet, had she been permitted to mingle with them, would that necessarily have polluted her belief in Yahweh as Japheth feared? Mightn't she instead have become a part-ner in his evangelizing? Did he hold her in such slight re-gard?

"Use only the slightest pinch," one of the women in-structed. "You have more than enough, no matter how long your imprisonment on the ark."

Imprisonment?

"And when you return," a young, dark-haired woman said, her small hand pressing Afene's arm, "we'll show you where they grow."

When she returned . . .

Afene recognized most of the spices. For those, Kyral al-ready had seedlings aboard.

"This one," and Afene indicated a packet of shriveled sil-ver leaves, "could you show me now?"

"Of course!" A plump, middle-aged woman stood. "I used it in my dish—perhaps you tasted some?—with sliced tubrous roots, baked until soft and brown, then garnished with dill." Breathless from her haste, she turned to look hopefully into Afene's face.

"It was delicious!"

Afene was rewarded with a bright smile, and her new friends led her to the growing place.

It was a low shrub huddling in shadow. Since they'd brought no tools, Afene knelt and carefully, digging with her fingers, coaxed a young shoot from the mossy soil. Preserv-ing the roots and as much rich earth as possible, she bun-dled it into her outer skirt. The other women carried her gifts as they left the wooded area and turned once more to-ward the ark.

It was a mammoth presence, dark and looming. Trying to interpret it through the eyes of her companions, Afene imagined that it represented more threat than promise.

"It's so immense," a younger woman breathed.

"And yet," a tall matron added with some bite to her words, "it will seem small enough with all of them crowded there for only the gods know how long!"

"And with those animals!" A shudder.

Afene knew they could never comprehend her contentment with that closeness, with her monopoly of Japheth.

Their silence—broken only by soft footfalls, disturbed pebbles, and the distant music—was almost comfortable.

A soft hand touched Afene's elbow. "I wish we'd known you earlier. You're really very nice!"

"As all of you are," Afene said, tears gathering in her eyes. How could Yahweh bear to snuff out these lives, when there were such obvious elements of goodness in each?

"When Noah releases you," a light voice said, "surely we can become better friends, sharing more than recipes."

"We'll introduce you to our gods!"

Afene's breath tightened, and when she stumbled, three hands reached to steady her.

No harm, she chided herself. No damage could accrue from the mere mention of their gods. After all, Japheth had spoken of them often.

"They're not as stuffy as yours." The voice, unheard before, was huskily musical. "They demand so little."

"And that is more pleasure than duty! In fact," the speaker's voice showed renewed excitement and she began an urgent pattering on Afene's shoulder, "we could take you now, this evening!"

The light phrases slowed, becoming almost secretive, sensual. "There is one whom I particularly serve. Alyra, goddess of fertility. Have you heard of her?"

Afene shook her head numbly.

The words continued, enclosing Afene as the woman's arms encircled her, stifled her, besieged her. "Her thighs are like the trunks of trees, sturdy and wonderfully muscled. Her womb forever bulges with young. And her breasts are *huge!*" She described with her hands.

"No!" Afene gasped, too brusquely not to disturb the friendliness that had involved them. Pausing she explained awkwardly into their stunned silence, "Yahweh is a jealous God. To look on such an idol would anger Him. Even to hear of such an abomination . . ." In her heart, she pled for His forgiveness.

Their laughter rippled.

"Just as we said, your god is stuffy and old. He forbids your enjoyment, while *our* gods encourage us to sing, to dance, to make love before them."

"Please." Afene's voice was ragged; her knees sagged. Once again, hands cupped her elbows, prevented her falling.

"We only want you to be one with us!"

"And when you return . . ."

"Oh, yes! We'll have such fun together! If you've never danced freely, casting your clothing to the wind, and . . ."

"The temple priests are so handsome!"

"Their bodies firm and hard, anointed with perfumed oils!"

"If ever there were men who have learned how to please a woman . . ."

A sigh of exaggerated ecstasy was echoed by the others.

"Please." Afene whispered, her mind seething. She choked on nausea.

A hand on her elbow grew insistent.

"Do come with us now, Afene! Once you've tasted the pleasures offered by *our* gods—"

"No! No! No!" She felt herself quivering, cowering, sinking to the earth. They huddled above her, and she shrank from their soft touches.

"It's all right, Afene," one said soothingly.

"We've pushed her too hard."

"Just imagine! All those years of harshness! Being taught that her body is evil, that physical pleasure must be shunned."

"Poor child. Poor child."

"Come, Afene." Someone lifted her. "We won't pressure you further. Let us take you to the ark, to your husband. There will be time enough, when old Noah tires of his madness and gives you back to us."

She allowed them to lead her. She was powerless to do otherwise. As her quivering mind renewed its ability to reason, she praised Yahweh that she had been sheltered from their foul worship, and prayed that He would be gentle with these women who, despite the training that had shaped their sinning, had so much of human kindness in their hearts.

There could no longer be any doubt. Yahweh was doing what He must if the world He'd created was to remain His. But, oh! What tragedy! How His heart must bleed. How it must have broken whenever they refused to hear of Him or to accept His love, when they laughed and hooted and ran simpering after idols and priests who glorified promiscuity and all excesses.

They'd reached the ark. Her lips trembling, Afene turned to the women, whose expressions showed only concern for her. "You've been kind to me," she said, "and I care for you." Once more they pressed the vials and packets and urns into her arms. It was with difficulty that she juggled them, the clumped skirt, and her heavy thoughts. "I'll pray for you," she promised. "I'll beg Yahweh's mercy on you."

One reached to kiss her cheek. Another hugged her warmly.

"And we will petition our gods for you!" one promised lightly. "In fact, we go this very moment to offer incense for your protection from this god of harshness and anger."

They seemed barely able to wait, they had such eagerness to be off. She gave them one last, longing look, then mounted the ramp to the comforting dimness of the ark. Perhaps Japheth had been right all along. Tiredly, she sank to a hard bench. Perhaps she could have been swayed, rather than swaying. She shivered. Certainly, her emotions would never have survived a day-after-day battering, as Japheth's had. No wonder he'd had so little left to give her!

It would be different, now. The ark would enclose them. Once the flood came, once the opportunity for evangelizing had passed, he could relax. He could be with her. Together they could plan for a future where false gods and their corruption would not exist.

Bowing, she prayed to Yahweh that it would be so.

Maelis joined her there. Finding Afene sobbing, she comforted her in that warm, accepting, motherly way only Maelis knew. "I know," she murmured. "I know, dear sister. I felt it, too—a wrenching sadness." They sat, Maelis rocking both herself and Afene.

Eventually, their last tears fallen and final sobs subsided, they slipped to their knees and prayed together. And though both felt Yahweh's nearness, neither could fully shake off the pressure of grief.

"How will we bear it?" Afene began, later.

"Yahweh will help us. He grieves with us."

"And Kyral. Perhaps Japheth."

"Shem will not grieve." Maelis sighed, touching her temple, as though the tense throbbing had resumed.

It was Afene's turn to comfort. Beyond them, in the gathering night, the music continued and increased, its tempo heightening.

They looked out to find the dancing more frenzied, more abandoned. They saw Noah, pausing with Kyral and Tamara beside him, scanning the crowd and peering into shadows made confusing by the flickering flames of a huge bonfire.

"We're here, Father Noah!" Maelis shouted—far too softly to be heard above the celebration.

Still, he turned, acknowledged them, and climbed stiffly, assisting Kyral, to the entryway where they waited.

Kyral's face was wan, streaked with evidence of fresh grieving. Maelis drew her into her arms.

But Tamara's face glowed, and her feet still danced, though she sobered, slightly, as she entered the finality of the ark. "I'm happy!" she said. "I was able to say goodbye, and to accept it as goodbye."

Afene sighed. Perhaps she, too, would find a greater acceptance, later.

Kyral murmured, "Some I already loved, but . . ." Her voice broke.

Just then, looming in the doorway, Shem said tightly, "It was a mistake to go, as I knew it must be."

"No mistake, my son." Noah's face, too, was drawn and weary.

Bristling, Shem gestured at the downcast group. But Japheth argued, "In those final moments, when the waters close above them . . ." The women shuddered. "Who knows what they may remember of all we've spoken tonight?"

Afene moved confidently into the circle of his arms. *Yes,* she thought. *Yes!* she prayed. *Surely, it will be so!* When the false gods themselves were destroyed, proven to be powerless, when the priests floundered, crying out in terror, when the people saw that only the ark stood firm, they'd know! And to those who cried out for forgiveness, even in those final moments, Yahweh surely would not turn a deaf ear.

Long past dusk and well into deepest night, the last music clattered into discord, then silenced. Dark figures tossed sand on the fire, and eventually only a few coals glowed as evidence of recent celebration.

In the dark entryway, Kyral stood alone, musing, worrying. Where could Doreya be? And Grena?

She paced restlessly, praying, resisting Noah's urging that she strengthen herself for the difficult weeks ahead.

"You rest, my love," she said. "I'm too churning with thoughts just now."

And he went, although reluctantly.

Spent with concern, she dozed, awakening suddenly when anyone passed near the ark. Drawing her breath in sharply, holding it against the potential for some new vandalism, she exhaled, breathing normally as dark figures passed on, often trailing tendrils of flirtatious laughter.

Sometimes she heard slurred muttering. Occasionally angry words erupted, and she stiffened again.

Still, toward morning, when she heard the swift pattering of bare feet, the rustling of garments, furtive whisperings, it never occurred to her to be afraid. More from habit than from necessity, she reached for a torch.

"No!" came a compelling, insistent whisper. Then, closer and more gently, "Please, my friend. Light would betray us." And Kyral's heart constricted.

Doreya's voice had never sounded more tense. And Grena—sweet, sunny child—wept softly, wretchedly.

"He's coming to claim her—at first light!"

Shumri! Kyral's skin crawled with revulsion.

"Saert will know we've come here," Doreya drew a shattering breath, "but there's nowhere else to go! There's no other friend who'd take such a risk, or see a reason for it."

Wordlessly, Kyral tried to stand. Slapping her legs, numb from long sitting, she urged, "Come!"

Grena's gasp alerted them—too late!

Accompanied by at least a dozen relatives—some swaggering, swinging clubs, others shambling, obviously half-asleep—Saert and Shumri approached the dock.

Dismayed, Kyral saw Morgine also approaching. How different his attitude, now, from when the night before he'd come as an emissary of friendship and good will. In truth, Kyral thought, he seemed a bit uncomfortable with this official role. Hanging back, his head bobbing erratically, he continually folded and refolded his arms in their too-long sleeves.

Yet his presence, whether willing or not, proved one thing. Saert and Shumri were determined that they be backed by the law.

If only Yahweh would intervene! Half-expectantly, Kyral pushed the suggestion toward Him, but sensed no response.

Behind her, she heard the shuffling of sandals. It was Noah, not troubling to cover his yawn, followed by the boys, looking somewhat more alert, but fully as puzzled.

Sobbing, Grena threw herself into Noah's arms.

He held her close, then ordered gently, "Hide."

Shaking her head, she sank even more deeply into his embrace. "They'll kill you! If only Yahweh would send the rains!" Mopping at her eyes with the hem of her robe and sniffling in a childlike manner that underlined her vulnerability, she peered into the sky, as though searching for rain clouds.

Kyral tried again. *Yahweh . . .*

Why couldn't He delay this evil until the rains began? Or until the ark was afloat with Grena and Doreya safely aboard? Though He gave no answer, she sensed His sadness, companion to her own. Still, impatience surged within her.

Was He all-powerful or not? When He planned to suspend the laws of nature with the flood, when He had promised to reverse all reason by saving a seed of humanity, of animals of each species, and of growing things, was it asking too much that He strike two evil men with temporary blindness or some other malady that would stop their evil pursuit?

Such a small request, my Lord . . .

"Come, Grena." Saert spoke softly, but assertively, from the foot of the ramp. "Now."

She whimpered against Noah.

When Shumri stepped forward, Kyral could sense the boys moving beside and past her, stopping before her, their feet widespread, their well-muscled arms at their sides.

Shumri stepped back, but raised his voice in oily entreaty. "I'll be a kind husband to you, my little one," he said. "And I've paid a generous price to your father."

Doreya, her voice shaping only shrill sounds of anguish, thrust herself past the boys and down the gangway.

"Doreya, no!" Kyral shouted.

Doreya never turned, never hesitated. Colliding with Shumri, she beat at his chest with her fists, while he, backing away, made pathetic cries of protest. But Saert, catching her cruelly, flung her into a heap on the dock.

He never looked at her, only at Grena, then at the boys. Determination sparked in his eyes and twisted his lips as he stooped to the grass and caught up a heavy length of timber.

Shem, Ham, and Japheth began a slow descent. Kyral wondered if a signal had been given, they moved in such concert.

Quickly Saert's companions not already armed found whatever lay at hand. One wrenched loose a plank from the walkway. Another claimed one of the forked supports used the evening before in roasting the goat. Shumri found a weapon in Noah's stone-headed sledge, left leaning against the ark's hull. Trying it, discarding it, he tested an ax, its iron edge honed to a sharp glitter.

Oh, Yahweh, Kyral thought miserably. *He never* was *one to put away his tools.* If their own sons stood in danger because of such neglect . . .

"Your sons are safe," Yahweh assured her heavily.

But Noah? She felt such quivering in her knees, she found it necessary to seek support against the solid doorjamb.

"My dear," Noah suggested, "go inside."

Instead she caught both him and Grena in a loose embrace.

"Grena!" Saert called more tightly, while, behind him, Doreya, stirring on the dock, moaned.

If only she'd lie still there, Kyral thought—and quietly—she might escape Saert's notice.

But Doreya reached out, almost languidly, catching Saert's leg in both hands, and jerked. Was she struggling to pull herself upright or trying to topple him to the dock? Kyral couldn't be certain. She knew only that Doreya, stunned and shaken, was no match for Saert. Easily, he shook her loose, then turned again to the ramp.

"Go home, fool," Shem said coldly. "Don't add to your sins by forcing this child into slavery."

Shumri's hands shook on the shaft of the ax; his pock-marked face flamed with angry color. "I offer her honorable marriage," he snarled, and again stepped forward, as though intending to challenge Shem.

Saert gave a signal, just a quick, sideways movement of

his head, but with whoops and curses and the enthusiasm of bloodlust, the charge began.

As the ramp, which had supported elephants and buffalo without damage, throbbed and pitched beneath the struggle, Kyral's concern moved from Grena and Doreya to her sons.

"Yahweh is with them," Noah said calmly. And of course Yahweh Himself assured her . . .

It seemed, as they forced the battle from ramp to dock, that the boys were holding their own. Though impromptu weapons cut many wild, swishing slashes through the air and grunts and groanings denoted great effort on the part of the attackers, few blows landed.

Almost comfortably, Kyral wondered whether that was due to Yahweh's intervention, or to inferior fighting skills.

The struggle moved from the dock to a grassy sward. *Good.* Perhaps with attention elsewhere, Grena and Doreya could find safety.

But Kyral's heart sank as she saw Shumri, standing alone, testing the edge of the ax across his fat thumb and staring up the gangway.

Would he attack Noah? An image, vivid and chilling, cut across Kyral's memory: Shumri, the day the animals had arrived, glaring pure hatred toward Noah. But surely Yahweh would protect Noah! He *needed* Noah. Still, the ark was complete, now. And Noah could no longer father sons.

Please, Yahweh!

Shumri took one slow step.

Grena drew a harsh, quivering breath as, the ax glinting in his hands, Shumri took another step, and another.

Handing Grena into Kyral's care, Noah stepped grimly forward.

"No!"

Kyral had screamed it, but so had someone else.

Grena, lurching beyond Kyral's reach, stumbled down the ramp.

Smiling, Shumri moved the ax to one hand, reaching the other toward the child in welcome.

But Grena, pushing past him, ran to kneel by her mother. Her face contorted, eyes streaming, she faced Shumri.

"I hate you!" she screamed. "Don't ever touch me! If you do, I'll spit on you!" She half-turned to tug at her mother, helping her to stand, but her bitter words continued. "I'll scratch out your eyes! I'll . . ."

That swiftly, Shumri tightened his grip on the ax and raised it above his head, then brought it down.

"Yahhhhwehhh!"

Kyral's scream extended, echoed. Her head buzzing with disbelief, she rushed down the ramp with Noah beside her.

"No! No! No!" Grena could not be lying there, her head severed, her blood gushing, drenching, pooling.

"No!"

Doreya eased from beneath her child, knelt over her, clutching at her, sobbing hysterically. Her words sounded like caresses, like curses, like prayers.

As the ax ascended again, Noah reached to grasp Shumri's forearm. The touch altered the upward arch and the ax veered. Turning, his eyes glazed and distended, Shumri seemed not to see, seemed not to feel the bloodied handle slip from his loosening grasp. Both gory hands groped slowly toward his throat. His mouth widened. A terrible gargling became foam, then blood, as he slumped to the deck, twitched horribly, and lay still.

Numb, Kyral watched as the battle ebbed into astonishment. Incapable of movement or reaction, she showed no response as Doreya brushed her shoulder in passing. She could absorb no further shock as her friend—scrambling, stumbling, sobbing—appeared on the second deck, then at the upper level of the ark. As Doreya mounted the bow, her arms lifted toward the open sky, Kyral watched abstractedly, as though she observed a dream.

Only when Doreya, shrieking the syllables of Yahweh's name, plummeted toward the rock-strewn shallows did Kyral's mind move from paralysis to heightened horror.

PART THREE

Now the flood was on the earth forty days. The waters increased and lifted up the ark, and it rose high above the earth.

Genesis 7:17

7

Her coverlet folded beneath her for softness, Kyral sat on the bench nearest the shadows. She had spread her mending about her, not that materials might be convenient, but that she might be alone.

Already Noah, then Maelis, and finally Japheth had come by, each asking if she wouldn't like to move closer to the light streaming from the high windows.

"I don't enjoy mending enough that I care to look at it," she'd answered. Maelis half-turned as though something further might need to be said, then shrugged and walked away. But the men, apparently feeling they had discharged their responsibility, disappeared at once. Kyral suspected they'd have done the same, whatever her answer.

All she'd truly wanted was for them to be off somewhere, anywhere. She needed to be alone to think and to heal. That morning, waking to unextinguished grief for Grena and Doreya, she'd known she must come to terms with what had been, what was to be. And, as she'd learned in the matter of her father and the shed, such solutions demanded an investment of time and trauma.

She wondered if Yahweh would join her, or if He might so respect her need for solitude that even He wouldn't intrude. She didn't think she'd mind His presence. Without Him she could never have cast off the demons of her youth. How else would she have learned that her father's atrocities had rooted in his own abused childhood?

For years, she'd expected to unsnarl that puzzle for herself, eventually. Unsnarl or perpetually avoid? She winced at her own thoughts. Such self-scrutiny probed as deftly as she might expect Yahweh's words to do!

Perhaps the questions originated with Him. Perhaps, having once led her through the steps to restoration, He would thrust small perceptions into the process, trusting her to adapt.

And yet pain was the only common factor. That other agony had tangled like ancient briars inexpertly woven by wind and small, burrowing animals and human passersby. This current wound was fresh, fairly clean, still bleeding. Perhaps it could respond to cures more traditional than those that had freed her from the cloying, suffocating fear of enclosure.

They are totally dissimilar, aren't they? This emptiness I feel, this draining grief. Surely, they'll pass. In time they'll dull.

When her mother lay dead, the delicate, unmoving baby sister still wrapped in afterbirth and curved in her silent embrace, how Kyral had wept! She'd searched for some movement in her mother's hands, some rising and falling to her breast, some alteration in that death-frozen smile. Lacking that, she waited for some stirring in the tiny body—a whimper growing to a wail as babies were expected to cry, in lusty, loud decrees.

She stared so long, so steadfastly, that—convinced of movement—she bent her head close to their chests to listen. If her mother should stir, should ask for anything—water, perhaps—she'd race to the clearest stream she knew and bring it. And should she require some promise, no sacrifice would be too dear, too difficult, if only it might ensure her mother's life. Kyral would care for the baby, if that were a need. Gladly she'd feed and wash it, tend to its windings, clean between the tiny toes, soothe its frenzied crying. If only it would cry!

Please cry! she pled, intensely silent, staring, command-ing. *You've got to cry! You can't be dead, not both of you. I can't bear it.*

For days after the burial, as far from their father's recent grave as her brothers could find a spot for digging, Kyral had kept a sodden vigil. And when the tears were gone, she watched in sullen silence.

In time grief had passed, and life surrounded her again, like water swirling around and over pebbles. And one day she'd caught herself laughing—and felt such guilt!

In moments of crisis, before she'd known of Yahweh's ex-istence, she'd often experienced a sense of unreality, as though she were two people, separate and unique. One was fully involved in whatever occurred; the other, detached and dispassionate, an observer and evaluator. Many times, as in the shed with her father, this dichotomy had spun a slender thread of deliverance. The pain became nearly endurable when divided between the real Kyral, who flinched beneath it, and that other, who watched almost dreamily, denying it tangibility.

Kyral had sensed some of that abstraction during Doreya's last moments. For a time, like a draught adminis-tered by a physician to deaden physical pain, disbelief had deadened the shock. For those terrible first moments, de-nial diluted the tragedy, slowing its entry into her aware-ness.

So it had been, years before, when she happened on a child caught in the jaws of a mastiff. As blood spurted from puncture wounds to the small head and slender neck and streamed down delicate shoulders, the Kyral who thought, who cared, who shrank from confrontation—that Kyral was worthless. It was the observer Kyral who caught up a staff, who stunned the brute with a series of blows to the neck and the nose, who forced open his jaws, dismissed his half-hearted snarling, and hurried the injured child to his par-ents.

I thank You, Yahweh, for this braver part of myself.

"Without qualification?"

Ah, He'd come to join her!

But surely there could be no question. And yet there had been times when such fragmentation had robbed her of life's richness.

When Noah had first spoken his love, as they walked along a path hot with sun and redolent of lemon blossoms, the observer, the more cynical Kyral, had stood to one side, her smile denying his words. Be realistic, she'd urged. How could such a one love such as you? Only look! He's handsome, strong, sought by many women. Then think of yourself. No rich dowry recommends you. And remember your image looking back from the reflection of the pool, the unmanageable hair, the thick wrists, the lumpy waist.

And when Noah—those marvelous eyes imploring her to believe him—insisted, "No pool can reflect with accuracy how the crinkles form in your cheeks when you smile," that other Kyral had caused her to mock him: "So I'm wrinkling! Already! Then think how you'll despise me when age furrows all my face with the texture of raisins!"

"I love your smile, sweet Kyral! Your teeth are so even. And the color and warmth of your eyes; such specks of light flicker there!"

Quieted and flushing, she turned quickly away, moved to lean against a tree, struggled with the need for escape. But he followed.

"You walk with the unconscious grace of, of a bird, flying."

"Surely a heron!" was her retort.

He said firmly, "Something soaring and altogether beautiful!"

And both Kyrals had collapsed in giggling to hide disbelief, embarrassment.

Why did I risk losing his love? She knew the answer. She'd believed herself unworthy and feared that one day he would, as well.

"You'd been taught to feel unworthy," Yahweh reminded her.

She nodded. Yet no matter how she'd mocked Noah's compliments or denied his vows of true affection, he had been as patient—and as stubborn—in his pursuit of her as, more recently, in his construction of the ark. And his devotion had never wavered since.

Surely Yahweh had had a hand in that! She pushed her gratitude toward Him.

"Aren't you patient with Noah, as well?"

Not patient enough. She picked up her mending and then, with searing intensity, remembered why she had placed herself in the shadows to be alone.

She remembered Grena: her bright attention to Noah's most casual words, her love for animals, her spirited assault on Calet for throwing pebbles at "Yahweh's lions."

Shumri had said he admired spirit in a woman. And Yahweh had predicted that Shumri would cause his own downfall. And he had.

She paused. She could muster no sympathy for Shumri's death, only a deep anguish that it had come moments too late.

She cringed, and behind her closed eyes again saw the cruel ax descending, again heard herself scream, *"No! No! No!"*

"Remember instead Doreya's friendship, her laughter, her warmth and hope."

And her bruises?

"No. Remember her hungering for a God who is real, her dying appeal to me."

Did you hear her prayer?

"Yes. They are with me."

It was only a whisper. Still, surely it had been Yahweh's answer, not merely her yearning.

More firmly, He said, "They are *both* with me."

Tears of gratitude stung Kyral's eyes. She could be at peace . . . until she remembered those other women, their men, and their children, whose lives still progressed as before. They marketed, cooked, quarreled, gave birth, and shrugged at what Noah insisted would soon occur.

And she could understand that.

Readily enough, she'd accepted the confines of the ark—the close proximity, the structure of daily tasks, the need to adapt. (Four women jostled elbows, when each, before, had commanded her own space.) What had seemed strange at first had quickly become routine, even a comfortable routine, for Kyral, her long-term fears conquered and nearly forgotten.

But it was more difficult to envision the panic the flood would create, to imagine the lifting of the ark from its moorings, to accept that the world—save for the ark and its contents—would be no more. Such knowledges lacked concreteness.

Forgive my doubting.

"I have dealt with your doubting before." His voice was gentle.

Sucking blood from a pricked finger, she laid her work aside in the hope that He would say more, but He was silent.

How could she still doubt, she wondered. How much evidence would she require?

When would the waiting end? It had been five days since they'd entered the ark—or had it been six?

Tamara traced back in memory. Yesterday, she and Ham had tried to pluck a tune from the lute. While they'd managed only discord, they had at least lightened the passing of time and provided a reason for laughter. Certainly that was preferable to the day before when Ham had milked goats and mended a fishermen's net, while she wandered aimlessly, searching for cobwebs she might point out for Afene's discomfort. It was better than the day before that, when Ham's father required him to shore up the elephants' stall, while she had wandered, seeing if she could find the little gray mouse who'd skittered across the floor during breakfast. And it was better than the day before that, when . . .

She yawned. Definitely, the experience with the lute had been the most pleasurable time since they'd come aboard!

The thought gave her pause. If that was the best she could look forward to—week after week and then year after year after year . . .

The day before the mouse search, while Ham had worked, somewhere, she'd toured the room where seedlings flourished despite the relative dimness. Endless sacks of grain lined the walls of the hull and leaned against arched inner timbers supporting the space between. One sack was torn at the corner, allowing a seepage of grain. She'd wondered later if that might not be the work of the mouse.

The day before that, they'd worried over the animals. Would the row of slender upper windows allow enough light and air to filter below deck to the animal cages? And when the rains came, and she was beginning to wonder again if they would, wouldn't the windows admit the flood, as well? In which case, they'd be no better off than those outside. Perhaps they'd be even more vulnerable, since they'd be so effectively trapped.

Had there been a day before that? She couldn't be sure.

Five (or six) endless days. Could the rain possibly be worse than the waiting? Only the promise of night made each day bearable.

Smiling, she crossed her hands far before her, rocked to her tiptoes, remembered Ham's arms about her and his warm words tickling her ear. She loved the bunks! At home their pallet had allowed distance. Once asleep, Ham often turned from her, seeking space in which to flop and flail and stretch. But now . . . She sighed with happiness. Now, since nighttime confinement encouraged a new closeness, quarrels could occur only in daylight hours.

How she loved that red-bearded husband of hers! In the first moments of their time together each night, his tantrums, his teasing, and his frustrating trickery were easily forgiven.

Who cared when the rains came? Or if they never came? Only let her time on the ark stretch into years!

She spun herself about like a child, until dizziness collapsed her to the floor. Laughing, hugging herself, she remained unaware of Afene's hostile observation.

Would that silly child ever comprehend the seriousness of their situation? Afene scoured the floor marred with new sandal prints, with dust, with chaff. Later, when the stables overflowed, there'd be dung.

She shuddered.

It wasn't that she minded cleaning; in fact, she had always rather enjoyed it. She did her best thinking on her knees, scrubbing. And there was a definable sense of fulfillment when, because of her, chaos transformed into order, when her hands caused dullness to shine and grime to surrender. Sometimes she felt that life was a series of battles between her and dust, rust, cobwebs, and clutter. Winning each skirmish filled her with the same sense of elation Noah had expressed when the ark was finally complete. Or the satisfied sense of accomplishment Shem exuded when a clay tablet was fully and accurately inscribed. Or the manner and gratitude Japheth might feel when he won a convert, if there'd ever been one. Cleaning filled her days with meaning and purpose.

But couldn't Tamara see that there was enough work for everyone? In the five days so far, she'd contributed nothing. While the men tended the animals and Mother Kyral worked with young plants and Maelis organized and cooked and she scrubbed and swept and scoured until her knuckles were inflamed and raw (not that she begrudged her efforts), Tamara wandered listlessly and sighed. Hadn't the foolish child learned that if she made her hands useful, time would pass more swiftly?

She came to life only when Ham's work was finished. Then they'd giggle and romp together like a pair of undisciplined puppies.

Certainly, at the close of his days, Japheth lacked the energy for foolishness. That led Afene to the only possible conclusion: that, like Tamara, Ham shirked his duties. Though when she suggested this to Japheth, on the second or third day, he answered, "Actually, Ham's surprised us all."

"Ham has always been a surprise," she said wryly.

"You misunderstand," Japheth replied. "When we're working, he's dependable and decisive." He laughed. "I think he has motivation beyond that of most men."

She didn't understand, and said so. Or was she perhaps afraid that she had understood too well?

"He knows what waits for him when our work is done." Japheth spoke the words calmly, evenly, as though Ham's enthusiastic desire to return to Tamara might be fully expected.

Afene drew a sharp breath, hopefully not prompted by jealousy for that bit of froth Ham had married! Tears stung her eyes. Tears of . . . if not envy, then what?

Betrayal! She'd never thought she would hear Japheth praise another woman to her detriment. And especially not Tamara, when he himself had so often spoken of her immaturity!

He noticed her tears. "You're overtired, my love," he said gently.

Shaking her head, she tried to control the trembling of her lips. It had ever been a matter of pride with her to hide her tears from him.

"You're doing the work of two," he insisted, "as you always do. Why don't you take Tamara to one side and talk to her like an older sister?"

He needn't have placed such stress on the word "older"! Stiffly, she turned away.

Drawing her to him, he massaged the rigid spot between her shoulder blades. "If she did her share, you could relax. Then *we* could play chase around the storeroom too!"

The idea was so ludicrous that she had to smile. How foolish she'd been to fear that someone of Japheth's qualities could be drawn to silly Tamara! And yet it had sounded . . .

He was laughing. "I might enjoy that," he said. "Think I could catch you?"

She turned in his arms, allowing herself to be pressed

even closer. "Never, if you gave me warning," she murmured against his cheek.

Unexpectedly, he sighed. "Why, when I'm younger than Ham, do I feel so . . . old?"

She reminded him of those exhausting months of evangelism and abuse. "Such responsibility. Such strain . . ."

"I suppose."

"And while you were draining yourself physically and emotionally, Ham and Tamara were . . ."

"Even then, endlessly chasing each other!" He chuckled.

"And quarreling," she reminded him, uncharitably.

"Yes, and quarreling."

He continued to hold her, and she relished his closeness, basked in his love.

"Maybe we should try quarreling," he said, but lightly, so that her pique had scarcely begun to gather before she quelled it.

You were coaxing a quarrel just then, my love, she thought.

Brokenly, he said, "I never want to quarrel with you!"

"Nor I with you."

"I thank Yahweh that He gave you to me!"

They stood in silence. Then tenderly, he drew away.

"Quarreling seems to work for Ham and Tamara. It would destroy me."

"They're still children," she said without tolerance.

"Perhaps . . . and yet . . ."

He never completed the thought. During the evening and into the early night, while he slept easily and she held herself rigid beside him, she tried a dozen different variations, none satisfactory, to understand what he'd begun to say. All her wondering only created more questions.

Maybe she *should* counsel Tamara on her responsibilities. Earlier, Tamara had seemed to want to be close, had even called Afene "dear sister." Perhaps if she talked with the child about the joy of accomplishment, the self-satisfaction of putting one's energies wholeheartedly into a task, no matter now mundane, Tamara would view work in a different light.

Only when she'd firmly committed herself to the action, could Afene surrender herself to sleep. But the next day, and the next, whenever she found respite from her work, Tamara was nowhere around. When they were together at meals, she hesitated to make a scene. And after cleanup, she lacked the energy. Besides, by then, she couldn't have spoken to Tamara except through Ham.

Finally there was the day of the music, if it could be called that. Afene had never heard such jangling, such caterwauling! She knew if she spoke to Tamara then, it would be in tones too clipped and shrill for civility.

It was obvious that the term on the ark would be more difficult than she'd envisioned. And the rain had not yet begun!

Over and over, she asked Yahweh "when?" and his answer never varied: "Soon." Well if anyone were to ask her, and no one had, "soon" had passed days before!

"My love?"

"What?" she snarled, glaring up, then bit her tongue. What an evil temper she was developing—thanks to Tamara! She sighed, "I'm sorry, dear Japheth." She scampered to her feet, drying her hands on her skirt. "You'll want to throw me overboard, if I snap at you like that! It's just . . ."

Opening his arms, he enfolded her, patting. "I know. I know. We're all feeling the same."

Not Tamara, she thought, but with uncharacteristic tolerance. How could she be cross at anyone when Japheth held her pressed against his heart?

Another flawed stitch! Kyral tossed her sewing into a heap, stood, and stretched. Her fingertips grazed timbers smoothed but not evened by pitch.

Pitch. What a large part the smelly, black substance had played in their lives. What an important role it would play in the months to come, when only the solidity of the ark protected them.

Unexpectedly she felt an echo of the old fear of confinement. Yahweh had healed her forever of that, and she praised Him daily, and yet . . . the dimness oppressed her.

I never considered how dark the ark would be! The windows admitted only blocks of light, dissipated long before reaching the lower levels. *I worry about the seedlings.*

Of course! She'd move them to where the greatest light occurred! It was a wonder she hadn't thought of it before and had Ham place them there at once. Perhaps it was better that she hadn't. The activity now might lessen the strain of waiting.

Another day passed.

Their arms entangled and bodies close, Tamara and Ham sat in the large open area beneath the windows and watched for the earliest star. When Noah or Kyral, working near the plants, blocked their view, the young couple giggled and moved as one to alter their position.

Kyral plucked yellow leaves from a vine. "Only see, Noah," she said, concerned at the hours he spent peering and frowning from the windows, "they grow so well, here in the light."

"Mmmmmmmmm," he answered, his gaze outward, remaining fixed.

Certain he hadn't heard, she sighed heavily.

Turning, he said, "Forgive me, m'love. I was listening to the crowd."

She swiped her hands down the sides of her skirt, then dusted them against one another. Though she'd grown accustomed to the taunting with which their lives had been laced for so many years, a familiar fear shortened her breathing, and her ears strained to catch unusual sounds.

"No, no, my dear. We're in no danger." He tucked her arm in his. "Haven't you learned yet to trust Yahweh?"

She bristled at the hint of reproach in his words, but of course he was right. She trusted Yahweh, yet she feared, and at times even doubted. Certainly she fretted that He'd allowed Grena and Doreya to die. And what of Noah? Had he never considered that but for his carelessness in leaving his ax about . . .

She shook herself, both mentally and physically. How could either of them, Noah or Yahweh, keep patience with her?

"I love you." Noah drew her close.

And that was the answer, for both of them, just as the answer for her was to love both of them and to question less often. And to think less?

No, merely to think in less convoluted patterns.

Leaning into Noah's love and Yahweh's providence, Kyral listened to the sounds from far below.

"How soon, do you think?" she asked. "Has Yahweh told you?"

"Soon."

The first star blinked into brilliance, acknowledged by Tamara's giggle and Kyral's quiet smile. Beyond the ark, day sounds had mellowed to meal preparation; soon night's rowdiness would begin. Beyond the bulk of the ship Kyral could see only the distant slopes. And, though she knew that fires of cooking and celebration must already be ignited, she could find no nearby glow. Later, when darkness intensified any light, the sky around the ark would be alive with flickering.

Hearing a muffled thud, she supposed that someone had struck the side of the ark, perhaps with a large stone. She noticed the taunting that followed, but it was short-lived. What amusement could there be in harassing them, when their reactions could only be guessed?

They stood quietly, content, Noah's arm loosely about her and his face so close that his beard nuzzled her cheek. When he'd been building and she busy with household chores and child-rearing and then with shaping relationships among their daughters-in-law, there'd been little time together, except when both were too weary to enjoy it.

He sighed. "Are you restless, my love?"

"I'm content to be with you."

He expelled another sigh, this one longer and more despairing than the first.

Concerned, she drew back to peer into his eyes. "And you?"

"I feel useless!" he complained. "All those years of building, solving structural problems, gathering pitch . . . There was so much to do then. But now . . ." His voice drained away. She felt a tremor of dread, but his quick kiss eased her mind.

"You'll get used to the leisure, my love, and perhaps come to enjoy it!" Besides, she told herself as they made their way to the lower level already rich with scents of hot oil and spice, there'd be more than enough for all of them to tend to once the rain began.

Sometime toward dawn, Kyral woke to a different sound. It was firm and loud, like wood banging and metal clicking.

Alert, holding her breath, she touched Noah's shoulder.

He didn't rouse, merely murmured, "Go back to sleep, love. It's only the door closing."

The door? Noah shrugged away from her tightening fingers.

Yahweh?

"No one has responded to the open door," Yahweh sighed into her mind, "and now, it's too late."

Too late.

The words sounded a knell in her mind. Earlier she'd chafed that Yahweh seemed to hesitate, that His *soon* was so long in coming. Now she grieved at its finality.

There's no pleasing me, she grumbled inwardly, and envied Noah's artless, contented snoring. But, try as she did to emulate his contentment, her throat tightened with tears.

Maelis was careful not to awaken Shem. The evening before, while he'd worked late over his clay tablets, lamplight had flickered such imprecise waverings over his work that she wondered how he kept the markings even. She slid from their bunk, lifted the curtain separating their sleeping area from the others and tiptoed through the central living space.

The animals stirred below. She found comfort in their soft shuffling, bleating, snorting, waking sounds. Birds twittered in drowsy counterpoint. An elephant cleared his throat. Someone (perhaps a lion) yawned. Just beyond the curtains, Father Noah's snoring rattled and rumbled in its unique, contented way, harmonizing with the lighter, slightly wheezing sound she recognized as Ham's.

She smiled. Maelis had always loved early morning. Even in the ark, she could enjoy the feeling of space. While the others slept, it was hers alone. More importantly, a comfortable emptiness stretched in her mind. Nothing pressured. No one's needs clamored. She had no nudging of guilt at what she'd not yet accomplished.

Surely a persistent need to achieve beyond human possibility was one of her deepest flaws, an obsession, even in childhood. Her mother often urged, "Whatever weaving isn't done today, we'll do tomorrow." And when she'd wept over the tiny plot she'd planted, her father insisted, "Your perfect rows will produce far more bountifully than mine, where seeds fly where they will!"

Dear parents! How they'd nurtured and consoled, even though obviously puzzled by her driving need to *do*. Always she'd needed to produce quantity and quality beyond both the span of time and her level of skill. And she'd projected these unattainable goals into adulthood.

On those few occasions when he'd lost patience with her, Shem had demanded, "Why is it that you must apologize for the space you occupy?" Then, remorsefully, with his arms about her, he said gently, "I worry about you, my love. You'll work yourself to an early death. And how can I live without you?"

But in the mornings, before her goals took shape, she was at peace with herself, with her world and her place in it.

She breathed deeply, catching the scent of hay, of animal warmth, of milk oozing from bloated bags waiting to be drained. She was aware of fur that had never thoroughly dispelled the hot odors of desert sand and dried blood spilled in hunts now submerged in memory. How marvelous, Maelis thought, that Yahweh had suspended the curse of death imposed after Eden. Even the fiercely carnivorous on board now ate only grain and hay. Glancing up, she saw Mother Kyral's plants in sharp relief against the gray squares of the windows.

Momentarily her mind refused to interpret a darkness too deep for dawning, a roiling movement in the heavens, a distant rumbling.

Then, soft as the breathing of a child, erratic as a newborn lamb's lapping, drops tapped on pitch-protected timbers, rattled on stretched-taut coverings, clattered on metal hinges.

The rain was beginning.

It was gentle during those early hours. Kyral could hear children shrieking their pleasure. She imagined their play—wading in new puddles, then stomping, testing to see how high the spray might fly. In her imagination she could see them lifting their faces to the cool droplets and tasting them on their tongues, shaking their heads like wet puppies, turning and twisting as wet tunics clung to their bodies. Of course they wriggled their toes in the deliciously sluggish, squishy mud. As children, Shem, Ham, and Japheth had loved to splash and paddle in the stream. But, oh, the difference!

Kyral's throat tightened. When would the panic begin? Those neighbors who'd prepared their feast and shared recipes and gaiety as well as those who'd ridiculed and damaged—when would they realize that "Noah's Folly" had been Yahweh's wisdom? When would they fully grasp that they would perish because of their disbelief?

No one releases life tranquilly, without reluctance or resistance. How could she bear it when they began to bang and batter at the door Yahweh had fastened so firmly?

Kyral had watched as Tamara tried the latch, had noted her expression of desperation turn to . . . relief?

Scanning the roomy ark, she sighed. They didn't require such space, just for the eight of them! Briefly, she pictured Doreya, resting on a bench and smiling as Grena ran from spot to spot, reaching toward the flowing sky, laughing her excitement.

How she missed them, grieved for them.

"They are with me," Yahweh had said, and that was comforting. But a small part of Kyral's heart insisted, *I would prefer them here—with me.*

The rhythm of the rain increased. No longer pattering, it rumbled. No longer tapping and breathing, it hammered and grumbled. Light slashed the heavens. Wind snapped a vine and swept it from the upper level.

Climbing swiftly, Ham and Japheth covered the windows. But they couldn't shut out the burgeoning sound—the shouts of terror, the curses of denial. All were drowned in a roaring, a rushing—from where? The hills? Was the stream rising? Yahweh had indicated many sources for the waters of the flood.

They came from above and from beneath, surrounding the ark. Even its massive timbers failed to diminish the roar, rumble, rush of the combining floods. Though the ark stood steady in its moorings, the din was pervasive, the pressure overwhelming!

Covering her ears with both hands, Tamara rushed to Ham's embrace. He held her, comforting. Afene, her eyes wide, moved to Japheth, and Shem came to Maelis.

Maelis heard another sound. Even above the violence of nature, she could hear the swelling shrieks, the frantic pounding on the ark's door.

Shem heard, too, she knew. His eyes, as he reached to enclose her, shone with victory. And she turned away.

Yahweh . . . she prayed, but went no further. He well knew her yearning, her grief, her empathy for those poor drowning souls outside the shelter of the ark. Even for the comfort of Shem's love, she couldn't approve his gloating.

Tears blurred Afene's vision, as well. In her mind, she could see the women who a little over a week before had joyously offered gifts of spices and recipes. Even their plan to corrupt her faith in Yahweh, they'd meant as kindness. Numbly, she turned her face into Japheth's chest and wept.

Too frightened for tears, Tamara clutched at Ham's shoulders. Carefully, although unsuccessfully, she tried to blank her thoughts of individuals. It was better to think of those outside as a teeming, nameless mass, not Elose or Armya, not . . . her mother . . . or Cloyren. Even for them, she felt no sense of vindication. Drowning was drowning; death was death. However many others struggled, each person would die alone.

Kyral thought of Sereda—such a generous woman. Married to Morgine, with his skinny neck and bobbing head, his uneasy pretension with his own importance, Sereda had still managed to be likable and human. And when she'd shown her caring that Noah was ill . . .

Be kind to Sereda, she prayed.

Since He'd welcomed Doreya and Grena, perhaps Yahweh could find space for Sereda, as well.

The floods continued. They poured from above and swelled beneath them. And slowly, almost unnoted, human sounds ceased.

Though the four couples huddled together, their thoughts were separate. They neither ate nor drank. The unabating violence of the storm had a numbing effect, even on the animals.

Tamara's eyes were wide, her mouth smaller than ever and quivering. Afene made no effort to wipe away tears. Kyral's lips moved in perpetual prayer. They slept, sitting.

And the flood continued.

When the ark first shifted, Afene cried out, then flushed with embarrassment. When the next swell came, it was stronger. Some animals snorted, trumpeted, roared. Both Tamara and Kyral screamed, and neither apologized.

Then came a series of swells, of rolls, of pitches. And with unexpected softness, the ark lifted. They felt the buoyant difference, the freedom. For moments, standing in breathless silence, they braced themselves against the unaccustomed movement.

Ham was the first to speak, but Noah—maintaining an attitude of careful listening—touched a finger to his lips.

Kyral imitated his stance, the quality of his attentiveness. She heard the lapping and the creaking of timber, felt the smooth rolling, noticed that the animals had quieted.

"Praise Yahweh!" Noah fell to his knees in reverence. "The ark will hold!"

This wasn't a time for celebration but for worshipful silence and fasting.

Drinking only water, they'd eaten nothing for two days. They had slept apart, walked apart, not touching, even with glances. Taking time only to tend the plants and animals, they had spent the hours in separate meditation.

But now, Yahweh had called them together.

There had been no audible command. Simply, each sensed the need for corporate worship.

Stretching their stiff muscles, they gathered in the central living area bordered by the curtained sleeping spaces, benches, and storage bins. With a common consent, they expressed their praise.

"Father Yahweh, all that You promised has come to pass," Noah began. And the women murmured in unison, "We are safe in the ark. Safe in Your care. Safe in our trust of You and our love for one another."

"You have vindicated us in the eyes of our enemies," Shem said, his voice holding an edge of triumph. "Their bloated bodies float before You."

"They have died for their unbelief," Japheth mourned, then pleaded, "yet they remain Your children, the seed of our father, Adam."

"We are safe in the ark, safe in Your care. May all those we loved and lost find knowledge in Your forgiveness."

"Comfort Doreya, nurture Grena," Kyral prayed, and other names flowed in a litany begging for mercy.

"Forgive Armya, Elose, even Nurilla."

"Accept Sudith, Arn, Sereda, Morgine, Jence."

"And those who gave love with a gift of spices."

"Teach those whose minds were corrupted, whose eyes were blinded to truth, whose ears accepted the false promises of idols. May knowledge gained in death annul the misconceptions acquired in life."

"Forgive them, Lord. Teach them."

"Father Yahweh, all that You promised has come to pass. The rain has come. The ark holds against the roaring floods. You have saved us to serve You."

"We are content in the ark, content in Your caring, content in our trust of You and our love for one another."

"You have vindicated Your truth in the shrieks of Your enemies!" Shem intruded impatiently. "Their voices are stilled! Their treasures lie rotting beneath surging floods. Their sightless eyes search for their fallen gods. Their spirits cry out for deliverance. And there is none!"

"Yet deliverance—like destruction—lies in Your hands alone. You strike down; You lift up; You pronounce judgment or show mercy as it pleases You. Show mercy, we pray, to those who merit no mercy."

"We are safe in the ark. We are safe in Your care. All that You promised has come to pass."

"And we praise You! Amen."

Will he never change? Maelis mused as she helped with preparations for the special meal Yahweh had commanded. *Will his anger—however righteous—ever mellow?* Could Shem not feel some shred of sympathy for those who lacked his training in truth? Or was his vindictiveness more righteous than Japheth's urge toward salvation or her own revulsion at the loss of any soul?

Or were all these—judgment, yearning, mercy—portions of Yahweh's plan?

Certainly, Yahweh's dealing with her had been nurturing. But what if she had worshiped false gods?

Her fingers, kneading dough, stilled. Her head throbbed from accumulated tension, from hunger, from grief. Still, she knew that she could never have knelt to idols of iron and stone!

But what if she had?

The answer was simple. If she had, she'd have perished in the flood.

And, before the flood, she'd have scoffed at Noah's "foolishness." Perhaps she would even have abused him. And she'd have participated in unspeakable acts. She'd have disobeyed, disappointed, and angered Yahweh. And Yahweh, as any parent, must discipline.

Yet what grievous discipline!

"It is essential discipline," Yahweh insisted gently. "When someone writhes in pain, when his system is fouled with poisons, it becomes necessary to purge the foulness."

Still, Maelis mourned. Why had *she* been spared, and so many others destroyed? Why had she—so far from perfection—attracted Shem's love and, therefore, assured her survival?

"You weren't spared merely because of Shem's love for you. As wonderful as it is to you, it is merely human love. Only I, the Lord your God, can love you enough to save you."

She found herself warming to His words, leaning into that love.

"You were chosen, my child, because you believe in me—as Shem believes." He paused.

"Be patient with Shem, my child. He is still growing, just as you are, and just as your children will."

My children?

"Yes, your children—yours and Shem's. From his seed and your womb, the new earth will be blessed beyond imagining."

Tamara had never been so famished! She nibbled a crumb of dried fruit from the plate she was arranging. The aroma of frying leeks assailed her nostrils. Cheese, round and golden, fell in slabs from Afene's knife. Tamara swallowed, and swallowed again, wondering how she could possibly endure waiting until the meal was ready and the men called. And then they'd have to bow while Father Noah intoned an endless prayer of thanks.

She blushed hotly. *Forgive me, Yahweh,* she murmured.

How could she resent the time it took for gratitude when all that they had—or would ever have—depended on His generosity? A portion of the morning's litany rose in her mind: "We are safe in the ark, safe in Your care."

Thank You, Yahweh, she mouthed the words without sound, *and please forgive my thoughtlessness.*

There. The cheese was sliced, the tubers sizzling and spitting. Testing their readiness, Afene reached for a packet of spice.

With painful intensity, spawned by her thoughts of the morning, her memory summoned the images—even the voices and movements—of the women who'd offered the spices and their friendship. Grief throbbed within her. She could grasp Yahweh's reasoning for the flood—a thorough sweeping of evil, of disbelief, of sin from the world. (She, of all people, understood the importance of careful cleansing.) Still . . .

She sighed, gauging through tears her accuracy as she sprinkled a measure of spice on the lentils. If only there could be some assurance, however slight, that the souls of those friendly women hadn't perished with their bodies.

"I am a jealous God."

She waited.

"I am the only true God."

She tried to imagine what it would be like to love your children, offering them life, and then endure their preference for death.

"When you care for children, you'll understand."

She gasped, half with pleasure. So they *were* to have children, she and Japheth! But then, He hadn't promised that the children she tended would be her own.

"Be patient, my child, and remember that some decisions are for me alone to make."

"Oh, my Lord . . ." she said aloud. The fragrance of spices intensified as she covered her mouth with both hands. Slowly, she lowered them. "I didn't mean . . ."

"Mean what, child?" Kyral glanced up from the table, where she was arranging places.

Still listening for Yahweh, Afene mumbled, "Nothing, Mother Kyral."

He asked, "Do you presume that I look only for flaws?

"I searched the world for righteousness, and found Noah. I looked for obedience, and found only Noah's household. I listened for voices raised in praise, and heard Noah's hymns, while elsewhere my name was reviled and worship rendered to mute figures made of metals and clay!" The voice gained in volume, until it became a roaring. "I AM A HOLY GOD! I WILL NOT TOLERATE EVIL! ITS SOUNDS OFFEND MY EARS! IT IS AN ABOMINATION IN MY SIGHT!"

She had bowed, holding her ears against the thundering pronouncement, and thereby containing it more fully.

"Are you ill, daughter?"

It was Noah, his voice strained.

"No, Father Noah," she gasped, and forced herself to a renewal of her tasks.

His voice, when He spoke again, was gentle. "And yet, yes, I value kindness. And those kind women, as the flood overtook them, remembered all you had told them of me. They renounced their promiscuity and their idolatry. They asked for forgiveness and mercy. They are with me."

Smiling and closing her eyes with relief, she sighed.

The meal exceeded even Tamara's expectations.

Not only was the food more savory, more satisfying, than any she'd eaten in recent memory, but the conversation was lighter. The smiles were broader and the eyes more glowing than at any moment since the rain first pelted the decks of the ark.

Smiling, loving each one with her eyes, Kyral looked about her small group. After the long waiting, after the tragedy, following their fasting, surely Yahweh had granted them this lightness, this joy, for the healing of their spirits. Perhaps He was saying, "Relax, my children. Enjoy one another—and me. Never again must you know such sadness . . ."

Or, she frowned, perhaps He allowed them this respite to gird them against even harsher times ahead.

Refusing to suppose that and joining in laughter at one of Ham's insane antics, she committed herself to celebration.

⇢⇢⇢ ⇠⇠⇠

Tamara huddled in the bunk with her arms over her ears.

Rain, rain, rain, rain. She was sick of the pounding, pelting, roaring, thumping, rattling! Dampness clung to her clothing. Overnight, mold covered the soles of her sandals. Moisture turned her hair to tangles. Clamminess, eroding every breath she drew and weighting her eyelids and lashes, enclosed her when she tried to sleep.

When would it stop?

How could Ham expect her to be herself, to be cheerful and dancing, when all she heard was rain, rain, rain? When all she saw, as she lifted the window coverings, was rain? Sliding, silver rain. Windswept, slashing rain. Rain bouncing from the decks of the ark. Rain dashing against the waves.

Rain. Always rain. Only rain.

Once the ark landed, once they'd begun their new lives, she planned to pray that she'd never have to look at rain again, or listen to it.

She pressed her palms to her ears. There was no way of shutting out the ceaseless sound. After a while, it seemed that the pulsing originated within her, was a part of her, as inseparable as the beating of her heart.

How many days, already, had it rained? She was afraid to ask. Noah said the rain would fall for forty days and forty nights. Surely, already it had been longer than that! It seemed a lifetime since she'd seen sunshine and any green, growing thing, save the pallid plants Mother Kyral struggled to keep alive.

Tamara was convinced Mother Kyral was wasting her time. The rain would never stop. They'd float in these endless waters, in the rain, until they arrived at the end of the world and simply fell off. Or until the timbers of the ark grew waterlogged—even with all that pitch—and the ark sank. In a way, they might have been better off simply dying with the others.

Caught by a quivering of conscience, she thought a half-apology to Yahweh.

"I am with you," He said gently.

She was grateful for that. But to stay with them when He didn't have to, He must like rain a great deal better than she did.

Opening a bag of meal, Afene carefully scooped out a measure into a bowl. If any spilled, not only would it waste a precious part of their supplies, but she'd have to clean it up. And in this dampness, sweeping was more difficult. Everything was more difficult.

She'd never realized, before, how emotions were tied to sunlight. At least hers were. She hadn't felt like singing as she worked for so long she couldn't remember the sound of her voice. She hadn't felt like working, either. She felt like sulking.

It was strange that Ham, who'd always been the sulker, now seemed jubilant, content. But Japheth, his potential for evangelizing ended, paced and glowered. Answering a simple question taxed his patience. He never had a civil comment for either of his brothers, and whenever he had to speak to his parents, he used the fewest possible words and the most formal attitude. And he never smiled, even at her. And yet, occasionally, she heard him talking to the animals.

Maybe he wasn't using words with them, either—just snarls and growls.

It must be difficult for the men, with their labor so limited by space. Women's work must go on, much as before, no matter the circumstance, except they couldn't hang their clothing to dry. Well, they could hang it. It just wouldn't dry, not in this dampness.

Their appetites had suffered, too, primarily from the ceaseless rain, but occasionally in response to the constant rolling, bouncing, pitching of the ark. Father Noah was looking so pale and his cheekbones so sunken that Afene was concerned. Mother Kyral, in trying to encourage his appetite, had neglected her own. Only Maelis and Ham seemed to maintain girth and color. Maelis, despite the fact that she ate little, and Ham, because he inhaled everything that seemed even remotely edible.

How strange, Kyral thought, that the dim, dark caverns of the lower ark, which had once caused her breathless panic, had become her haven. These dark places of confinement were her refuge for quiet, for aloneness, for uninterrupted conversation with Yahweh. Many times, as she sat or walked there, watching the play of shadows cast by flares, she thanked Him for her healing.

If only, sometime during all those years when enclosed space had oppressed her, she'd thought to ask His help. And yet, perhaps a malady must exceed human endurance before its healing could be fully appreciated.

Had the thought come from Yahweh or from herself? Did it truly matter?

How comforting was this recurring sense of oneness with Yahweh! Why had it eluded her before the ark? Was such closeness impossible in a sound-filled life, busy with color and movement and filled with options, each demanding decision?

"It isn't impossible . . ." A pause. "Only improbable."

She smiled, wanting to confide how it delighted her, now that it had been achieved. But she felt too languid, too content for speech. And, of course, He knew, as He knew all her thoughts.

She strolled past the storerooms to the ladder, mounted easily, and slowly and quietly entered one of the stables. Lofty, evoking images of endless space, it deserved a grander title. But Yahweh was silent.

Then "stable" it would remain.

The place hummed with buzzings and murmurings and cooings and purrings. A cub, its eyes squinched shut, submitted to the rough, cleansing tongue of the lioness.

Kyral inhaled sharply as a lamb, squeezing between the bars of its own straw-strewn enclosure, scurried along the littered walkway, its tiny hooves beating a staccato that drew the lethargic attention of the lions. The male stood, shook his mane, and yawned noisily as the lamb entered his lair.

Kyral shuddered. Should she intervene?

"Wait. Watch."

Without altering the rhythm of her lapping, the lioness licked the lamb's pert face. Its bleating was soft and accepting. Even its mother, watching without wariness, seemed trustful.

Kyral relaxed. She'd forgotten, for the moment, that Yahweh had suspended nature's normal laws.

The lamb wriggled into the warm abrasion of the lapping tongue until its fleece was as wet as the cub's coat. Then both babies lay within the huge circling paws and drooped in napping. Yawning again, the male sighed, flicked his tail and stretched full-length in the straw.

"The lion shall lie down with the lamb," Yahweh said softly. "Such will be my world again, one day."

Contentment flooded Kyral's soul with warm, sun-filled images. *When the ark lands, my Lord?*

"Not for thousands of years beyond that."

Oh, my Lord . . .

Heaviness supplanted her peace. What, then, was the purpose of the flood, if old patterns would perpetuate? And through the seed of Noah and herself!

You could force us to obedience.

"Forced obedience, like forced love, is a contradiction of terms."

Of course. Love taken, not given, was plainly rape. Obedience demanded would be rape of the spirit. But, oh, how it hurt her to sense Yahweh's pain!

Suddenly the shadows of the stables oppressed her. The lamb, rousing, pattered back to the ewe. And, as she mounted the stairway to the next level, Kyral heard Ham's voice, raised in teasing, again.

❧❧❧ ❦❦❦

Relentlessly the rain continued.

Carefully, Tamara moved from the sleeping area to the stairway and then to the upper level. Lifting the window covering, she peered out. The turbulence above and beneath and surrounding them had become familiar, almost dependable. She'd learned to adjust her walking and her sitting to accommodate the rolls and pitches. Even in their bunk at night, she could anticipate the upheavals of the ark rather than fighting against them with sudden fear.

She gazed in awe at the dark clouds, boiling across the sky, and the dark sea, heaving to meet them. Great, driving curtains of rain, ribbons of rain, walls of rain, joined dark to dark. Crests of mountainous waves tossed so high it seemed they would swallow the ark, its hugeness diminished by their vast dimensions.

If Armya and Elose could have seen this, if somehow she might have convinced them how immense was Yahweh's power . . . But she hadn't known herself, until now. Remembering her anemic pleas to her friends and the sturdiness of their rejection, she whimpered, the tears starting. "Elose . . . Armya . . ."

She hadn't expected to miss them so sharply. As a child, her shy reserve a contrast to their effervescence, she'd imitated their most reckless actions. On learning just a few forbidden words, they'd joyously practiced, giggling in the secrecy of their "cave" made of fallen grapevines and the vast trunks of gopher trees felled long before the construction of the ark. Sometimes, gathering anemones to be strung as garlands, they linked arms on impulse and swung until their laughter evolved into hiccoughs and the world swooped and blurred, while their ears rang and whistled.

Mourning the sunshine of those lost days and her innocent forays into the boundaries of evil, Tamara tasted resentment.

Resentment of . . . what? And whom?

Resentment of Yahweh? For allowing evil to seem more attractive than innocence? Of Ham? For luring her with his love to a righteous household? Of both? For choosing her for survival, while her friends were doomed to drowning? She hadn't known that losing them would hurt so much.

Her mother, too, had perished in the flood.

Inwardly she shrugged, then warmed with shame. Would she ever be able to forgive her mother's harshness, or even to understand it? Was it possible that she'd emulate it when she and Ham had children, if they preferred him as passionately as she'd worshiped her own dear father?

She choked on tears. Even now, she grieved for that sweet man. Had he lived, she could never have entered the ark if it meant leaving him behind. Ham would have had to choose someone else.

The suddenness of her next notion jolted her so that she nearly lost her balance. Gripping the window rail, she explored the thought further. She knew well that Yahweh was aware of all thoughts—even this traitorous speculation she now pursued. Knowing her great love for her father, her total dependence on his adoration, had Yahweh *caused* him to die?

She closed her eyes against the pain.

Yet surely her father would have been worthy of salvation? Certainly there was room enough on the ark for him!

Yahweh? Why did my father die? And my mother and Elose and Armya—why did they die when I'm here?

"My child, do you doubt my wisdom?"

Mother Kyral has said that Your wisdom is infinite.

"Do you believe that?"

I believe. But I don't understand. Elose was pretty and Armya was playful and fun. Ham might've chosen either of them. If he had, she would be here now instead of me. Why does he love me when I am sometimes . . . so silly?

"Love is like that."

But . . .

"My child, your father loved you. And I love you, only my love is greater than a father or a husband can feel."

Did you love Armya and Elose too?

"Yes."

And my mother and my father?

"Yes."

Then, why . . .

"Armya and Elose rejected me when they chose to worship false gods. And your mother hardened her heart, even against you. But you believed in me. You learned to be obedient, just as Noah and Kyral and Ham and the others believe in me and are obedient.

You mean all these years, in spite of the teasing and the thrown rocks and the . . . That's why they kept on?

"Yes."

But I tried to escape . . .

"I know. I knew you would and I knew you would come back to me. Just as when you were young and tempted, you chose to resist the pagan ways; you chose to be obedient and follow my desires for you—to marry Ham and to enter the ark. And one day, when the rain has ended and the waters have receded you'll leave the ark, you and Ham together, and be a part of my new world.

Then everything will be perfect in the new world?

"Just as my world was perfect in the beginning, one day it will be again. But not yet."

It would be perfect if my father were there.

She wanted to talk further, but her thoughts quavered. If Yahweh were to confirm her fear that her father had died because of her, she wouldn't be able to bear it.

In memory, she could still see him falling, still hear his

screams, still hear Ham say, "No house is worth this." How could anyone ever stop grieving for a father such as hers?

Old Noah's father, Lamech, had died only months before the flood. There hadn't been a willful daughter at fault, so Yahweh must have had another reason. Had He thought the hardships of the ark too severe for someone so old?

Perhaps. Even though old Noah was younger than Lamech by nearly two centuries, stress and fatigue frequently lined his face, dulled his eyes, and robbed him of erectness.

Tamara wondered if he still grieved for his grandfather, Methuselah. The few times she'd seen him, she'd thought him a crotchety old man—always grumbling, discouraging conversation. Before the flood, Mother Kyral and old Noah had gone to help gather his few belongings, to move him and them into the ark. But shambling off toward the hills, to the stream and then to the woods, he'd waved them back and mumbled something about following "Yahweh's instructions." They hadn't seen him since, and repeated searching of the fields and woodlands had yielded no clue.

He'd always said his death would be the signal for the rains to begin. And the others, especially when they couldn't find him either alive or dead, accepted his disappearance as that signal. Maelis had suggested that Yahweh might have taken old Methusaleh like his father, Enoch, who long before had walked with Yahweh and never tasted death. But old Noah hadn't said so, and surely he would have known.

Had Methusaleh perhaps chosen not to be a burden, and so simply allowed the flood to take him? Or had there been some secret sin that despite his venerable age, prohibited his passage? Of course, brigands might have murdered him and hidden the body.

She sighed. Her thoughts were as endless, as monotonous as the rain.

Would it never stop? It had been so long since she'd seen a mountain, except for some occasional small mound of jagged rock, protruding from the loftiest peaks.

Would the sun ever shine again?

Would she ever stop grieving for her father or ever learn to grieve for her mother? Would these things continue to trouble her in the new world?

Yahweh had called her "his child" and said she was obedient. She wouldn't forget Elose and Armya or her mother, and certainly not her father, but the ache in her heart had diminished.

≫≫ ≪≪

Maelis smiled.

The mingled scents of oil and spices and vegetables energized her. The tubers were still firm under her fingers and beneath the blade of her knife. And she could ignore the withered texture of those legumes and apricots plucked unripe just prior to their entry into the ark.

Briskly, rhythmically, the blade sliced, releasing a fragrance reminiscent of the hours she'd spent in the garden. She could feel the moist soil on her fingertips and the touch of sunshine on her shoulders and hair. She hummed a song from her childhood. While the words wouldn't arrange themselves in her memory, the images were clear. Birds floated on currents of cerulean skies and flowers, exuding perfume, merged scarlet with mauve and ocher with citron. She could see the dragonflies, their wings like ornate spiderwebs.

A cleared throat, just behind her, drew her sharply around, her knife arcing in midair.

Noah smiled, drawing back in mock alarm.

Chuckling, she placed the knife on the cutting board. How she loved this gentle old man!

"You sound happy, my dear."

"I was remembering my childhood."

Laugh-lines crinkled his eyes nearly shut. "You haven't nearly so far to remember as I." He frowned slightly. "I would ask a small favor."

"Anything you ask, Father Noah, I will gladly do!"

Those lines, again, were puckering the corners of his eyes. "It is rather something I would have you *refrain* from doing!"

"Oh, Father Noah! I have . . . displeased you?"

"Never, my dear one!" He paused. "It is only . . ." He reached for the packet of spice, turning it in his hand, inhaling its fragrance, sighing.

"Could you omit the oil and spice on my portions, daughter? The blame doesn't lie with your peerless cooking but merely with my ancient system. My eyes, nose, and tongue welcome the spicy flavors, but my bowels turn to flame."

Her joy congealed. She should have noticed, should have guessed.

His bony hands curved in pleading. "Don't look stricken, child! It's due to your delicate feelings that I've hesitated to speak. But," and his eyes crinkled again, inviting shared amusement, "I fear that one of these days, the fire in my belly will set the ark ablaze. And there are no longer any shores to which we might swim!"

She smiled and, impulsively, hugged him.

❯❯❯ ❮❮❮

Afene awoke, stretched, smiled.

Despite the cramped quarters of the bunk, despite Japheth's arm heavy across her throat, she felt more rested than she had in weeks.

How dark it was, and quiet.

She'd slipped from the bunk and was straightening her robe about her before she noticed how extraordinary the quietness. She could hear only Japheth's deep breathing, rattling occasionally into a snore, and the creaking of timbers, a sound so omnipresent that she paid no more attention to it than to the rain.

The rain!

Stretching into the silence, she listened for the sounds of rain.

The stillness throbbed and spun.

"Japheth!" She shook him. "Japheth!"

He grumbled something unintelligible that ended with "m'love."

Sighing she decided to be sure before she thoroughly wakened him, or anyone. She pattered into the open area beneath the windows. Despite their coverings they showed scant gray light.

Again, she strained her ears. Again, the creaking, the shifting, the lapping, but . . . there was no sound of rain!

She hurried up the steps, lifted the cover from one window completely and reached out a hand.

No rain! No rain!

"Praise Yahweh!" she shouted, then bit her lip as she heard startled grunts from each of the sleeping compartments.

Ham, his bright hair disheveled, his eyes puffy with sleep, emerged first. "Hmmm? Uh?" seemed to be the best he could manage.

"What's wrong? Who? Where?" Japheth was turning about, stumbling.

Shem just stood, blinking.

But Father Noah smiled, nodded. "As Yahweh promised," he said contentedly, "forty days and forty nights—now the rain has ended."

9

Leaning against the rough rail, Tamara watched scudding white clouds, the play of sunlight on rippling water. She listened to the slap of waves on wood, the braying, snorting, barking, squawking, roaring of the animals, and knew that no sounds, no sunlight, nothing could be more beautiful or more hopeful.

She was pregnant!

She'd suspected when her "seasickness" occurred after the waters quieted. She was certain (almost) when her monthly sign was late and then more hopeful when it hadn't appeared at all.

But now, there was no doubt!

She lifted her face to the warmth of the sunlight and to the presence of the God she not only acknowledged, but had learned to worship fully.

"Thank You," she whispered. "Thank You!"

There'd been a time when she'd have been selfishly thrilled to conceive before either Maelis or Afene. But now she only wished them such joy as hers. There'd been a time when the thought of bearing a child caused her to begrudge the abuse of pregnancy to her figure. Now, squinting, pushing her belly out, she tried to imagine its marvelous and mammoth dimensions in only a few months.

She wanted to dance around the deck, tra-la-la-ing. She wanted to share her joy with someone.

Sighing, she gazed across the endless waters and knew that, if he were living, she'd tell her father first. And he would be so happy, so proud, so sweetly concerned.

She should tell Ham.

But he'd been carefully cold for two days and, involved with her new hope, she hadn't troubled to coax him for the cause. That had almost certainly deepened his sulking.

Let him sulk as long as he pleased. Maybe by the time the baby was born, he'd be over it. But, oh! if he'd only tire of sulking soon, and share her joy.

What a perverse man he was, anyway. During those endless days of rain, with the constant wind and rumbling and pitching and jerking, when the others suffered from the dampness, darkness, and confinement, he'd been persistently, annoyingly cheerful. But now, when the rain had stopped and the sun could be seen every day, was a time for joy, for looking forward with enthusiasm. And Ham was sulking. She might never understand him.

She could tell Afene. But Afene would think the news far less important than spotless benches or a newly scrubbed floor. She might confide in Maelis, but Maelis shared everything with Shem, unfailingly, and Shem would surely take offense that the behavior required for this condition had occurred on Yahweh's ark.

Shem was so stuffy. She could enjoy shocking him . . . Still, Ham should be told first. But he was sulking.

Old Noah would rejoice that Yahweh had so quickly blessed them with a new babe—the first toward the repopulation of His devastated earth. And He had chosen her to bear it!

But how could she speak to Ham's wizened father of a woman's most private joy?

Mother Kyral, then? She played that through her imagination.

Yes! Mother Kyral would be the perfect confidante. She'd be as pleased as Noah but more approachable, more prudent. And Tamara would burst if she couldn't tell someone.

Then, as though Yahweh Himself had reinforced the decision, Mother Kyral, dusting flour from her skirt, emerged from a dim doorway.

"What a lovely day!" she called in greeting.

"Lovelier than you might ever guess!" Tamara answered, and giggled.

Kyral gave her a quizzical look that Tamara interpreted as "What a strange young person she is!" or "I just don't understand young people these days!" or perhaps even "No wonder Ham's so moody, when he must deal with such a one!"

Tamara giggled again, and Kyral reached to embrace her.

"I'm so pleased," she said, warmly, richly, tenderly.

Drawing back, Tamara stared into Mother Kyral's eyes.

"How do I know?" Kyral laughed gently. "My child, how could I *not* know?"

They parted only slightly to observe the sky, the waves, the ark.

"By the time the child walks," Kyral mused, "there may be butterflies to chase once again, and grass growing beneath trees, if the trees aren't gone."

"If they are," Tamara comforted, "you'll plant new ones from your pots of seedlings."

"That would take so long. So long . . . When will you tell Ham?"

"How did you know I hadn't?"

"Even he couldn't sulk, with news like this."

Tamara sighed. "I *would* have told him first, but . . ."

"Child," Kyral paused thoughtfully, "Ham is my son, and I dote on him. But we both know, you and I, that when your babe is born it will mean simply that you have two children to raise."

"Surely, when he's a father . . ,"

"He's a prankster; he'll always be a child. Years ago, to save my sanity, I resigned myself to that. I fear you must do the same." Her soft hand rested on Tamara's shoulder. "I'm sorry."

"I love him," Tamara said simply. Then, "Perhaps we can raise him together, you and I!"

Kyral laughed comfortably. "Do you know how fond I am of you, child?"

Tamara kissed the soft, wrinkled cheek. "And I could never measure my growing affection for you."

Smiling at the odd mixture of emotions churning within her, Kyral went to the storeroom to be alone. There, pretending to count and arrange sacks of provender, she attempted to turn sensations into concepts. Noah would be jubilant. There was to be a child—Yahweh's promise made tangible. As wonderful as that was, as overwhelming (and she would praise Yahweh for it forever) she couldn't deny her personal joy at the thought of a baby to tend, to watch grow, to enjoy.

So, Tamara was first to conceive! She'd thought, hoped, one of the others—both more . . . prepared for nurturing—would be first. Well, Yahweh knew best, of course.

The girl was delighted. And it had been obvious for months that she was becoming more a woman and less a spoiled child. Still, pregnancy, even under the best conditions, drained emotional as well as physical energy. And, Kyral sighed heavily, it required a husband's strong support.

How did we fail with Ham? she asked, as she had asked over and over through the years. *Yahweh, as Ham's parents, what did we do wrong?*

What had instructed the other boys had only created challenges for Ham. No matter what the lesson, always Ham had understood only the excuse and opportunity for yet another prank. And some of his pranks . . .

She shook her head, smiling even now.

The sand in the salt bin had been no laughing matter. She'd tried to make him understand both with whacks to his small rounded bottom and her insistence that he eat from the spoiled baking. And he'd been so contrite!

Was that her weakness? Because his remorse touched her heart, had she been too quick to forgive?

With other pranks—the frog in her sleeping pallet, the hem of her robe tied in knots, her oven crammed with flowers—even as she scolded, she'd had to laugh.

Had *that* been her fatal flaw?

Of course Noah had always been too preoccupied to take a hand. Had that been the problem? If so, why hadn't Noah's distraction affected the other boys? Certainly when Shem and Japheth were young, he'd been fully as busy. Still they'd become mature, responsible, dependable young men, while Ham had grown in body but not in maturity.

Now Ham was to be a father. He'd have to share Tamara's time and attention with a child. He'd need to learn patience, gentleness, forbearance, *wisdom*.

She breathed another sigh, this one beginning in her toes.

Yahweh knew best, of course.

If one of the others had delivered first, so that Tamara could have watched and helped, she could have learned . . .

When Afene heard, she would be desolate. She prattled endlessly of dust and dirt and their defeat when the others would listen, but to Kyral she confided her deepest yearnings, her continuing fear of barrenness.

But, of course, Yahweh knew best.

Surely only He could untangle Kyral's own jumbled emotions—teaching her how to comfort Afene, support Tamara, and lecture Ham in some long-needed tenets of adulthood.

"Help us, Yahweh," she murmured aloud. Surely they'd be off the ark before the birthing, wouldn't they?

She listened, hoping to hear His assurance, but there were only the familiar sounds of creaking timbers, shifting stores, and restless animals.

"Surely?" she asked again.

Still there was no answer.

Yahweh knows best. She must continue reminding herself of that.

Afene dipped the bucket, time and again, pouring water

into the large wooden wash barrel. In one bucketful she caught a fish. Holding it by its wriggling tail with her thumb and forefinger, she tossed it back.

Shuddering, scouring her hand down the side of her skirt, she didn't pause to consider how the fish—making its home in the very water she'd confidently use for washing the bed-clothes—could possibly be dirty. Still, it had been beautiful, a sparkling arc of silver scales curving through sunlight.

She leaned on the rail. When they had children, she and Japheth, she'd tell of this moment of peace and beauty.

If they had children . . .

Disgruntled, she dumped the fish-tainted water over the railing and captured another bucketful. This one was clear, sparkling, and empty of creatures.

Of *course* they'd have children.

"Would Yahweh have chosen you as Japheth's wife, if you were barren?" Mother Kyral had reminded her on more than one occasion. "Approach Him about it!" she urged. "Ask for His affirmation! And remember our reason for being here—to begin a new world with those who will worship Yahweh. Placing a barren woman on His ark would be like . . . like storing useless seed for later planting!"

On one occasion, perhaps weary of the frequency of Afene's doubting, Kyral challenged, "Do you presume that Yahweh placed you here only to clean? Had we required a housemaid, surely He'd have found one capable of bearing both children and a mop!"

Mother Kyral's frustration caused Afene shame. She knew Mother Kyral's love and patience, and that if she ever spoke sharply, it was because she had explained and consoled until her endurance was exhausted. But as the weeks and months of marriage passed, and there had been no babies, not one, what could Afene think but that she was incapable?

Jerking herself from that pain, Afene approved the level of water in the barrel and began to dip and rub and scrub a bed cover. Only then did she permit herself to recall another even less comfortable moment when Yahweh Himself had given an assurance not even Afene could doubt.

They'd been afloat for less than a month when the dreams began. At first she and Japheth cuddled a newborn. Awakening, realizing that the babe might be someone else's child—a niece or nephew—she decided it hadn't been a sign.

In another dream, she lay in labor. Twisting with pain, yet glowing with its glory, she felt the miracle of giving birth. But when she awoke, aware of a residual pain in her belly, she couldn't be sure whether this dream was a promise of childbearing or merely the aftermath of Tamara's cooking the evening before.

But in a third dream, a cooing child had sought her breast and suckled there.

Assured at last, she'd awakened, stretching and smiling. Then fully alert, she'd alternated between accepting the dreams as Yahweh's clear promise and believing them symptoms of her own deep longing. In the midst of her doubting, Yahweh spoke to her.

"How long will you doubt me, Afene?" His voice, though firm and a bit chiding, carried the quality of patience.

She fell to her knees in fear.

"Do you know who I am?" He asked.

She nodded, cleared her throat, croaked, "Certainly, my Lord! We've spoken before." Did He think she could have forgotten?

He paused. "Then you won't doubt, later, that I am speaking to you now?"

How could she doubt, when the ark's floorboards pressed hard beneath her knees, and rain, a constant reality, beat and hammered and dinned?

She shook her head. *I will not doubt, my Lord.*

"You doubted the dreams," He reminded her.

It was only because my yearning is so intense. I did not want to imagine a promise that You haven't made.

"I know your yearning. That is why I came to you in dreams, so you would have no doubt. But still you doubt."

No, my Lord! She flushed with the memory of that other

confrontation and of the discomfort it had caused her, the pressure of His words filling her mind. *It isn't that I've doubted You, but only that I've recognized my lack of worth . . .*

"You have doubted me."

Forgive me, my Lord.

"You have great worth, my child, far beyond your abilities to clean and keep order. You will have great value in my new world. And, you will have many children, and they will multiply."

Many children? My Lord, I would be overjoyed with just one.

"*Many* children," He repeated.

She began to rise with excitement, wanting to rush to tell someone. Then, reconsidering, she sank to her knees again.

Oh, my Lord Yahweh, she said, her gladness a tangible thing, *How can I thank You? How can I sufficiently praise You?*

"By believing me this time."

Oh, I believe, my Lord. Can't You read my thoughts?

"Yes, my child. For the moment you do believe. I know."

How could I doubt?

He answered gently. "It is in your nature to doubt."

She wanted to argue, but she knew herself too well and *He* knew her better even than she knew herself.

Forgive me, Lord.

"Of course, my child. And to help you as your faith grows, I will give you this sign."

She felt a touch on her forehead. Placing a fingertip there, she sensed a spot of warmth.

"You must learn patience, my child. These matters are in my control. You must not question my wisdom."

Oh, my Lord, I promise. I will remember. I will not doubt. I will have faith. I will be patient.

Again she touched the spot on her forehead, and again she felt the warmth. Many children—Yahweh had said she would have many children! She yearned to shout her news to the world. Then, remembering that the world had shrunk, she wanted to share it with all on the ark, but perhaps . . . she should wait.

Uncomfortably, she wondered if her hesitance were itself a manifestation of doubt. Surely not. She was only being patient, just as Yahweh had instructed. And He had given no indication of *when*. It would surely be unkind to draw everyone else into her tense waiting, watching, and wondering.

Remembering that vivid interview with Yahweh, now long past, Afene touched a wet fingertip to her forehead, and felt the warmth. Always, when this occurred, she sensed a need to find Mother Kyral, and to share with her, at last, the full flavor of Yahweh's promise.

Perhaps today she would do it, for seldom had the inner urging been so strong. Mother Kyral, a partner in her pain almost from the beginning, deserved to know!

Yes, today she would tell Mother Kyral. But not just yet. First there was the laundry to complete.

She set to work with renewed energy. Yahweh had said she would have many children, but in all this time there'd been no indication of even one. Yahweh had mentioned her worth, but she wasn't aware of any value beyond her ability to clean floors and walls and benches, chasing away cobwebs and dirt, washing, scrubbing, sweeping.

But when she had children . . . that's when she would have value, purpose, a reason to live. A woman's purpose was to keep order in the home and rear children . . . but there must be children to rear!

She'd promised she would be patient, but it was *so* hard.

The sounds of brisk footsteps and whistling caught her attention. She hadn't heard Ham whistle since the rain stopped! He approached, grinning cheerfully.

"Have you heard the news, dear sister?" he called. "Have you heard that my beautiful wife is making me a father?"

She'd reached to retrieve the bedclothes she'd just dropped into the barrel. Now she felt the wet lump slip from her numbed grasp. *Tamara? Having a child . . . before me? She's only a child herself. That's not fair . . .*

Afene covered her confusion by fishing in the barrel for the laundry, by keeping her head bent until she could control her features, and her voice.

"Wonderful!" she said at last—proud of her prowess in feigning joy. "You must be very happy. Both of you!"

"Ecstatic!" Ham said and swung along the deck; his whistling resumed.

She watched him around the corner. Then, dispiritedly, she scrubbed at a spot already fully clean. Tears drizzled down her cheeks and splatted into the barrel—dimpling the surface, then widening into rings. And a gentle voice whispered like a thread of summer breeze.

"Dear Afene. I never promised that your children would be the first!"

Maelis lay apart, her body curled, tears seeping, a sob struggling to break free. The more rigidly she held herself and the more adamantly she strove to contain the aching in her throat, the closer she came to losing quiet control. Never had she been more aware of her bulk and of the bunk's inadequate dimensions than when, yearning for the fetal position, she fought against childlike weeping. Were Shem to awaken—which appeared unlikely, judging from his deep, even breathing and the occasional snore that rattled the night's stillness—she'd be hard-pressed to explain this grief which, increasingly, overtook her without warning. One minute she was cheerful and the next she'd be weeping without cause.

Unreasonable, Shem called it. Further evidence of women's instability, and another argument in favor of men's preeminence as heads of households and leaders in government, he'd said.

Shem was so arrogant! She clenched her fists, and the sob escaped.

Carefully silent, she exerted firm control, until the quiet was broken by another snore.

He hadn't heard! Relieved, knowing she'd avoided giving Shem an explanation that wouldn't convince even her, she approached Yahweh in her thoughts.

Probably You can't understand me, either, my Lord. After all this time—the rains ceased long ago—why do I still grieve? At unexpected moments, when I'm content in my own life, why do the death agonies of those poor souls oppress me so?

"Your compassion is a blessing, my child. As keeper of the faith, Shem must be unwavering. But sometimes he is too rigid, too judgmental. He needs the balance of your sorrow for the sufferings of others. It helps him to be more human."

But Yahweh, my Lord, I weep so easily now . . .

She was pleading for answers. Once, Shem had admired her for her stability and her clear reasoning. But now . . .

"It's hard for an active man—or woman—to be patient in confinement."

Confinement? Were they both at odds with themselves because they were restricted to the ark? Was that why Shem was more . . . "unwavering" than before and she so often wept without warning?

"It is the reason for Shem."

Yahweh paused. Maelis waited. She heard a chuckle. Had Yahweh chuckled?

"Have you noticed . . . nothing?"

She felt a surge of impatience. How, in such an unusual situation with so many strange sensations and concerns, could she fail to notice many things?

She'd noticed that the rain had ceased and the sun, no longer hidden by storm clouds, warmed them every day. That had lifted their spirits. But Ham, the perpetual child, always ready to play his senseless jokes and pranks, had responded to the change by sulking. She'd noticed that Tamara had matured somewhat. Although her cooking still fell far short of the skill displayed by the other women, at least she'd shown some responsibility in helping prepare their meals. Afene had plunged new energies into her cleaning as though a spotless ark would somehow hasten the end of their sojourn.

Father Noah and Mother Kyral had become more quiet. He was withdrawn, as though distracted by a battle raging within himself, and Mother Kyral, growing thin from her worries about him, seemed less buoyant, less focused on the new world they would experience when the waters had dried up.

She'd noticed that the animals, although still living in the harmony of Yahweh's suspension of their natural survival instincts, were expectant, as though they sensed that the end of their contentment with one another drew nearer. And she'd noticed that Shem had become more rigid, speaking more often of the rules they must follow in worship of Yahweh.

"Yes. All those things are true," Yahweh agreed. "But about yourself—have you noticed something . . . new . . . within you?"

I weep, my Lord.

She waited, but Yahweh did not speak again. *What else is there?* she wondered.

Unexpectedly she felt a fluttering, a stirring, in her lower body. There was a focused sensitivity there, as though all of her senses centered on that area and its potential. She put her hand on her stomach and felt the fluttering again. It was a definite sense of movement.

Pregnant? she wondered. Then, sitting bolt upright, she said it aloud. "Pregnant?"

Shem stirred. "Did you say somethhh . . . m'love . . ." he murmured, rolled over, and resumed his deep breathing.

She wanted to shake him awake, to tell him of her discovery. But, newly wakened, Shem was fuzzy at best. When she told him, she would want his full attention, would want to watch realization spread across his face as he grasped the meaning of her news. She would need him to share the joy he would surely feel. Until then, it would be her blissful, wonderful secret.

Perhaps he would notice a change in her demeanor and guess the reason. If not, she wouldn't wait long to tell him, only until the time was right.

Hugging herself, she imagined how it might happen, and when, and where—and how she would tell Mother Kyral.

Of them all, Mother Kyral would be the most delighted.

Moonlight brightened the opened porthole, silvering all it touched. There was a majesty, a magic, about moonlight. It was so clean.

Smiling to herself, Afene snuggled beneath the cover.

Japheth was pacing again. As he moved past the bunk, to the window, his muscular silhouette was outlined by brilliance. When he moved away, her eyes—assaulted by renewed light—retained his wavering image. She could transfer it about the tiny cubicle wherever she pleased, to the overhead timbers, to the wall, to the pale coverlet. Just as she'd always desired, she could see Japheth wherever she turned her eyes.

Smiling, she stretched and sighed. The covers were pleasantly cool and the moonlight perfect for sleeping. The soft lapping of endless waters under and about them formed a familiar lullaby.

All she lacked was Japheth beside her, and he would come soon, she knew. But now he both paced and sighed.

"My love," she invited softly, turning back the cover on his side of the narrow bunk.

He negotiated the tiny circumference of their cubicle twice more before he came—reluctantly, it seemed—to sit on the bunk's edge.

She reached to touch him, to stroke his arm.

"By daylight," he murmured, "I can manage. There's enough to do, then, that I can forget."

"Forget?" she prompted.

"The excitement," he mumbled.

Quickly she withdrew her hand. Surely he didn't mean the "excitement" of the flood, with its destructive force! She shuddered.

"You can't even imagine what it was like," he continued thoughtfully, and she felt his weight easing down beside her. "You were always at home, where it was safe—and, I suppose—dull. But out there, speaking of Yahweh . . ."

Her hand found his arm again. "I'm sorry, my love."

"Sorry . . . ?" The word hung in the air as though he sought its meaning. "Oh! You grieve that no one accepted Yahweh. It was a deep sorrow in my own heart as well."

"*Was* a deep sorrow?"

"Yahweh has healed it," he said comfortably, then sighed still again. "What He has not healed is . . . my restlessness, my discontent."

Knowing herself so content now, with the rocking of the ark and the transformation of moonlight and with Japheth never far away, she found it difficult to sympathize.

"For a man, it's frustrating to be confined," he said, and added carelessly, "Women are always inside."

She felt a small burst of annoyance. "Women don't necessarily choose to be 'always inside.'"

"Patience, my love." He reached for her, and his words contained laughter. "I don't always phrase my thoughts diplomatically."

Though his fingers still stroked her forearm, she knew that in his mind he had left her. He was transported, once more, to that thread of the Euphrates, with its banks and docks, and to the town they had known so well. The hub of streets, expanding to the valleys and woodlands surrounding it, had once been alive with movement and sound. Now all was obliterated, stilled, silenced.

"The worst of it is," he whispered, almost plaintively, "my work is done. There will no longer be a reason—or an audience—for evangelizing."

Poor Japheth, she thought, with more than a touch of sarcasm. Was the fact that his time "on stage" was past the greatest concern he could muster?

"I suspect," she said tightly, "that Yahweh will have other work for you to do."

"I suppose." Turning toward her, he adjusted their bodies to the confines of the bunk.

She would have preferred to draw away, now that contentment was shattered. But the ark's heavy wooden framework was rigid against her spine, and the covers too warm, now, for leaving.

That is, until she heard the pattering of small feet across the floor, a high, ecstatic chirping, and the swish of an animal's swinging from some rope or other. (Later she discovered it was the belt of Japheth's tunic hanging from a peg.)

A monkey! The filthy creature was wandering around in their sleeping quarters, having done who knows what in the cooking area! Hadn't she enough to clean, without scraping monkey droppings from the floors and walls, or picking animal hair and fleas from her clothing and bedding?

Grumbling, she removed herself from Japheth's embrace, scrambled over him—ignoring his grunts of surprise—and stepped from the bunk to the floor. The monkey, hanging at the porthole, chattered to the moonlight. His dissertation rose to high, scolding screeches as she caught him none too gently, held him at arm's length, and bore him purposefully along dim passageways and down shadowed stairways.

"Horrible beast!" she said, her fingers feeling soothed by his silky hair. When he fixed her with those large eyes— barely discernible, save when they passed a torch—and, his fingers to his lips, coaxed like a begging child, she had to smile. "Charmer!" she accused more softly, but refused to hold him closer. Already her arms and neck crawled with the prospect of fleas. Still, both then and moments later, when she dropped him into the cage with his relatives, she recognized that less of her anger was with him than with Japheth.

When she'd spoken of the sameness of her days, he hadn't tried to understand. "Visit my mother" was the best he could suggest. But now, simply because there was no one left to hear him preach, she was expected to offer him consolation.

Men, she thought resentfully. *What self-centered creatures they are!*

She was glad, when she crawled carefully into bed, that Japheth was already deeply asleep.

Kyral sighed.

Noah had changed. He had lost his zest for life and, apparently, for her. In the early years of their marriage, he had coveted her company, solicited her conversation. Even in those years when the ark demanded his energies by day and his thoughts much of each evening, she'd often sensed his glance upon her. She could feel his eyes following her about her tasks, warming her with a smile that smoothed his expression and glowed in his eyes.

How she'd loved him! And she'd known his love for her then was as deep as the waters on which the ark now floated.

Pausing in her work and observing Noah slumped astride a bench, she searched for those characteristics she admired. His straightness, the clarity of his eye, the perpetual traces of humor about his mouth were all gone, smudged by surliness.

And her love and respect had been damaged, as well. She could nearly despise the dull-eyed husk huddling there.

She missed his lightness and the elasticity of his step as fully as she yearned for his tenderness. Why was he so morose, so defeated, so joyless? Why, except when speech was mandatory, did he move silently, heavily about the ark?

It was he whom Yahweh had selected from all the earth as the righteous man. It was he to whom Yahweh had spoken first and most consistently. Wasn't this present peevishness a denial of that heavenly favor?

She was aghast. How dare she, Noah's wife, experience such revulsion! Could she, when his spontaneity returned, express anything of what she felt? Suppose it didn't return. Was she doomed to spend her days with this unfeeling stranger?

Noah was rousing.

No, he only shifted to a deeper slump—his eyes nearly closed and deep sighs rumbling. She turned away in distaste, as when, that afternoon, she'd fished a cockroach from her bin of grain.

Why, of all the creatures they'd brought aboard, was it the unsavory that flourished? Cockroaches, flies, bedbugs, ticks, mosquitoes—all had propagated alarmingly. And she—unsure at first whether she had the right to kill any at all—had withheld her foot, her hand, her duster until surely it was too late to control their burgeoning numbers.

Her advice to Yahweh, had He requested it, would have been to abandon all such pests to the flood. And the rats (she shuddered) and snakes of most varieties, and . . .

Noah's lurching reclaimed her attention. He'd fallen asleep, his expression smooth and open. Unexpectedly, she smiled, and before his head could crack against the creaking floorboards, she caught him, then eased him, shapeless as a half-full sack of grain, to safety on the floor. She untied her overskirt and covered him gently, as she would any helpless child.

Then, resuming her work with fervor, she firmed a decision. She would speak to Noah. In the morning, she'd draw him apart, explaining how she missed his companionship, how her respect faltered in the face of his dejection.

Or perhaps she'd wait until some night, when he held her, murmuring love words.

Or, far more likely, she would remain a coward, not wanting to offend him, or endanger his love for her—whatever of his love had survived his depression.

PART FOUR

And God said, "This is the sign of the covenant which I make between Me and you, and every living creature that is with you, for perpetual generations: I set my rainbow in the cloud, and it shall be a sign of a covenant between Me and the earth."

Genesis 9:12–13

»»» 10 «««

Kyral, standing on an upper deck and bracing herself against the laving of a warm wind, drew a deep breath of satisfaction.

Surely the waters were shrinking! It wasn't just that they stretched quiet and still, moving only in gentle heavings that swayed and glittered into infinity; they seemed somehow less dense. The ark remained a tiny, bobbing speck on the surface of a vast sea that curved to the edges of the earth. But, occasionally, as at this sunlit moment, it passed over the rearing monument of a mountaintop, its points and planes and dark crevasses discernible through the clear, deep water.

It was strange how that shifting sheen of water caused images to waver. Kyral knew, of course, that the rocks were solid, firmly-rooted far below. It was the sea that moved and altered, causing the peaks to seem now close, now removed, now leaning, now insubstantial.

She thought she could perceive, still deeper in that vast, clear pool, something else. Those vacillating peaks and slopes seemed to hold the litter of shattered trees, cast up, then anchored by the frenzy of the flood. But there was more than trees, some further debris. Could it be broken ships? The remnants of what once had been . . . homes?

Swallowing, she determined not to dwell on ancient

griefs. She would not consider what other relics of a discarded world also lay beyond her sight.

Just below, Noah and the boys struggled with the heavy anchor. They were testing it, readying it for later use. Ham slipped. Muttering, he kicked at the chain, then howled, holding his injured foot, while hopping on the other. She sighed. Only a fool would kick such a massive chain in anger. There could be only one result.

He limped off—surely to seek Tamara's comfort and salve—and Kyral resumed her peaceful scrutiny. Morning light pattered across glittering objects. Glancing at the men, too busy with their coiling of the heavy chain to notice, Kyral strolled to the bow, leaned as far over the rail as safety permitted, and shaded her eyes.

Strange, those patches of gleaming white and those bright points of brilliance, shifting as the sun's position altered with the turning of the ark. Could her eyes be deceived? Was there movement under the water?

Sharply, she inhaled and looked again.

There was a flapping, a swaying, faded colors, something white. Could anything still live? It seemed too stationary for fish, for any creature at home in the sea.

Frowning, she turned to summon Noah, then remembered that his eyes were even older than hers. Smiling, Shem approached. His arms enclosed her in a brief, grunting hug.

"My son," she said, returning the embrace. Then, pointing, "What is it? Can you tell?"

He peered intently, his glance following the direction her finger ordered. And she, narrowing her eyes, still could interpret only patterns and that scant, mysterious, persistent movement. But somehow the apparition seemed less alarming with Shem beside her. Besides, of all aboard, his eyes were keenest.

"Can you tell what it is?" she asked again.

He chuckled. "Yahweh's enemies," he said, his voice deep and grimly satisfied.

She gasped, staring into his hard eyes.

With one strong arm about her shoulders, he prodded a forefinger toward the thick, moving layers of water. "There . . . human bones picked clean by scavengers."

That was the white . . . she thought, tasting nausea.

"And there," Shem continued, "their once-fine garments, bleached and frayed."

Fabric, then, accounted for the movement. Perhaps it still embraced skeletal arms and shoulders, giving the sleeves and skirts to the water's play . . .

"And that brilliance . . ." Shem was pointing and her glance followed. It seemed she had no choice and besides any image supplanting those already in her thoughts must be an improvement! "Bracelets," he said, "silver and gold—of little use to harlots now in Hell!"

His chuckles had become laughter, his harshness almost a shout of victory. And she felt for him—this son she had borne, this son she loved—a revulsion beyond that she'd known for the whole of sinning, suffering humanity. Stiffly she pulled away, shivering, ignoring his solicitude (was she all right?), shaking her head at his suggestion that he see her to her quarters.

"Go," she said. It was all she could manage, but she delayed to make certain he obeyed.

Then, shuddering, she stumbled only a few awkward steps before leaning over the rail to vomit into the sea.

It was a sight that occurred with increasing frequency as the waters lowered, and it was one to which Kyral could never grow accustomed. But she could, with care, avoid it. And so, whenever she observed mountaintops beneath the water's surface, she remembered compelling tasks within the ark.

Her daughters-in-law did the same. It was a subject none of them mentioned. But all were unfailingly quieter at such times, and sadness renewed itself in their eyes, in their wanness, in the thin, straight lines of their lips.

Once, Kyral found Tamara, huddled—as tightly as her growing womb permitted—near the newest hutch, necessitated by a burgeoning rabbit population. She was cuddling a young rabbit, stroking its deep gray fur that was pitted, in spots, by tears, their wet tracks still staining Tamara's cheeks. Her eyes were puffy, reddened. The rabbit's ears flicked and twitched and wobbled as Tamara whispered, "I keep wondering what I'd feel if . . . if by some chance I saw her."

By some flash of intuition or perhaps by Yahweh's nudging, Kyral knew that Tamara spoke of her mother. It was the first symptom of softness she'd seen in that direction. Wishing that Tamara had chosen to grieve on a bench, she eased to the floor, awkwardly.

"There, there," she said, casting about in her thoughts for something more directly tuned to the moment. Unable to find more comforting words, she shrugged. "There, there, now," she said again.

"I hated her," Tamara admitted, sniffling. "I may still hate her. That's the worst part."

Kyral, working to arrange her legs in some non-cramping position, knew that admitting this combination of hatred and grief was healthy. How many years the coldness of her own loathing and contempt, unrelieved by tears, had weighted her, crippled her, rendering her incapable of the self-liking essential if love for others is to be open and freely expressed. That other Kyral, the cool observer, the callous survivor—while she'd seemed a savior during times of greatest trauma—had, in reality, become an anchor, dragging at Kyral's movement toward a life beyond abuse.

But Tamara—finding her healing in this huddling, these tears—wouldn't require another, "coping" self.

But how would she teach this to Tamara?

"In every parent-child relationship . . ." Yahweh suggested and Kyral picked up the thread, repeating it.

"In every parent-child relationship, there's a duality. Always there is something of love and something of hate."

Tamara, her hands tightening on the rabbit's small body, insisted, "I never felt hate toward my father."

"Perhaps not that you recall. But when you were small, when he denied you something . . ."

"He denied me nothing."

"Poor child, poor child."

While she patted as though supporting Tamara's grief for this man she perceived to be perfect, Kyral recalled that true parental love requires refusal of some whims. How that poor woman must have battered her emotions against those closed ranks—the doting father and the undisciplined daughter!

"And Mother," Tamara's voice congealed, "Mother denied me *everything*. She took such joy in my tears." She straightened, suddenly, and the rabbit squirmed in reaction. "If she could see me now, she'd be delighted."

"I wonder. I wonder . . ." Kyral was still patting. "She'd be delighted, perhaps, that you're safe? That you're happily married . . . and giving her a grandchild?"

Tamara sat quietly. "She'd hate my being happy." But the sentence evolved without vehemence. It was lacking even in resoluteness.

She'd turn that in her mind, Kyral knew. And she'd consider the possibility that her mother might have been more complicated than she'd thought, perhaps even less evil when compared with her father's good.

It will take time . . . Kyral heaved heavily to her feet and stretched to quench the sparks and flickers that signaled rousing muscles.

Everything takes time. *See how slowly the waters recede, revealing their gruesome hoards. Just as cautiously, relics in memory yield to study. The mind holds and turns them, revealing new facets, re-interpreting concepts considered solid before. Only through this evolving process can maturity occur.*

"Come, daughter," she urged gently, and Tamara rose in one movement, though not as gracefully as some months before. Carefully she replaced the rabbit and smiled at its twitch-nosed exploration of its siblings and its tentative hops. Turning, she dropped a kiss on Kyral's cheek.

"If my mother had known you better," she whispered, "you'd have taught her to love without anger."

It's a start, Kyral thought warmly, as she limped in the wake of Tamara's half-running and wished that her foot could come awake without such prickles of pain.

How she loved them, these daughters! Tamara, always walking proudly, her shoulders thrust back and her rounded belly far forward. Maelis huddled a bit, her arms sometimes encircling her growing child, already cradling it, her lips often pursed as though she already crooned a lullaby.

And Afene. She'd disclosed her pregnancy only a week earlier in tones that throbbed between joy and disbelief and escalated to something much like triumph. Tamara, seeking Ham with laughing eyes, had almost hidden a giggle behind her hand. But Maelis, smiling quietly, had lingeringly embraced Afene.

What a change there'd been in Afene! Her expression had softened. Her eyes glowed. The edges of her temper had smoothed. Perhaps the most obvious change came in her moderated obsession with cleaning!

Kyral prayed for all of them, of course—that their babes would be full-term and healthy and their deliveries easy.

Well . . . deliveries were seldom *easy*. She prayed they would, at least, be quick and free of complications.

But she prayed especially for Afene—that she hadn't been so eager to prove her fertility that she'd imagined pregnancy. She wouldn't have feigned it purposely! But Kyral had heard of more than one woman whose body had played such tricks.

Especially she remembered Synha, who, time after time, announced to her husband and neighbors that she was with child. And, time after time, her belly and feet had swollen, and her face had plumped and freckled as morning sickness gave way to cravings as diverse as fried eels and raw turnips. And, time after time, no child resulted. Once she'd worn her inflated body for months past a normal delivery.

Poor thing. *Poor thing.* She was ridiculed by those women whose bodies bore actual fruit and beaten by her husband for his humiliation when other men derided him, mocking at his seed—apparently empty, they charged—as they parodied his wife's awkward gait.

At last, Synha was banished to the temple and assigned a prostitute's role. But that, so Kyral had heard, had ended with her next false pregnancy. She'd been whipped and, judged unworthy of sacrifice—since her lack might neutralize the power of those deities specializing in fertility—was cast alive to the dogs. Poor, tragic Synha. Kyral had always found her a kind, gentle woman, unassuming, thoughtful...

How tragic if Afene should carry an imagined child! Of the three girls, Afene *required* pregnancy. For Tamara, her swelling body was an ornament, accentuating youth and beauty. Maelis wore pregnancy sweetly, quietly. Certainly Shem's love for her would have been as all-encompassing had she never borne a child. (If only, Kyral thought with a sigh, he could extend a fragment of such love to perished humanity.) With a shudder, she recalled that moment on the deck, when he'd triumphed so callously over the fragments of dead pagans.

But for Afene, motherhood had always seemed an affirmation of self-worth. No matter how much any of them praised her, loved her, comforted and encouraged and cherished her, it was never enough.

Chilled by a new thought, Kyral considered the possible fate of the children of such a mother. Would Afene expect from them the same perfection she demanded of herself?

Yahweh, Kyral sighed. *How complicated you have shaped us to be!*

"And yet how elemental," came His answer. "All women yearn for children."

But between yearning and an obsession such as Afene's...

"And what of your obsession with her obsession?"

She smiled. How well He knew her!

"Afene will have a child," He assured her, "when you have

left the ark, built shelter, and watched some of your seedlings grow to bearing."

She breathed deeply, relieved. He'd answered two questions at once! While allaying her fears for Afene, he'd also
limited their term on the ark. At least it couldn't continue
for more than nine more months! Unless . . .

He was chuckling. "No, I wasn't referring to some future
pregnancy. Afene is with child *now*."

⋙ ⋘

When a child, Maelis had nearly drowned.

Her mother, doing laundry beside the stream, had been
singing a song without words and with minimal melody, a
fragment of a tune that repeated and repeated and repeated.
Or perhaps the scene had replayed in memory so often, so
slowly, so vivid in its detail, that the song only *seemed* repet-
itive.

In this second drowning, there was no music save the lapping, surging, gurgling, flowing of the water.

Maelis turned lazily. The waves washed over her comfort-
ingly. Languidly, she moved her arms, experiencing the cool
caress of ripples, of eddies, of kelp. She felt her hair floating
on the endless waters. But the water would support her
only until her arms tired. She knew that when she could no
longer stroke the swells, she would sink and drown.

Shouldn't the possibility of drowning distress her? How
could she know such inner warmth? Such peace?

That first time, she'd felt this same lassitude. *So this is
what it's like to drown,* she'd mused, *this peaceful.* The water closed over her head, pressing her down, almost playfully. She stretched her toes to push up from pebbles and
silt—not because she must, but because it seemed expected,
because it was enjoyable. The elasticity of the water rendered her graceful. Its texture and temperature made her feel
immortal.

Down. Up. Down. Up.

This time the waters, deep enough to submerge mountains, were far too deep for that mandatory bouncing. This time there was no mother, her eyes widening in panic, and no melody turning into an ineffectual scream as forgotten laundry, splashing into shallow shoreline water, created prismatic arcs of crystal droplets. Maelis had watched, enchanted, smiling, as she bounced down, pushed up, her hair floating, her thoughts floating, too.

Her mind was at ease this second, more serious time in the deeper waters with Shem's child within her womb. (Did the babe experience this same peace, this comforting weariness?) For this drowning, there was no shore, only the ark. And it was too distant for reaching, since her mind wouldn't dictate the movements required for swimming.

Such sluggishness possessed her.

Perhaps this was only a dream, a remembering of the childhood event with an image of the ark superimposed. She giggled tiredly and yawned. Soon, she would drown, unless she could bounce.

She imagined herself sliding down, pushing up, gliding down . . . So soothing.

What her thoughts entertained, her body yearned to imitate. But before the downward glide could begin, a scream shattered her peace (not her scream or her mother's), and a splash (not dumped laundry, suddenly inconsequential).

Frowning, she looked toward the interruption, her arms forgetting the circular movement essential to buoyancy. She slipped, effortlessly, comfortably, and the water began closing over her mouth. Straining upward, she spat. And saw Shem, swimming toward her! His expression was frightened, anguished.

Don't worry, Shem! she thought toward him. *It's only a dream.* Smiling, she waved. And the waters claimed her. Down. Down. Down.

She hadn't expected that, just yet. But what exhilaration! Her toes stretched for bouncing surface, and found none. Greens and blues rushed by. She felt weightless and invincible. *Marvelous!* Entranced, she stared upward to study the line of bubbles growing from her lips.

She laughed, gasped, inhaled water. Something had caught her hair, was tugging her upward. Even foreshortened, she recognized that arm and those muscular legs, kicking, their normal hue paled by the blue of the water, their fine dark hairs disturbed and swirling.

Shem.

You're hurting me, Shem! She wanted to shout it, but she strangled, choked, coughed. And the word remained a red, unshaped wildness in her mind.

When he released her hair—finally—his arms closed tightly, much too tightly, across her chest as he lifted her up, up, up, until they surfaced, sputtering.

Sunlight assaulted her eyes; the air seemed too thick for breathing. Still, she could glare. His panic had shattered her peace. Why hadn't he left her alone with the cool greenness?

Desperately, struggling to return, she strove to convince him that it was only a dream—*her* dream! But the combined power of his arms and the demands of her coughing allowed only strangling sounds.

She twisted, wrenched, clawed, fighting to return to the peacefulness of drowning.

He slapped her! And her head snapped back, striking something hard, something unyielding. Wood? The ark? Fragments of thought spun through explosions of light. Wood? He'd never struck her before! The ark? Shem! *Shem!*

Again, she slipped beneath the treacherous waters. So *this* was drowning! *SHEMMMMmmmmmm . . .*

She awoke, coughing and sputtering, her head throbbing. Her ribs were certainly crushed, her emotions in turmoil. The water! Where was the water? The cool, welcoming, deceptive, destructive water . . .

"Shem."

"Don't fight me!"

Was he trying to kill her? What of their unborn child?

"Shem!"

Through sobs, his anguished words exploded. "I can't . . . let you perish . . . in the flood!"

She softened in his arms, wiped his cheeks with her hair, soothed him with words. "My love. My dear, sweet Shem. It's only a dream."

Still he struggled, but weakly, and, gasping for breath, he whispered, "If only . . . we'd listened. If only . . . we'd believed."

His arms convulsed. Words of agony, of hopelessness, grated through his clenched teeth. "The waters are too much for me! Forgive me, my love! And may Yahweh forgive us our unbelief!

He lay so still, then, that she listened for his breathing. It was there, though slow and shallow.

She woke him.

Despite her gentleness, he started, jerked upright. "What? Where?" Then, slumping, sobbing again, he drew her toward him.

"Oh, my love. Can you ever forgive . . .?"

Her ribs and her head would heal. She stroked his hair.

He was whispering. "I've been so arrogant, so self-righteous, so judgmental. Even against you, my love, when you mourned those poor souls who perished."

She drew a deep breath of amazement. His apology, then, was not for the violence. Perhaps he didn't even realize he'd struck her. But oh! how thrilling the realization that had, at last, come to him!

Thank You, Yahweh, she breathed. It would have been miracle enough to give them the identical dream, allowing Shem to realize the tragedy and horror of losing a loved one to drowning.

But You did more . . .

"Shem was growing harsher."

"I know. I know." She said it aloud, and Shem leaned into her soothing.

Yahweh continued, "It was essential that he experience their *spiritual* desperation."

In Shem's dream, he was a pagan?—unsaved, scoffing at Noah, rejecting Japheth's appeals.

"How could he have functioned as keeper of the faith

without such understanding? Without humility? Without gratitude for the miracle of his own salvation?" He sighed.

Maelis comforted. *You did only what was needed.*

She knew she'd spoken truly. Just as it had been necessary to wipe false gods and their worshipers from His earth, it had been crucial that Yahweh correct Shem. And her measureless love for Yahweh deepened as she realized again that such disciplining gave Him no pleasure.

❯❯❯ ❮❮❮

The shuttle clicked, swished, whooshed. Singularly comforting sounds, Kyral thought, especially when paired with the stroking of gentle waves against the hull of the ark, the sleepy afternoon murmurings of animals, and Afene's humming. Was it only through the long scarcity of anything remotely musical that Afene's tones seemed truer now, more melodious?

For a moment, Kyral experienced a twinge of loss. She had told Yahweh that she'd miss music. But there was so much of promise in her life that it seemed ungrateful to dwell on those elements that were absent.

Swish. Whoosh. Creak.

Pausing to study the emerging pattern of soft blue against creamy white, she imagined the small garments she'd fashion once the length was completed. There would be three of each, just alike. She smiled in anticipation. How marvelous to care for babies again! No wonder Afene hummed as she embroidered flowers on a tiny robe. No wonder that Maelis and Shem conversed quietly, touching often and lingeringly, as they shaped and smoothed a cradle.

How different Shem had grown! His expression softened, he was speaking of a talented woodworker he'd admired as a child.

"An old man," he said, "or so he seemed at the time, though as I remember, his hands were misshapen from accidents rather than twisted by age. There was a scar near the wrist, where a chisel had slipped. The ends of several fingers were missing. He told us his wife had cut them off when he reached for another slice of bread without asking. And we believed him, until we observed the reckless way he handled knives and her clucking gentleness as she patched him up." He paused to sight along an edge. "And of course his fingernails were blackened from hammerblows, as Father's were all those years when I was growing up."

Kyral chuckled, remembering those nails, sometimes drawing back from the cuticle and falling completely away.

Looking up, smiling, Shem and Maelis included her in their conversation.

"Do you remember, Mother? He lived not far from the dock. And his wife made a bread carved with deep, slanted cuts, and black seeds scattered over.

"Poppyseeds?" Maelis guessed.

Kyral nodded. "His name was Muranthis."

"Muranthis." Shem seemed to be tasting the word. "I'm afraid we simply called him 'Old Woodcarver.'"

Swish. Swoosh. Click.

"He was younger than your father," Kyral corrected comfortably, "not much older than I."

Shem said easily, "Everyone looked ancient in those days." He rubbed his thumb over a curve in the rocker, and held it there as a marker while he reached for pumice. "He made toys for us. Did you know that, Mother?"

"I remember."

"Such hours he must have spent on them! I realize that, now."

"And then, you left them underfoot."

Shem sighed. "So much goes unappreciated when we're young."

A thundering of footsteps sounded on the lower stairs. An elephant trumpeted a protest, and monkeys chittered encouragement.

"No, Ham! No!"

Kyral protected the loom as they raced past, Tamara shrieking, Ham chortling as he swatted her rump with a flexible switch used to chase away flies.

Breaking off her song, Afene clucked disapproval.

Afene's child, Kyral knew, would never be allowed to run and shriek. A shame. But she agreed that Ham and Tamara should long ago have outgrown their childish playing. Footsteps pounded up another set of stairs and rumbled across the upper floor. Dust sifted down, drifting, some landing on Kyral's weaving.

She glanced at Afene, wondering if she'd noticed. But in recent weeks Afene had grown more casual about dust.

There was banging, and another shriek, shrill and warning.

What if they injure the child? Kyral demanded in her thoughts.

"They're children themselves," Yahweh murmured.

Yet . . . and she hoped she was masking her reproof, *she was first to conceive.*

He chuckled quietly.

She jerked the shuttle on its course. It just didn't make sense—children bearing children. What kind of example would those two set for their tiny ones if they persisted in scuffling like puppies?

The resounding thump, overhead, failed to surprise her.

See, she thought uncharitably, *it won't be so laughable if she miscarries.*

"She won't miscarry," and suddenly His voice seemed weary, "although generations to follow might prefer it."

She shivered. What could He mean?

She sensed His withdrawal. She wouldn't have asked, anyway. Sometimes it was better not to know what lay ahead. But the chill remained.

Joy had gone from her work.

She anchored the shuttle, stood, stretched, and went to see if Tamara would be crying, again.

Tamara rocked back and forth on the hard floor, hugging her knees, her tear-wet face hidden in her skirt.

"You've changed," Ham accused, sullenly.

And you haven't! she thought.

"Of *course* I've changed! I'm pregnant." Dull pain throbbed in her womb.

He shrugged. "You used to enjoy playing."

"We were children, then," she whispered.

"You were old enough to seduce me."

Straightening, she felt a surge of anger that overshadowed physical discomfort. She'd never seduced him, or anyone! Then, with swift shame, she remembered how she'd once carried herself, how she'd studied each movement, plotting its effect on others—on men, on Cloyren.

Ham was nodding grimly.

She repeated, "We were children." And Ham still was, and might always be. But she'd never again allow him to force *her* backward to immaturity. There was the babe to consider.

Clutching below the baby, supporting its bulk, she controlled her groaning with a grimace and managed to stand, without Ham's help.

He still sat on the floor, cross-legged, drawing his finger along a toolmark in the wood. "I liked you better then," he said spitefully.

And of course he would have.

"I liked you, too . . . then," she said carefully and refused to look at him, to acknowledge his tightening expression, to react to his stamping exit.

When he was gone, she sighed. Gingerly pressing the spot where pain still gathered, she prayed to Yahweh that the child hadn't been injured by their foolishness. *Ham's* foolishness, she amended.

Reminding him of her condition, she'd begged him not to chase her. But he'd teased and scoffed and pushed playfully as he always had. And she'd given in, as she always had.

No longer! And she wouldn't seek him out, this time, or (perhaps) ever again. Let him come to her, or not, as he chose. She could find companionship with others on the ark. With Maelis, who'd teach her more of herbs and spices. With Mother Kyral, learning to water and prune the plants. Even with Afene, if she could endure that constant humming, though she preferred even the humming to the song of the bird who died of cold.

She could sit alone, crooning to her unborn babe. She could visit the stables and watch other mothers with their young. Already the gray rabbit expected a litter. Imagine! That day Tamara had cuddled her she'd been little more than a baby herself. That had been the time she'd feared her reaction if suddenly the sea should shrink enough and the ark would unexpectedly cross a valley, and there, below, she'd see her mother's corpse splayed out in death—perhaps her sightless eyes still mocking, still accusing.

Forcibly she returned her thoughts to the rabbits and the ewes and their lambs, to that ugly, small hippopotamus, pink and round and uncertain on its newborn legs. Yet its mother was as proud as any mother who'd ever given birth!

It was strange, the peace she felt, knowing she didn't really need Ham. She could live without his admiration, even without his nighttime cuddling, if she must. She had the child.

Unexpectedly she remembered her father and their oneness. She and her baby would be as close, as loving, as all-sufficient. *Dear, dear Father . . .* It was one of the few times she'd remembered him with love and warmth unmarred by wrenching grief.

❯❯❯ ❮❮❮

Kyral watched as the shrinking yet still-endless waters quenched the fire and molten gold of the setting sun. She could almost hear it sizzle.

Shem and Ham lowered the anchor.

Where was Noah?

Even from this distance, she could see the twitch of Ham's firmed jaw. He was still sulking. How long had it been since she'd seen him with Tamara? Two days? She'd wondered that first night, if the closeness of the bunk would force a reconciliation. She should have known better. After all, hadn't she herself suffered Ham's stubborn displeasure over and over during his childhood? She should have guessed that he'd sleep on the floor or some hard bench to "punish" Tamara.

He would always be a child.

She paused, suspending her thinking, hoping that Yahweh might disagree with her, but He was silent.

She sighed.

Where was Noah? He usually helped with the anchor. It was essential now, with numerous ranges looming closer and closer to the surface, an occasional crag jutting above. Soon, one might catch and rend the hull. And then . . .

Where could he be? With the waters receding, he should devote constant attention to their possible peril.

"Yahweh will care for us."

She looked about quickly. "Noah?"

She was alone. It had been her memory, recalling his confident words spoken months before.

How different he'd been then! Sometimes brooding, with his major work completed, but largely affirmative and loving. How long it had been since he'd held her for no reason . . . nuzzled her cheek . . . declared his love. Shrugging, she admitted her inability to read his current moods.

The voice of Yahweh intruded. "So many days of endless waters! Remember, my child, how inactivity enervates men."

And the women, of course, hadn't been inactive. She had often noted that while men must sometimes leave their work behind, work clung to women like burrs. Perhaps the very pervasiveness of women's tasks, their interminableness, shaped proof against whatever now afflicted Noah. *Please give me patience . . .*

"I, too, must exercise patience with Noah." He paused. "You've never spoken to him about his despondency, that it threatens your love for him."

She flushed, then dared to ask, *Have You?*

There was a beat of silence. "It doesn't affect my love."

How she shrank from approaching Noah, offering her reproach! *It would mean so much more, my Lord, coming from You.*

"You underestimate the power of his love for you."

Well, she thought dryly, she'd seen no evidence of his consuming passion these recent weeks! Much of the time, she hadn't even known where he was.

"How often have you searched him out?"

New warmth invaded her cheeks. *There's been the weaving,* she explained, *and always the cooking. Surely the seedlings can't live much longer, my Lord, without proper replanting. They require my constant care.*

While He didn't say the words, she sensed His thinking, His reminder that marriage required nurturing, too. Noah was far more precious to Him, and surely to her, than any number of tiny plants could possibly be.

Yet when she found Noah, slumped slack-legged near a stack of empty grainsacks, she wanted to scold, as she would have the children. She wanted to ask, "How can you sit idle! Don't you hear the goats, begging to be milked? What is it you want from me, from our sons? Such ingratitude you present to Yahweh, with your frowning and moaning. Surely he regrets preserving you . . . and us!"

The words surged toward utterance. She wondered if Yahweh inspired them. Yet she couldn't . . . she wouldn't . . . speak so to Noah. Despite this unexpected weakness, he was a good man. Perhaps it was his goodness that weighed on him now, his delayed grief for those who'd perished, or his postponed grief for Grena, or . . .

Only Yahweh could know what darkness walked through anyone's thoughts. And if He expected her to speak to Noah, to lighten his dread, why didn't He instruct her more specifically?

As for herself, she had work to do.

Quietly—not that Noah'd have noticed or cared if she'd trampled like a team of water buffalo—she withdrew.

Later, struggling with her irritation, she allowed a brief memory of her own father, of his coarseness and his cruelty. While periods of gloom had refined his malevolence, nothing she remembered of him could cause her to find the same hurtfulness in a man such as Noah. Still, if the downward spiral continued, Noah would injure himself. There might well be nothing she could do to ease his depression, yet, looking at him and remembering the love she still held for him, she knew she must try. She must help him—if only she knew how.

❧❧❧ ❧❧❧

What a beautiful day—pleasant, with a gentle, warm breeze, and singing with sunshine.

Ham laughed as he brutalized the out of tune strings of the lute. His sulking suspended temporarily and his attention diverted from his childish insistence that Tamara "play" with him, he'd discovered the instrument hidden weeks before by someone whose ears could no longer stand his "music." But this day was too lovely to be marred even by Ham's off-key singing or the discordant, rhythmless sounds he plucked from the lute. Recognizing the song he attempted by the words, they laughed and sang along.

Kyral hummed as she listened to their varied voices. Afene's was sometimes sure and pleasant enough, although it lacked the warmth of Maelis's and the crystalline beauty of Tamara's. Shem sang in a booming monotone. Japheth's nasal sounds were undeservedly assertive. And Noah's singing was reedy and wandering.

We're not exactly a heavenly choir, she thought, *but willingness counts for something.* Allowing herself to reach into memory to recall stirring sounds she had stored there, she imagined the racket surrounding her into the harmonies replaying in her mind.

Warming, she linked her arm in Noah's. His eyes crinkled with amusement. "If it were up to us to preserve music, it would be gone forever. Fortunately Yahweh has a better plan." Laughing that deep, rich laughter that Kyral had despaired of ever hearing again, he swung her in dizzying spirals. Shem began to lead Maelis in cautious steps bounded by benches, shelves overflowing with utensils, and stacks of half-empty sacks.

Ham raised an eyebrow of invitation in Tamara's direction, but she, peering demurely through her lashes, shook her head and pointed to her considerable bulk. When Afene indicated she was too comfortable to stir, Japheth placed his fingertips on her shoulder and danced around her in a strange assortment of jubilant hops and leaps. Afene rolled her eyes in mock dismay, while the breadth of her smile showed her pleasure.

This is wonderful, Kyral mused. The shared experiences of tragedy and these endless days afloat had forged them into a unit. Surely they had become inseparable, were incapable of further wrangling.

"Not quite," Yahweh warned softly.

But they'd changed, matured, become less obsessive. Even Noah had put aside his depression, and Ham . . . well, she could imagine some slight improvement in him as well. For the moment, at least, she could not ask for more.

Giggling with dizziness, collapsing on a bench, she tugged Noah with her. Maelis and Shem, their arms entwined, rested on another bench. And Kyral's heart swelled with renewed gratitude at the depth of their love.

Perhaps Shem had changed more than any of the others. His rigidity moderated, he showed a measure of compassion absent before. Maelis' influence had been good for him. Yahweh's wisdom in bringing these two together was boundless, but then Yahweh's wisdom always was.

"And now," Ham announced, strumming the lute discordantly, "let me entertain you with . . ."

"Silence?" Tamara asked, pure pleading in her tone.

Everyone, even Ham, laughed. And Kyral exchanged glances with Noah. She loved that wheezing prelude to his heartiest laughter.

Squeezing his arm, she wriggled closer—needing in some way to express a pulsing passion moving in her. It was a surging tangibility that had never been stronger, even in the magic of their marriage night. How was it possible for emotion to expand, multiply, inhabit her heart, and govern her mind so that the thought of even momentary separation became intolerable?

She'd never loved him more! Nor could she love him less, except when he embraced dejection. Sighing, she moved to extricate her arm, but he kept it captive.

"Now is the time," Yahweh prodded. "You should tell him of your feelings." And she cleared her throat in preparation. But the joy in Noah's eyes was so pure, his love for her so naked, that she hadn't the heart for reproof.

Later, she suggested, and wondered in her heart if there might be no need, now, to broach the tender topic, since Noah was so obviously happy.

The moon, full and golden, cast a molten sheen to all it touched. Preferring to observe its magic than be swathed in it, Kyral sat in the shadows. The others had gone to bed. She assumed that Noah had, as well, until she felt his presence near her, his glance warm and loving. Turning, smiling, she invited him to join her. Delighting in his nearness, she had no need for speech. Nor, it seemed, had he.

He sank behind her, his arms encircling her waist, and cradled her head against his shoulder. They sat for a length of time which seemed comfortably endless. The moonlight lost its richest gleam. There were no sounds save for the laving of water against wood, contented snores from the sleeping compartments, and the stirrings of resting animals.

Noah's fingertips stroked her arm; his lips brushed her cheek and her ear. When finally he released her and stood—reluctantly, it seemed—she knew she wanted him to hold her until morning. Surely he would when, later, she joined him in their bunk. Expectancy both chilled and warmed her. If only she didn't linger too long.

She sensed Yahweh's presence. Surely he'd come to share her joy.

He said, "Noah feels the end of the journey is near."

And there'll be no further periods of frustration?

"So he hopes."

Her heart sank. *But if the months of waiting are ended...*
"Not ended. Not yet."
Perhaps I should still ...
"Perhaps you should."
But she hadn't the heart for it tonight. After the joy of the evening and her gratification at Noah's renewed affection, now came this deadening disappointment. How could she marshal her thoughts, how convince Noah to look forward to his place in the new world, no matter how long they must wait?
Later, she said, without the tenor of a promise.

It was during the night that Kyral woke to heightened movement. The ark seemed to be racing. The danger of rearing peaks ... "Noah!"
Reaching for her, he mumbled, "Yahweh ..."
Exasperated, she swung her feet to the floor and stood, not knowing what she could accomplish. How could Noah sleep? How could he ignore the danger? All he ever said was "Yahweh is in control." Yes, she knew that, but didn't Yahweh expect them to participate? Wasn't that why they had minds, the ability to think?
The increasing speed brought thoughts of rising mountaintops. Surely they'd ram against one and the ark would be destroyed.
The ship shuddered to a stop! The suddenness caused her to fall backward, across Noah. Fear gripped her as she listened for sounds of breaking timbers and gushing water. But there were no sounds, except for Noah's even breathing and the contented sleeping of the animals.
And there was no movement—no swaying as if the ark were anchored—but a rigidity that seemed to be total, a stability that she recognized only from memory.
Noah enclosed her in his arms. "Yahweh has brought the ark to rest on Mount Ararat," he said. "Our journey is complete. Once the waters recede from the land, the world begins afresh."
Smiling into the darkness, she relaxed in Noah's embrace.

Soon, she thought. *Soon we will walk on solid ground and feel the springing of grass beneath our feet, the sponginess of moss. We will loosen the soil, preparing it to receive seedlings. We'll climb hills and view distant mountaintops stained with sunset color. We'll watch small animals scamper freely in the meadow and pick wildflowers, and hear the music of swooping songbirds . . . Soon!*

"Not all that soon." Yahweh whispered a gentle reminder. "Such things take time."

➤➤➤ 11 ◀◀◀

Smiling, Kyral bent stiffly to a row of lentils, their shells silvered with ripeness. It's strange how moments or months dissolve in celebration or in joyful work, she mused. Yet on other occasions time seems more sluggish than blossoms becoming fruit. It's even stranger that in memory a certain span of time can seem to have been both swift and laggard, depending solely upon those particular memories tapped.

Still, fleeting or slow, the passage of months and years can be read by reliable signs. Knees no longer flex without conscious command. Fingers freeze at times into configurations molded by pain. Breathlessness fragments phrases, and wheezing occurs in the midst of singing. Memory fails with more recent events, while the past etches itself in ever more crystalline detail.

And of course the passage of time could be marked in the ways their lives had evolved since the ark.

It had been ten years since that door, once closed and locked by Yahweh, had opened—since the gangway, propped and firmed against an ice-skimmed declivity, had borne their footsteps. Kyral had stroked that pitch-coated hull and felt the sting of illogical tears.

Why am I weeping? she'd asked Yahweh, but He hadn't answered. She wondered if He shared the opinion of many men—that women's tears were incomprehensible and, therefore, seldom worthy of notice. In this case, she'd agreed. There was nothing about the ark she wanted to experience longer, even for one additional moment.

What a relief it was to breathe fresh air, and in such quantities! She'd never before fully appreciated air! *Thank You for air* . . .

Even though it might be a bit brisk, particularly with that edge of ice causing her teeth to chatter, she was sure she could never breathe deeply enough, nor often enough, to erase the memory of the fetid closeness of those final months in the ark.

And the space!

Thank You for space . . .

Even now, remembering, squinting her eyes toward Ararat, she marveled at the magnitude of Yahweh's world. During those endless last months, she'd felt like a moth trapped forever in its crysalis or an animal in an unyielding womb, which, instead of opening toward birth, closed ever more tightly—constricting, petrifying, nullifying. She'd thought she'd never again be able to stretch out both her arms without bumping someone or something. And even now her vision must stretch, must expand, must strain to find its boundaries!

It was ten years since the ark, since Ararat. On clear, moonlit nights, the bulk of the ark became one with the mountain, the clean line of its prow seeming merely an additional formation of dark granite. In autumn, its contours were often obscured by haze. Now, as rising sunlight ignited its encasement of perpetual ice, upper Ararat seemed some element of fantasy.

"Grandmother . . ."

Startled, she spun from her dreaming and nearly succeeded in ignoring the breathlessness any swift movement now caused her. She tried not to show chagrin as Asshur, toddling in the wake of his older cousin, managed to obliterate several blooming tendrils of melon vine. She welcomed Gomer, perhaps her favorite of the grandchildren, then made room in her embrace for Asshur, as well.

Shy and sensitive, with little of Japheth's fire or Afene's

zeal for cleanliness, Gomer seemed at home with the earth. He loved to work beside Kyral, quietly coaxing the soil to bearing. And he loved equally to rummage in moss or undergrowth for crawling creatures or tiny treasures of shell, shattered and deposited by the flood.

Squirming, he pointed toward Ararat. "There it is, Asshur. See? It's the ark. It's where everyone who was alive then lived, and the animals, too, for months and months and months. All the land was covered up with water. But Yahweh had told Grandfather to build the ark and he did. And then the animals came and they all got inside and the rains started and covered up everything and they were saved."

Asshur bounced and giggled in the contagion of excitement. "Tell us again, Grandmother, what the animals were like," Gomer begged, "and how long it was before the waters dried up."

She'd thought the days and days of rain unendurable, and those months of limitless waters endless. But nothing had prepared her for the interminable period on Ararat.

Lodged among the jutting rocks, the ark motionless at last, she'd felt a deep sense of relief, of fulfillment, of growth beyond loss—for a day or so. And then Yahweh's words, "Such things take time," assumed new meaning.

Each morning she rushed to the deck—yearning for obvious change, only to discover little discernible difference in the watery landscape—morning, after morning, after morning.

Day after day she steeled herself against annoyances that had once been endurable. She was so weary of crickets! Their interminably cheerful chittering and their insouciant presence startled her when she spread the bedcovers, when she opened the flour bin, when she rested on the steps. She was certain she would always loathe crickets, although she had no more bitter a hatred for them than she bore a thousand other crawling, jumping, hopping creatures! And, while she thought of it, she despised the arrogant llamas, looking down their sneering noses, spitting—even sometimes at Noah!—and the ignorant donkeys, with their wheezing, belching brays. What possible use could there be for donkeys, anyway? They were such stupid beasts!

Yet when she'd confided these feelings to Yahweh, He had assured her mildly that the donkey would hold a very important position in the future. She couldn't imagine why or how! They could bear burdens and that was all. Surely the horse could do so with more grace, greater speed, and less balking. And the elephant—although abrasive, too, when he trumpeted—could carry much more weight.

"I have chosen the donkey," Yahweh said.

There was no way to understand. And, to tell the truth, she was weary of trying.

But it wasn't only the animals that grated on her nerves.

Day after day tempers—including her own—frayed and flared. Snappish words had become more common than kind ones, but even those were preferable to the long, grim silences, when narrowed eyes refused to make contact, when utensils were often set more firmly than necessary. She was tired of deep sighs and stompings. She was tired of trying to soothe Afene's fears and to staunch Tamara's weeping. (How did the child *produce* so many tears?) She was weary of trying to ignore Japheth's pacing, Shem's grumbling, Ham's sulking, and Noah's depression.

Only Maelis maintained equilibrium, attaining peace through work and solitude. Her calmness was a silent rebuke, though surely unintended, to Kyral's own inability to cope. Guiltily she knew that Maelis annoyed her as much as anyone—except Noah.

With increasing frequency, came periods of withdrawal when he seemed unaware of his surroundings. He stared into space through clouded eyes, while his body heaved with heavy sighs, until gradually a deep malaise settled and he slept.

"Did you ever mention . . ."

There seemed no need, once he'd shown improvement, she responded stiffly.

"It was brief."

Yet it happened more than once. Surely it proved his intention.

"He needs your help and your understanding. He needs to tell someone how he feels."

My Lord, it's not right for a wife to question a man about his feelings. Shouldn't that be something he would tell You?

"I made men and women to need one another. And not just in marriage for the purpose of rearing children, but for the sharing of their souls. Noah speaks to me often of the feelings in his heart, and of his frustrations and longings, but he needs to talk about all these things with you, his companion."

It's just that the frustration of the endless days at sea were nothing compared to our experience now. You mentioned that Yourself.

"You could talk to him."

And what would she say, if she did? Considering her own frustrations and ill temper, she couldn't help sounding shrewish.

Am I the cause of his depression? she wondered, scarcely breathing as she waited for an answer, but there was no answer just then.

She sighed. She feared she would drive herself to melancholy if they should spend many more weeks on the stalled ark. While they were moving, at least the landscape had altered somewhat. Waves, whipped by wind or responding to other forces of nature, had risen in pseudo-peaks sculptured of water and foam. And occasionally a school of dolphins might break the glassy green-blue surface of calmer seas. Arched in glistening dark and white wetness, they reentered with a descending grace no dancer of any lost culture could have equalled. But dolphins, no matter how adventurous or playful, were unlikely to hazard the submerged peaks of Ararat simply to entertain Kyral.

And if they had, she'd have resented their freedom.

She hated this fractious side of her personality and feared how it might deteriorate further. When she was with Yahweh and those others she surely still loved, she longed to be more like Maelis.

I do still love them. Don't I?

"Of course you do!"

And I'll be myself again—once this waiting is past?

"Of course."

And that will be . . .

"These things take time. Try to be patient."

And she tried, but she couldn't bring herself to speak to Noah about his moods while her own were so mercurial.

Still, there were landmark events to break the monotony and resurrect hope. When Noah discovered in the distance another set of emerging peaks, that was cause for celebration. To think that *his* old eyes should be the first to sight such a wonder! For days, he strode the decks with new enthusiasm.

But his buoyancy soon evaporated, and again he was despondent.

And Kyral's hope dissipated in renewed frustration. If those were peaks, how long—how unendurably long—would it be until valleys emerged? When would the water recede, leaving the earth traversable? When, at last, would they be able to move all their necessities, all their belongings—all those *animals!*—to some habitable space? There would be so much to do then that no one would have time or energy for moodiness!

Night after restless night, Kyral visualized the process step by step. Night after night, she fretted that little could even be begun until the waters had fully abated.

During that time, knowing she was poor company, she sought Yahweh's companionship only occasionally. She feared any conversation between them might deteriorate into whining. And, certainly, there was whining enough already!

"Will this baby *never* come?" Tamara whined with sickening regularity. "Was it necessary that Yahweh send so *much* water, when surely His enemies died in the early deluge?" Shem whined frequently before hurrying quickly to prayer, surely seeking absolution. "How can our stores possibly last until we see a first harvest!" Japheth whined at meal times and Ham echoed the thought. And daily Afene whined, "Such filth! No matter how I scrub and scour..."

Kyral tried to shape her own thoughts, When? When? When? When? WHEN?, toward anger to avoid any appearance of querulousness.

❱❱❱ ❰❰❰

It was a month past Noah's sighting of the mountaintops when Tamara entered labor.

Enchanted by the earliest twinges of pain, she became nervous at the later, more insistent pressures and terrorized during those final hours.

At first, Ham stayed nearby, stroking her small hands and pressing one, then the other, to his cheek, while he murmured assurances. But, as her anguish deepened, he seemed grateful for banishment to the lower levels of the ark where the other men already waited.

It was a relatively short labor, but vicious, convulsing Tamara's small frame, contorting her lovely face, shaping her slender fingers into rigid claws. But Cush's lusty birth cry, determined and self-assured, restored her.

Kyral's eyes misted as she cleansed him. He was beautiful, rosy-colored and sturdy. And his eyes, when he decided to explore his world, rather than to berate it, were like his mother's—as deep and clear as endless waters.

For that moment, Kyral forgot her frustration with water and with waiting. Remembering only Yahweh's provision, she praised Him for this tangible promise of the future.

And now Cush was ten! He and the other children often begged to hear about the launching of the raven and then the dove, how the dove had returned from her second flight with an olive leaf! Kyral's voice always relived that excitement when she retold the story of how Noah had accepted the leaf carefully and, his eyes sparkling, handed it to her.

She'd stroked it gently, admiring green in its natural vivid-
ness—not diluted and sickly, as in her ark-bound seedlings,
or dark and watery and streaming with algae, as in the
dying sea. They had passed the precious leaf from one to another, to another, each studying it, smelling it, sighing, smiling with tremulous hope.

At that point in her retelling, Kyral might pause, lost in
thought. "And then, after another seven days . . ." some
young voice would prompt.

"In another seven days, the dove flew off again and never
returned. Your grandfather uncovered the ark, and sunlight
flooded in." (The plants had seemed to stretch for it, she remembered. They'd seemed to inhale its warmth and its fire.
And so had she!)

"Your parents reached their arms high, like this." They
would imitate her movement; then, giggling, dance about.
Her own days for dancing long past, she would recall with
mingled wonder and disbelief how Noah had swung her in
celebration ten years before, and how, glowing, she'd offered her arms for more.

Then another child would prompt: "And then you praised
Yahweh."

"Yes. We praised Yahweh."

"And when you first stepped from the ark . . ."

"How strange it was to walk on *ground!* I lost my balance,
and if your grandfather hadn't steadied me . . ."

"You'd have tumbled down the mountainside, head over
heels, down and down and down! And landed *splat!*
Wouldn't you?" This was sometimes offered with clumsy
choreography and more than appropriate glee. But she always smiled. "I well might have, but for your grandfather."

"And the rocks were dry, weren't they, Grandmother?"

"Except where ice and frost held, they were dry. And
where the slopes were covered with earth, it was dry. And
farther down on the mountain, and in the valley . . ."

"You could see green!"

"Yes, green grass. The animals smelled it . . ."

"You could tell, 'cause they started to bellow and screech

and baa and, and make every other noise animals know!"

"But you didn't let them leave just then. First, Grandfather built a . . . a . . ."

"An altar."

"Did my father help?"

"And mine?"

"And did my mother?"

They all clustered closer. "We all helped!" she said, and the children gave a communal sigh of contentment.

"And it's still there, isn't it, Grandmother?"

"It will always be there," she said softly. "And we must always remember to praise Yahweh, for all that we have are His precious gifts."

"Even us!"

Laughing, she'd gather them close. *"Especially* you! All of you, and all those yet to come!"

"We *do* praise Him," Gomer assured her, his head nuzzling her neck.

"I know you do, dear," she answered, but absently. Once again her mind was skittering across the ten-year span to that season of praise by the altar.

⟫⟫⟫ ⟪⟪⟪

When the altar, spattered and streaked with sacrificial blood, sent its fragrant smoke heavenward, Noah began the litany:

Who are we to praise Yahweh—we whose hands are weak, while His move the stars in their courses?

We are His chosen people.

How are we to praise Yahweh when our voices are pale, when even His breeze overwhelms them?

We praise Him from our hearts, wherein He dwells.

Then let us praise Him indeed.
How numberless are the works of our Lord:

Who has created the beasts of the field, after their kind,
and creeping things, after their kind,
and plants of the plains and the woodlands after their
* kinds,*
and leviathan, of the deep,
and even us, O Yahweh, whom You choose to serve and
* praise You.*

How marvelous are the works of our Lord:

Who stretches out His arm and mountains rise in obedi-
* ence;*
Who populates the heavens with stars;
Who spreads His hand over mighty oceans, whose wa-
* ters move or still at His command;*
Who draws His finger from cloud to cloud, from horizon
* to horizon, and sets His sun and His moon for our*
* lights there.*

How wondrous are the works of our Lord:

Whose Ararat rears to the heavens; rending ramparts of
* clouds;*
Whose power slashes His skies with lightning, and rum-
* bles in the depths of His sea with the thunder of many*
* waters, and in the bowels of His earth with the voice*
* of volcanoes;*
The roar of Whose lions resounds through His valleys
* and within His deep caverns,*
causing all ears who hear to tremble at such a fierce maj-
* esty!*

Yet how merciful are the works of our Lord:

Who sees our weakness and our weeping and strength-
* ens us;*
Who knows our fears and soothes them;
Who hears our pleas and praises and honors them;
Who touches us in guidance, in healing, in forgiveness;
Who has chosen us—even us—to be His people.
We shall ever serve and praise Him!

When she remembered that thrilling time of worship, Kyral lost touch with all other reality—as she had here, ten years later, with her grandchildren. They were clutching, patting, encouraging her to continue.

Of all her memories, they inquired most often and most urgently about the rainbow.

❯❯❯ ❮❮❮

Tamara looked upward through shadows flecked by sunlight. Drops of moisture on a spray of leaves produced miniature dancing rainbows. Sighing, she smiled.

It had been twelve years since Cush's birth, since the altar, since Yahweh's promise. A promise, she sometimes felt, He had made more to Himself than to them.

How marvelous that first rainbow had been. As it spanned the sky they'd stood enthralled, then had fallen to their knees in worship, continued from the recent litany near the altar. Even tiny Cush, in her arms, had cooed and pointed toward those brilliant, arching hues.

There'd been other rainbows since, but they were like echoes, reminders. Though again, whether to them or to Yahweh, she couldn't be sure. But she was certain that there would never again be a rainbow so brilliant, so all-encompassing, so awe-inspiring as that first one.

In her arms, tiny Canaan roused, and she guided her breast to his mouth. While he sucked noisily, appreciatively, his small hands patted and stroked. How she loved him! And Phut, resting nearby on a threadbare cream and blue blanket Mother Kyral had woven while the ark still floated. And she loved Mizraim and Cush, off somewhere with their father.

It was no wonder they sought Ham's company. He was more their older brother than their father. Usually he was down on all fours, yapping like a wolf cub, or flapping his arms and crowing like a rooster, or playing hiding games.

She sighed, but without rancor. She'd matured in these twelve years. And though Ham insisted that she was as lovely as ever, she could see the physical changes wrought by time, childbearing, and work. But the greater changes lay within.

She'd outgrown her childhood confusions. Carrying her babes within her, caring for them, watching as they scurried from her side to romp with Ham, she had come to understand her mother. She'd come to pity her, to forgive her, almost to love her.

Recalling her mother's face, she could interpret those unhappy lines in a new light, could realize that the shrill voice communicated frustration rather than dislike, could believe that the sarcasm spoke primarily the pain of repeated rejection.

We were unfair to her, Father, she thought. But with his entrance into her mind, old preferences were renewed. If her parents were to walk toward her together in that moment, she knew she'd run past her mother into her father's arms.

Forgive me, Mother.

Yet, how she'd loved him! How she still did. In her heart, he filled a spot no one could ever preempt. Additional guilt nudged her.

As hard as she'd tried, she still hadn't been able to call Noah "Father." And, because lifelong training prohibited her using his name without a preface, she called him nothing. Because of it, each day uncomfortable situations occurred. To gain his attention, she had to catch his glance or touch his shoulder or resort to saying something such as, "Ham, have you yet told your father . . .?"

Shouting voices—two young and light and joyous, the other Ham's—broke into her reverie. Canaan, releasing her nipple, waved his small arms in excitement. So soon they wanted to play with Ham!

Tugging her robe over her leaking breast, Tamara sighed. Perhaps the next child would be a girl, and she'd have a companion too.

Before laying Madai down to sleep, Afene swept the packed earth floor of the tent. Shaking the blanket thoroughly, she examined it for clinging bugs or flecks of dirt.

Japheth, bouncing their youngest on his knee, looked up to smile, and at her gesture settled the child on his stomach. His rump elevated, his small fingers gathering the blanket, Madai mumbled his contentment. Afene bent to straighten the blanket, but Japheth caught her close.

"You're so beautiful!" he said, and she praised Yahweh for her husband's lack of discrimination. She knew all too well that she was more angular than ever. And sometimes—though not often—her unplanned retorts were as sharp as her bone structure. Her only requirements for happiness seemed to be Japheth's nearness, his contentment with his work, and his obvious delight in his family—and cleanliness, of course.

It was more difficult to achieve now than in the old life, though not as impossible as on the ark. Shuddering, she remembered how relieved she'd been to see the last of the animals. First they had leaped and then had slid and faltered down the slopes of Ararat. Finally they stood, confused and wary, in the valley, sniffing the breezes before setting off in various directions. Some still walked two by two; others went with their young trailing behind or nudging alongside.

Of each of the "clean" animals, Father Noah had chosen the most perfect for sacrifice. He'd encouraged many of the remainder of those species to stay nearby, and most did, at least for a time. Some of the less savory creatures established nests or dens nearby, as well. And since Yahweh had restored the instincts suspended just prior to the flood, on still nights Afene often cringed at the sounds of the chase and the chilling screams of death.

Even considering that, Afene could find little to criticize in this post-ark life. Her days were buoyant now, and the children healthy and loving. Most importantly, Japheth was usually nearby.

Her sigh of contentment ended in a gasp as a fly lit on Madai's cheek. She swooped to catch it in her skirt, dashed

it to the ground, crushed it beneath her sandal, and gingerly
removed the corpse.

>>> <<<

Plucking a ripe apricot and admiring its blush, Kyral
sighed in perfect happiness. The sun was warm, the earth
fruitful, and her family—if not all in immediate view—were
certainly within easy calling. It especially pleased her to see
Noah in his vineyards. She knew that most of the grapes
would be washed for present eating, as she preferred, or
dried as raisins, which delighted the children. How Noah's
pleasure echoed theirs as they munched and murmured!
Then, too, a portion of each crop would be crushed and fer-
mented into wine, both for treatment of upset stomachs and
for libation during sacrifice. That, too, added to the whole-
ness of their lives.

Indeed, it seemed that everything about this new life
pleased him. It had been years since she'd known him to
surrender more than momentarily to dejection. And that,
she thought a bit smugly, without any interference from her.
Praise Yahweh!

Yahweh didn't comment, but that wasn't surprising. He
spoke to them less frequently now. Perhaps He felt they required less comforting. Or (as she often suspected) perhaps
they were too busy with their broadening lives to seek Him
with such constancy.

She must remember, in the quiet of this very evening,
when there were time and room for stretching the elbows
and the mind, to approach Him. Then she would thank Him
more formally for Noah's cheerfulness, for their sons and
daughters-in-law and the growing cluster of grandchildren,
for the bounty of His earth, and for its beauty, for the mel-
lowing memories of past terrors and losses.

For some reason, Doreya and Grena had been strong in
her thoughts that day. She'd discuss that with Yahweh, as
well, and praise Him that her raw grief had smoothed and
that even her residual aching had eased long years ago. Now

when they came to mind, she cherished unconditionally her sure knowledge of their presence with Him, their perfect joy, their awaiting her eventual arrival.

How pleasant it would be—when she'd woven her final coverlet, harvested her final garden, baked her final loaf of bread, and tucked in a grandchild for the very last time—to relax with Doreya. Perhaps they'd sit on the bank of a stream where no ants crawled and seaweed never stained a newly-fashioned garment. Giggling as minnows nibbled their toes, they'd move their feet in the coolness of the flowing water, while Grena led Noah on a walk through wildflowers. None of them would recall that such evil as Saert and Shumri (or Kyral's father) had ever existed.

She heard a rippling sound, saw sunbeams.

Never before had her imagination exerted such power! It was as though she'd summoned the scene to reality, for there, just beyond her vision, surely she heard Doreya's laughter—light, joyous, carefree, inviting.

Noah still tended his vines. Hadn't he heard?

That *was* Noah, wasn't it? Before his image could fade completely, she savored one last, long look. He stood straight and confident.

As for the others—Maelis's comfortable bulk, Afene's stick-thinness, Tamara's slender, now-slightly-stooping beauty, the sturdy muscularity of her sons, the vivid aliveness, the flexible energy, the musical laughter of her grandchildren—all quickly blended and grew indistinguishable.

Dreamily, Kyral shook her head to clear her vision, but all that was close, however dear, lacked focus; it was only that distant spot—emerging from shimmering—that projected tangibility.

The laughter, warm and contagious, enclosed her. There were two figures. No, there were three. One, slight and agile, swirled in green, the green of new young leaves in spring; that particular green that marks the deeper, clearer stream when sunlight probes; the green of vibrant, yearning life; the green of an olive leaf, borne by a dove. The second, taller, bending to pluck a vivid blossom, laughed Doreya's laughter, stabilized by safety, refined by love.

The third figure was swathed in light. Carefully, tremulously, Kyral inhaled.

Surely it's not . . . surely . . .

As one, they turned and moved toward her, their arms extended, welcoming her. And beneath her the rough ground leveled and dropped away. She knew a weightlessness of mind and body, an effervescent joy, a consummate peace. It was a rightness exceeding any perfection possible in less-than-perfect worlds.

Doreya, never so beautiful, tucked the bright blossom in Kyral's hair and kissed her. Grena hugged them both.

"And Noah?" Kyral asked, but without concern.

"Soon," Yahweh said.

Comfortably, into the pulsing light, Kyral said, "I'd planned to find some time tonight, to talk with You."

They laughed together, for of course time would never again be a consideration.

⇒⇒⇒ ⇐⇐⇐

It was spring again.

Nursing Lud, enjoying the tug of his strong, hard gums on her flowing breast, Maelis knew she would never lose her enchantment with new life. The gold-greens of springtime, the blossoming herbs, the bounding waters freed from winter's ice always reminded her of Yahweh's power and His care.

Often she and Shem walked within view of the ark lodged near Ararat's summit. At times, when they lay at certain angles, the sun's rays pierced the crystalline covering, and she could see the glow of darkened wood. She would never forget their experiences there and she would never tire of Shem's hand, strong at her shoulder, firm across the small of her back, gentle as he stroked her cheek, unwavering when he guided her across rough terrain. She'd never lose her contentment at nestling against him or working beside him.

The time since the ark had passed quickly. And now, when she reflected on those years before the flood, the grief she'd felt for those who died, the shock of the total devastation Yahweh had caused in His Creation, she was overwhelmed with His care for them since. She was at peace.

Certainly they all missed Mother Kyral. But the young couples, comforted by the peacefulness of her death and by Yahweh's assurance that she was with Him, had come to accept her absence. In her own grieving, Maelis had moved from questioning why someone so loved and needed should be taken to praising Yahweh for the blessings of Kyral's life. She was thankful for the support and gentle comfort Mother Kyral had given all of them, for her cheerfulness, which seldom flagged, and especially for her wisdom. Often she found herself remembering Mother Kyral's words and using them as though Mother Kyral still lived in her.

Gradually life had regained balance. Kyral's sons worked. Afene scrubbed and sang. Tamara, her serenity increasing each day, it seemed, contentedly performed all the tasks that fell to her. She wove, tended the children, and pruned and weeded Kyral's garden. And the children played until they dropped, spent and panting, then asked for stories of the past—always the same stories which must be told as Grandmother had told them, with no detail neglected and no inflection missed.

But Father Noah had not done well since Mother Kyral's death. Stooping to his vines, he spent long, motionless moments in grim silence. And more and more often he turned from his work and disappeared.

At such times, Shem frowned, Japheth knelt in prayer or pressed his lips in displeasure, and Ham found release in foolishness.

Yahweh, Maelis had begun more than once, *when You knew what her death would do to Father Noah* . . . But she lacked the arrogance to actually ask, "Why did you take her?"

And sooner or later, Father Noah would return and continue his leaden work.

Please, Yahweh. This is the man You have loved, the man You have led. When You searched the world for righteousness, it was in Father Noah that You found it. She broke off. How dare she censure Yahweh?

"Questioning is not censuring, my child."

She squirmed.

"I could forcibly end Noah's mourning," he continued.

Then, please . . .

"My daughter, Noah chose to be righteous. He chose to follow me, even with the certainty of ridicule. Now he is grieving, but not just for his wife. There's more . . ."

He sighed and Maelis felt Yahweh's sadness.

"Noah is a wise and obedient man, my child. He fears he has failed me. He knows why I destroyed my world, and he also knows that sin remains. That weighs heavily on him."

Sin? Here? Now, in us?

"Yes, my child, even in you."

Then, You'll . . .?

"No. Rainbows will remind my children of my covenant that never again will I destroy all things. In the generations to come there will be those who believe as you do. Some will be as righteous as Noah. And there will be those who will reject me, who harden their hearts, who turn their backs on me. But I will not destroy them. They will destroy themselves.

"That is why Noah grieves."

On an autumn afternoon, with a strangled cry, which might have been freshened grief or accumulated rage, Noah flung his trimming tool to the earth. Raising trembling hands toward the sunlit skies, he ran blindly from the vineyard.

Tamara lifted a fruit-stained hand to her throat. "Father Noah!" she shrieked. *"Father Noah!"*

Unaware that for the first time she'd called him by name, she recognized only that this grief was different, more crucial. "Ham!" she spoke with gentle urgency. "Stop him."

Ham's face betrayed a matching fear before settling into stubborn lines.

"Follow him," Yahweh whispered in her mind, and Tamara obeyed. But what would she say? How could she plead with Noah? How could she remind him that Yahweh and Mother Kyral loved him and understood his grief?

Maelis, breathing heavily, joined her. Afene passed both of them easily and then waited.

"I fear for him," someone panted. Perhaps all of them had said it. Surely all of them had felt it.

Glancing over her shoulder, Tamara saw their husbands still watching. Their postures betrayed an equal concern coupled with the paralysis of indecision.

You're his sons, Tamara thought coldly.

They'd reached Noah, but not because his pace had slackened or his determination diminished, only because he'd paused at his tent. He was reaching for a wineskin when Tamara caught his arm. How thin it was beneath the rough sleeve of his tunic! And how gray his face.

"Father Noah," she sobbed. "Please . . ."

A fleeting expression of surprise warmed his tortured eyes.

"He realizes," Yahweh whispered, "that you have finally called him 'Father.'"

She had called him "Father." She had cared with that depth, had grown to that love! Shock, dropping her hand away, cost her the opportunity to take advantage of his softness.

"Father Noah," she pled again, but by then he had shrugged away from all their clutching hands, and was scrambling up a rocky slope to a cave, topped by dying underbrush and filled with shadowed darkness.

When it was morning, still dark and chill, Noah hadn't returned. Lighting a torch, Ham went to find him, and Shem and Japheth said they'd follow. But first they paused to gather bread and cheese in the event their father hungered. They prepared also a packet of grapes and apricots and a skin of fresh water for his thirst.

The women huddled together. Except in their startled first grief for Mother Kyral, they'd never known such oneness. Together, they heard Yahweh's words of comfort. "Be at peace. It is done. Find joy in your families, in your love, in your work. As long as my earth abides, it will be peopled by your descendants. It will blossom under their touch. They will breathe its perfumes. Their ears will delight in its musics, and their eyes will exult continually in its wonders. Their souls will feast upon its harvests."

Afene nodded and smiled.

Maelis murmured, "Thank You, Yahweh!"

Though Tamara endeavored to echo their praise, a strange tightness had caught her throat. Their oneness had dissipated. Maelis and Afene seemed together, while she was alone and separate.

She shivered and hugged her arms closely across her chest. "I am with you," Yahweh said, and she sensed that these words were for her only.

She stood and walked slowly apart. Some cold, shapeless knowledge had invaded her heart. Ham would have reached the cave by then. Surely Father Noah couldn't be dead! And Ham, finding him . . .

"Noah lives. Be at peace, my child. You are strong, and I am with you."

Puzzling, she turned her eyes toward the cave. In the slightly dimming gray of predawn, the entrance remained the sooty hue of raven's wings, the somber tone of mourning, the unrelenting blackness of pitch.

Shuddering, she clung to Yahweh's assurances. Father Noah lived. Yahweh was with them.

But Japheth and Shem would have reached Ham by now. When all carried torches to light their way, why did no glimmer relieve the darkness of that entrance or the darkness of her spirit?

Had Maelis and Afene experienced this same disquietude?

But no, they still knelt together, praising, apparently oblivious of her departure, of this chill disruption of her peace.

She'd go to the cave.

Somehow her feet found safe footing. Somehow her hands moved without thought to shield her eyes from snatching twigs, to disentangle her skirt from briars. Her thoughts became a roar in her mind, a tangible frenzy and a leaden dread.

She met Ham as he emerged from a wooded glade. All was shadow—beneath the trees, beyond the trees, in her fears, in Ham's face—contorted with grief, twisted in a parody of laughter.

"We must leave this place," he said. "Father has cursed me and all our children and their children and theirs."

Tamara's throat tightened. What terrible thing had Ham done to cause such anger that Father Noah could curse her sweet children?

Ham continued heavily, "He's an old man now, humorless and vindictive."

And grieving, she wanted to add, but she willed herself to be quiet, to hear his next stiff words.

"We'll go somewhere else, and there we'll live to please ourselves." His voice broke. "And we'll never speak of my father again!"

Never again to speak of Father Noah? Never to mention the ark, never to tell Phut and Canaan the stories they were still too young to understand—the ones Cush and Mizraim loved so much . . .

"Gather our things. We'll leave at once!" Already Ham faced away from their home, away from Ararat.

Bidding tearful goodbyes to Afene and Japheth, Maelis and Shem, and all their children, Tamara left with Ham, her heart once again heavy with grieving. Still, long ago, Yahweh had chosen her to be Ham's wife, and ever since He'd revealed His purpose for her life, she'd known His reassuring presence.

And so she went peacefully, with Yahweh always near, just as He had promised.

About the Author

Evelyn Minshull is a writer, public speaker, leader of writing workshops and conferences, and portraitist, and is retired from public school teaching. She holds a bachelor's degree in art education from Edinboro State University and a master's in English from Slippery Rock University.

She has published hundreds of articles, short stories, plays, and poems and sixteen books, including *But I Thought You Really Loved Me, The Steps to My Best Friend's House,* and *The Cornhusk Doll. Eve,* released in 1990 was her first biblical novel.

A life-long resident of Pennsylvania, she lives in Mercer with her husband, Fred. They are the parents of Valerie, Melanie, and Robin.